CALGARY PUBLIC LIBRARY

JUL   2017

NO GOOD DEED

NO GOOD DEED

KARA CONNOLLY

Delacorte Press

This is a work of fiction. All incidents and dialogue, and all characters with the exception of some well-known historical and public figures, are products of the author's imagination and are not to be construed as real. Where real-life historical or public figures appear, the situations, incidents, and dialogues concerning those persons are fictional and are not intended to depict actual events or to change the fictional nature of the work. In all other respects, any resemblance to persons living or dead is entirely coincidental.

Text copyright © 2017 by Rosemary Clement
Jacket photographs copyright © 2017 by Getty Images and Shutterstock
Jacket design by Angela Carlino

All rights reserved. Published in the United States by Delacorte Press, an imprint of Random House Children's Books, a division of Penguin Random House LLC, New York.

Delacorte Press is a registered trademark and the colophon is a trademark of Penguin Random House LLC.

Visit us on the Web! randomhouseteens.com

Educators and librarians, for a variety of teaching tools, visit us at RHTeachersLibrarians.com

Library of Congress Cataloging-in-Publication Data
Names: Connolly, Kara, author.
Title: No good deed / Kara Connolly.
Description: First edition. | New York : Delacorte Press, [2017] | Summary: "Ellie is USA's best shot at Olympic gold in archery, but one wrong turn in Nottingham on her day off from the trials and she's somehow been transported back to the Middle Ages. Amidst an evil sheriff who wants to lock her up, a knight who might not be who he says he is, and an assassination plot, she must not only find her way back to the present, but fight to survive and not change history"—Provided by publisher.
Identifiers: LCCN 2016032251 | ISBN 978-0-385-74393-8 (hc) | ISBN 978-0-375-99140-0 (glb) | ISBN 978-0-385-37323-4 (el)
Subjects: | CYAC: Archery—Fiction. | Time travel—Fiction. | Knights and knighthood—Fiction. | Middle Ages—Fiction. | Great Britain—History— Richard I, 1189–1199—Fiction.
Classification: LCC PZ7.1.C6468 No 2017 | DDC [Fic]—dc23

The text of this book is set in 12-point Bembo.
Interior design by Ken Crossland

Printed in the United States of America
10 9 8 7 6 5 4 3 2 1
First Edition

Random House Children's Books supports the First Amendment and celebrates the right to read.

For Peter, who really wanted
me to write this book

CHAPTER ONE

⁊ↄℂↄⅇ

Time stretched with the draw of my bow. Ancient ages whispered in the slide of the arrow on the rest, and all possibilities collected in that suspended instant when my breath slowed, my knuckle kissed the corner of my mouth, I loosed the shot—

And someone's cell phone went off in the spectator stands.

I got the shot off, but the bowstring smacked my arm above the guard. The sting ran all the way up to behind my eyes. I did a little it-hurts-but-I-can't-curse dance but recovered quickly because, one, I did the same thing a couple of times a week, and two, Dr. Hudson's Third Law of Competition Dynamics was "Never let them see you lose your cool."

Maybe Dad didn't put it quite that way, but it was what he meant. So I put my game face on and ignored the troubling fact that I'd let a cell phone distract me amid all the general tweeting and pinging and hubbub.

God, Ellie. Just because everyone's watching to see when you crack . . .

Even before I peered through the scope set up beside me, I knew it was a poor shot. But it was good enough that I could recover with a high-scoring arrow and make it to the medal round.

Hudson's Second Law of Competition Dynamics was "There is no such thing as *good enough*." There's *ten points* and there's *try harder.*

With the Olympic qualifying trials coming up, and as the second-highest-ranked woman in the United States, fifth or sixth internationally, it was time to make my move up the rungs of the competitive ladder. That was what I was supposed to be doing in Nottingham. Not shooting like a reasonably accomplished summer camp counselor.

But then, Rob was supposed to be here, not his alternate.

Focus.

That was Dr. Hudson's First Law. Its corollary was "Stay in the moment." Don't think about the last shot, or the next shot, only about *this* shot.

One arrow left in my quiver and two minutes on the clock. I took my time fitting the nock to the string, trying to narrow the prismatic scatter of my thoughts. I visualized myself on the podium, the way the team sports psychiatrist had suggested. But what my brain called up was Rob and me on the stand, the way the U.S. Archery Team had run our picture after my first national medal.

Crap. Instead of slowing its roll, my head game was about to go off the rails. I mentally swiped the image of Rob and me off the screen and zoomed in on the ten-point X in the middle of the target. Just that. No flags and no nations, no babel of languages from officials and spectators. I focused until everything blurred except me and the target—

And the bizarrely dressed man between us.

"Hold!" I shouted, lowering my bow and slacking the string. Years of safety standards kicked in before I fully processed what I'd seen. "Man downrange!"

The firing captain echoed my shout in three languages, and all the archers on the shooting line immediately complied. A confused murmur rippled through the spectators, and when I blinked myself back to the larger picture, I saw why. There was nothing between me and the targets, stretched out like a row of unblinking eyes.

The officials conferred on their headsets, checking that the range was clear. The delay wasn't long, but I could feel the murmur of annoyance trickling through the shooters.

Finally the firing captain gestured for me to come off the line to talk to him—pretty much the equivalent of getting called into the principal's office. As I stepped away from my spot, the North Korean girl shooting next to me—my major competition for the podium—made a comment as I passed. It needed no translation.

Before the official could reach me, Coach jogged over with a look of serious concern. "What happened, Ellie?"

I had my bow in one hand, and I spread the other in a palm-up shrug. "There was someone downrange."

Coach had brought Olympic medalists and world champions to the podium before. My brother was one of them. Coach was almost family. "Was it an official? A spectator?" he asked.

Honesty made me pause. "I'm not sure." Safety had been drilled into me from my first archery lesson, and I knew calling a halt was the right thing to do, but I hadn't really processed what or who I'd seen. I couldn't even be sure if it was a man or a woman. I had the impression of a light-colored dress or robe, like a costume. But I wasn't about to say that, because that was just plain weird and I didn't want to end up seeing a *real* psychiatrist. "I only saw him for a second, and then I yelled, and by the time I did that, he was gone."

When the line captain reached us, we had almost the exact same conversation, except in French. After I explained, he still looked doubtful but got on the radio and instructed security to watch for someone dressed in light-colored clothes. Then he had the field captain signal for shooting to begin again.

"Hey!" I protested. "I'm not on the line yet."

"Then I suggest you get there, Mademoiselle Hudson," the official said flatly, "instead of distracting your competitors with this delay."

He left, and I spun to face Coach and vent my indignation. "What was I supposed to do? Keep quiet and hope this figment of my imagination didn't get hit with an imaginary arrow?"

Coach made a calming gesture. "Ellie, this isn't important. You're wasting shooting time."

"Not important?" I flapped a hand toward the French official. "I just got called off the line for doing the right thing! How is that not important?"

"*Arguing* about it isn't important," he said before physically turning me around and adding, "The time warning is flashing."

It was, and I was still behind the ready line. It was bad sportsmanship to step up while my neighbor from North Korea was at full draw, so I had to watch the time count down while she held her shot much longer than necessary. She played a good head game, cranking up the pressure. Then, before she let loose, the woman to my right lifted *her* bow, holding me back another precious few seconds.

She loosed with six seconds on the clock. All the other shooters were finished, so I leapt to the line with my arrow already in my hand.

Five.

I fitted the arrow's nock to the string.

Four.

I put my eye on the target and lifted my bow.

Three.

I brought the bow down and drew back in the same motion.

Two.

My knuckle touched the corner of my mouth.

One.

I let fly.

The scores took forever for the target captain to tally, and I sweated it out on the field, where only shooters and coaches were allowed, unable to face my parents until I knew whether I'd screwed up or *really* screwed up.

By the time I got the news and went back to the field

house, a lot of the women had already left, but the men were getting ready to shoot their qualifying rounds. Marco Canales paused in his stretching to give me some good-natured hell. "Real dramatic, Ellie. Auditioning for a movie?"

"Courting the cameras, more like." Erik Murray didn't look up from adjusting the stabilizer on his bow. "The video is probably already on your fan page."

I pulled off the sweaty headband keeping my shortish hair out of my face and shot Marco a "very droll" look. I ignored Erik Murray. He was something like nineteen going on a hundred and fifty; his younger brother had to set up his Facebook page. The thing is, my unofficial fan page was a little embarrassing, but Mom and I tacitly supported it with exclusive videos and interviews because the moderators donated any ad revenue to the Women's Sports Foundation.

Someone threw their arm around my neck. I jumped, but settled down when I saw the red, white, and blue manicure. Angela Torres was my closest friend on the team, as well as my closest competition. She was six years older than me but had never treated me like a kid, even when I'd been one. "What happened, Hudson? I was too far down the line to see."

It was pretty quiet with the field house clearing out, so I set my equipment bag across two benches. "I barely squeaked by to the finals."

She folded her arms and leaned against the wall, watching me disassemble my bow and pack up. "I heard you cracked under pressure. That's why I'm not gloating about being ahead of you in points."

"Enjoy it while it lasts, Torres." I bantered on autopilot

because I was thinking about what Angela had said. *Had* I cracked? I knew that'd be the gossip. Some bloggers had been just waiting for it to happen. I'd been training intensely, and competition was brutal even without any family drama. But if I was going to lose it and start seeing things, why would it be something so random?

"Are you going to tell me?" Angela prodded. "I promise not to tweet it."

That made one. It was a matter of record anyway. "I saw someone downrange, walking across the field." I didn't mention the weird clothes, which were the one thing that kept me from believing the whole thing had been some kind of optical illusion, like I'd seen someone on the sidelines out of the corner of my eye and just . . .

Just cracked.

Angela took my tone as a sign I didn't want to talk about it, which I didn't. She straightened, then brushed off her track pants and nodded to the door. "Are you going to come watch the men's rounds with me?"

"No." It would be too hard watching Rob's alternate. "I just want to go back to the hotel and take a shower."

"Good plan," she said, wrapping me in a hug, acknowledging my reasons without saying anything. "Get some rest. I only want to take the title from you fair and square."

"Keep dreaming, grandma."

Ruffling my hair—hat-head: the struggle is real—Angela left me alone and went toward the field. I fluffed my bob, shouldered my bag, picked up my bow case, and headed to the portico out front, where, no surprise, Dad was waiting.

"Eleanor Nikola," he began, and I knew I was in trouble. Dad is a theoretical physicist, so there was an obvious "going nuclear" joke I could have made, but I didn't think it would defuse the situation. "What were you thinking, arguing with an official?"

"I was thinking I didn't want anyone to get hurt." I almost managed not to sound defensive and whiny when I said that. "He was the one being totally unfair."

"So what?" Dad asked, level and logical as always. "It's not the first time an official has been an asshole. What happened to Iron Ellie?" A blogger had called me that once— I must have had a really good day—and it stuck, as annoying nicknames do. "If you'd been concentrating on the timer, you wouldn't have lost your temper."

I was about to lose my temper again, but instead I opted to draw upon my dignity. "He called me off the line for doing the right thing, Dad."

"Which sucks," he said without sympathy. "But if you hadn't lost your cool, you could have gotten back in place in time to finish properly."

"But I made the shot!"

"But you shouldn't have had to rush it." He spoke calmly, with his "I'm very disappointed in you" look, which killed me. I wished he'd just yell. "Your coach says you have more natural talent than anyone he's trained. You should be at the top of the board for the next round, not the bottom."

"It doesn't matter, Dad." I knew he was right, but would it kill him to congratulate me on advancing and not keep taking shots at the same worn-out target? "The scores will reset with the next round."

"It matters, Eleanor," he said, finally heating up. "Your performance matters. You slide by on your talent when, if you would just—"

"Focus," I chimed in, because I was so sick of hearing it.

"Yes, focus," he snapped. "If you had *half* your brother's focus, you could walk away with this championship."

Bull's-eye.

I couldn't breathe, it hurt so badly. I actually looked down, *literally* looked down, to make sure there wasn't an arrow sticking out of my chest. In my peripheral vision, people went by, and maybe they said hello or goodbye, but I couldn't hear them over the noise in my head. Was I wheezing? I felt like I was wheezing.

"Are you two still here?" It was Coach, his voice pitched to disperse the tension. I didn't know if he'd heard any of the conversation, but he'd heard versions of it. He'd *given* versions of it, if not to me, then to Rob. "I saw the other Dr. Hudson looking for you," Coach said to Dad. "You might want to head her off before she gets to the car park."

"Thank you, George," Dad said awkwardly. He glanced at me. He was aware he'd crossed a line but seemed caught between wanting to soothe my feelings and not wanting to undermine his point. I was glad when he left it at "Stay here and I'll find your mom."

Coach put his hand on my shoulder and said, "Breathe, Hudson." I did, and he squeezed my shoulder—gently. "Don't

9

let him get into your head. Yes, you allowed yourself to be distracted, but you pulled it together and stayed in the game."

Without looking at him I said, "I really did see someone, Coach."

"I believe you, kiddo."

"Maybe it was an optical illusion."

"Forget about it," he said. "It's done. Tell me all that exists when you go out there on Thursday?"

"My eye and the target and one hundred and forty-four arrows."

"Good."

A tall blond woman hurried toward us, wearing Team USA colors and soccer-mom hair. My mom, the other professor Hudson. I laughed, realizing Coach had sent Dad off on a wild-goose chase.

"Eleanor, darling!" Mom cried, enveloping me in her arms, the way only she could. "I'm so proud of you! Advancing to the next round with a last-second save. You're such a rock star."

I laughed again, softly, and just for a second, allowed myself to relax into that maternal pride, as if I could be the girl satisfied with good enough, the rock star with a bow and a new day and a clean slate for the grand finale.

But that would take turning back time. And if I could do that, I would go back far enough to tell Rob not to go to a war zone. I would tell him not to be a hero.

Or at least I would tell him goodbye.

CHAPTER TWO

෨ාc෧

M<small>OM LURED ME TO</small> N<small>OTTINGHAM WITH HER THE NEXT DAY</small>, promising she'd treat me to lunch. She was meeting with a colleague at the university there, and I didn't want to spend my off day in the hotel in Leeds, alone with my thoughts. Plus, free lunch. And because Dad wasn't there, I ordered a big plate of deliciously greasy fish-and-chips, soaked it in malt vinegar, and washed it down with a half-pint of cider, in spite of the shoot tomorrow. Carbs with a side of salt and a glass of fructose, please. It tasted like truancy.

"This inn," Mom said, picking up a chip, "is reputed to be the oldest in England."

I set down my glass and looked around. More convincing than the *giant* sign outside that Mom had just quoted were the cumulative details of the place—the twisty stairs and awkward levels, the uneven floors and low doorways. The obvious stuff, though—whitewashed walls, dark wood, brass taps—was a bit Ye Olde English Theme Restaurant. "Don't tell me the espresso machine is original," I said.

Mom gave me her Professor Hudson look but otherwise ignored my comment. "Nottingham was one of the last stops in England for crusaders on their way to the Holy Land. It's plausible that by the Third Crusade there was an inn here. The caves in and around Nottingham were certainly used by the local monks to— Don't *sigh,* Eleanor. I'm making conversation."

"I'm not sighing," I insisted, though I probably had. Mom taught medieval history at Notre Dame, and though I went to school there, I didn't take any of her classes because mealtime conversations like this had allowed me to test out of the freshman-level history requirements. "Here's my question. Was there really an evil sheriff, like in the stories?"

"A number of them. Often as brutal as the one in the Robin Hood legend. Nottingham Castle has all kinds of treachery in its past."

I leaned forward, elbows on the table. "Really?"

"Oh yes," she said with enthusiasm. Treachery was one of her favorite topics. "Plots and rebellion and assassination. You should tour the castle while I'm at my meeting. Though, sadly, there's not much left of the original structure that William the Conqueror began."

"Wait, wait, I know this. What is the Norman Conquest," I said, like it was a Double *Jeopardy!* question. "Which started with the Battle of Hastings in 1066."

"Correct," Mom said, half professor, half proud parent.

I shrugged it off. "I only remember because that king got shot in the eye with an arrow."

She frowned. "Why do you do that? Don't dismiss your intelligence. Dad and I raised you and Rob to be athletes, not . . . jocks."

That was a painful but fair hit. How many kids get impromptu lectures on quantum physics and the Plantagenet royal family during the same dinner? I just really did not want to have another parental conversation about things I always did. "So, William the Conqueror . . . ?"

Mom was easily diverted. "Remember, there were Anglo-Saxons in this area before the Normans came across the English Channel. The Normans made a settlement here near the castle, and to the east, where the Lace Market is now, was the Anglo-Saxon town of Snottingham, which gave the new town its name."

I snickered into my cider. "Snottingham."

Mom tried to look annoyed. "Really, Eleanor. Don't be juvenile."

"Did they make lace hankies there? In Snottingham?"

She finally laughed. Then she moved her glass to the side in an obviously preparatory move. "By the way, Eleanor, your dad and I talked last night. He is sorry for comparing you to Robert." I know I sighed that time, but Mom didn't call me out. "You're *both* so talented, and you've worked so hard in your own right. Maybe too hard."

Great. Mom thought I'd cracked because I was too focused, and Dad thought I'd flaked because I wasn't focused enough. They might both be right. "Mom, I didn't imagine that I saw someone. He was dressed in white, or off-white, and it was sort of like a monk's habit, you know, with the—"

I'd raised my hands to show a kind of cowl, but Mom's expression stopped me. She sat pale-faced with her hands knit together on the table in front of her. I looked from her bloodless knuckles to the crucifix she always wore and made an intuitive leap. Reaching across the table, I covered her hands with mine. "Oh no, Mom. It wasn't Rob. It wasn't his ghost, wasn't any kind of angelic harbinger of his death. I swear."

She looked away, embarrassed. "When you put it that way, it sounds silly."

I rubbed her cold and clenched hands. "It's not silly. He is missing in a dangerous part of the world, but if he were dead, I'd know."

Her color came back as she turned her hands to clasp mine. "Of course. You two have always been so close ..." Then she laughed, shaky but genuine. "Oh my God, Ellie, I sound like a superstitious nut, not a history professor."

I squeezed her hands one last time. "You could be on *Haunted History*."

She made a face, but continued with a new thought. "You know, your description reminds me: the sports center where you shot yesterday was once the site of a Cistercian monastery. Only a corner of the foundation is left. It's not in the brochure."

"Then how do you know about it?" I asked.

"There's this new thing called the Internet." Deadpan, she

14

took a sip of her cider. And she thinks I get all my snark from Dad. "You can see the ruins of the foundation if you get close enough on Google Earth. *Anyway,* the Cistercians were called the white friars because of their undyed robes."

I gave her an intensely skeptical look. "You *should* be on *Haunted History.*"

She raised her hands, pleading innocence. "I'm just relating information. It's up to you to form a theory with it. Like your father says, 'Just because it hasn't been proven yet doesn't mean it's impossible.'"

"Yeah, but he was talking about the scientists at CERN creating enough antimatter to implode the universe."

She waved that away. "He said the same thing about the Red Sox winning the World Series, and I've yet to hear the end of it. My point is, keep an open mind. It could be a subconscious recollection of the abbey's history, or a psychic echo from the past. Maybe you were even glimpsing a parallel universe."

I narrowed my eyes, sure she was joking. Pretty sure, at least. She'd been genuinely frightened that I'd seen my brother's ghost. "I think you read way too many science-fiction novels."

"Well, life can't be crusades, treason, and Black Death *all* the time." She wadded up her napkin and tucked it into her empty glass. "Ready to go?"

"Yeah," I said, slinging my messenger bag over my shoulder and leaving the rest of my fish-and-chips on the plate. "Funny how mention of the bubonic plague always kills my appetite."

15

Outside, the sky was a mottled blue-gray. Or gray-blue, if you were a glass-half-empty sort of person.

Mom checked her watch. "Good Lord. I'm going to have to grab a taxi to make my meeting. Now, head straight up this road and it will take you to the castle."

I pointed straight up. "I'm guessing it's that big stone thing I saw at the top of the cliff."

She pinched my cheek a little too hard. "Didn't I say you were bright? Meet at the market square about five?"

"Sure thing," I said, hoping I didn't sound like I was eager to get rid of her. "Have a good meeting."

I watched her cross the street and catch a cab at the end of the block, before starting up the hill. The Trip to Old Jerusalem was at the base of a big sandstone cliff and Nottingham Castle was at the top—a defensive advantage that became evident in my thighs pretty quickly. I ran regularly, but on the level track at school or in the training center.

Maybe if I stopped climbing the hill like I was being chased by my own ghosts . . . I shook off that ominous word choice, slowed down, and actually looked around at where I was. Across the street was a small churchyard and another pub, the Friar Tuck Inn. Between them ran Maid Marian Lane. I sensed a theme. Ahead of me, on the left and cut into the cliff, was a paved park, and in the center of it stood a bronze statue of an archer. There was probably a sign, but it didn't take a genius to work out who it was.

Robin Hood, the famed outlaw of Sherwood himself.

The bronze was weathered to an appropriate shade of

green. The statue must have been a bit of a landmark, because a family was taking pictures in front of it. At least, the mom was urging her two kids to smile at the same time instead of swinging from the archer's arm and pretending to sword fight each other. Sibling shenanigans. My parents have a bazillion pics of Rob and me giving each other noogies in front of historic locations.

Nuts. I stared up the cliff so I could blame my stinging eyes on the watery sunlight. It's not the times you expect to miss someone that are hard, it's the ambushes.

Other people's brothers rebel by partying too hard, or becoming socialists, or joining an indie hipster band. Mine joined the Peace Corps. Left school, the archery circuit, his gold medals for me to hold on to until he came back.

I'd been furious at Rob for leaving—I mean, the freaking *Peace Corps*. Like it wasn't already hard enough being his sister.

"I want to do something that *matters,*" he'd tried to explain the night he let me in on his plan. We were in his bedroom, talking in whispers because he hadn't told our parents yet. I could still feel that tight-throated ache from keeping my voice down, holding in my emotions. Rob and I had done everything together—or him first, then me—my whole life. What would I do if I wasn't following in his footsteps?

What would I do without Rob?

The ache had spread from my throat to my jaw and temples and down to my sternum and my heart behind it. The pain made me panic, and panic made me angry.

"What do you call that?" I had pointed to his wall of

17

medals and trophies. "What do you call the international championships, or the World Archery Federation title? That doesn't matter?"

"I mean something big-picture important," he answered calmly.

"The freaking *Olympics* aren't big picture?" I jumped up and paced in the tiny space between his twin bed and the desk, because you can't be truly furious sitting down. "How is digging ditches more big picture than that?"

"Because people *need* ditches," Rob snapped. And then there was a weighted, awful, awkward silence while what he didn't say—no one *needs* an Olympic medal—expanded between us, sucking up the oxygen and pushing us apart.

"Fine," I said, loosing the word from the taut bowstring of fear and anger. "Then you won't mind my selling your medals on eBay if you don't come back."

It wasn't the last thing I said to him, but it might as well have been, the way it ran like a loop in my head.

This tournament mattered because my teammates were relying on me—for a team win, and for the medal tally—and because I wanted to qualify for the Olympics, and that meant medaling in the women's individual event. But I'd walk away from the tournament tomorrow if that would somehow bring Rob back.

"Excuse me, would you like me to take your picture?" asked the mother of the statue-climbing siblings. I glanced around before realizing she was talking to me.

"Oh. Um, no, I'm good," I said, feeling conspicuous. And

18

I wasn't sure a solo pic would help this acute flare-up of Rob-lessness.

"Come on, now. You can't come to Nottingham and *not* take a snap with old Robin," said the mom, holding out her hand and wiggling her fingers. "Do you have a mobile?"

Well, at least it wasn't a selfie. I posed self-consciously in front of the statue as the lady took the picture, then thanked her before she and her kids headed off.

I glanced at the screen. Most pictures of me came from tournaments, when I had zinc oxide on my nose and my hair was plastered down by sweat and the band of my sun visor. Today I'd tried to dress like a normal person, which in England in spring meant skinny jeans, a hooded green sweater, and a scarf knotted around my neck. My short blond hair was wavy in the damp air. Bronze Robin Hood and I could share the same stylist, actually, except I was wearing Chuck Taylors instead of boots.

Probably should have gone with the boots.

Dumb luck made me glance up from my phone in time to see a white-robed monk hurrying past. With the really old church across the street, it didn't strike me as strange until the monk had crossed Maid Marian Lane and continued uphill, at which point the rest of my brain caught up with my eyeballs.

Hold everything. I was not imagining this guy—this monk—or his similarity to the guy I'd seen yesterday. Now that he was on my side of Castle Street, I could see the texture of his robe's fabric, the color variations in the warp and weft, the dirt on its hem. His cowl bunched around his neck, and the sun glinted off the circle of damp, shaved scalp at the top of his head. I couldn't hear his sandals on the pavement or the click of the wooden rosary beads hanging from his belt, but maybe that was only because of a loud bus going up the next street. He was moving at a good clip, and passed out of sight before I'd gathered my shock-scattered thoughts. But once I did, I took off after him.

By the time I reached the sidewalk, the monk was just a flick of fabric going around the corner and into the castle courtyard. I followed him to the twin towers of the gate-house, but could only glimpse through the fenced area to the terraced garden leading still farther up, to the building at the top.

I ran into the gift shop, where a woman was straightening rows of green-capped teddy bears and Nottingham lace bookmarks. "Did you see a monk going by here?" I asked, only a little winded. "Into the castle?"

"A monk?" She took her time thinking about it. "No. I don't think so, dear. We have a couple of Robin Hoods who do tours, and one sheriff of Nottingham, but no Friar Tucks."

The man I saw had been lean and fair-haired, and his robe was white, nothing like the fat friar from folklore. Maybe this guy was role-playing a cleric from a video game. Or, crazy idea, he could be an actual monk. But really . . . how could I let him go without finding out?

I dug into my messenger bag for some change. "I need a ticket."

"Easy, love," said the woman, amused and so very *slow.*

"The castle has been here for a thousand years. It's not going anywhere in the next minute." She chuckled at her own joke.

Maybe not, but I had a wild goose to chase. I slapped enough money onto the counter for admission plus a brochure and threw a quick "Cheers" over my shoulder.

When I came out of the gatehouse, I didn't spot a robed figure, but all paths led uphill, so that was the way I went. When I topped the last terrace, I stopped to get my bearings and my breath. To my left loomed a blocky Italianate building. To my right was a flat field, roped off from pedestrian traffic. There was a modern play fort on the far side; around the curve of the promontory stood a wooden framework. I consulted the brochure and read that the construction was a replica of what the eleventh-century outbuildings would have looked like, on the site of the original timber and stone tower. The only remaining medieval structures were the gatehouse, which I'd passed through, and the caves beneath the castle.

There was clearly no monk in the open field, so I struck out on the path that circled the existing building. The pamphlet said it was built in the 1600s—modern, as castles go, I supposed. The terrace gave a spectacular view of the city and the surrounding countryside, but I didn't pay it much attention as I suddenly spotted the monk.

Or rather, I spotted the top of the monk's head, which was hard to mistake for that of a tourist. The rest of him was hidden by the terrace wall and slowly slipping out of view. He was going down a sloped path on the cliff face, and I was about to lose him.

I ran along the wall and found an iron gate with a sign that said CAVES ACCESSIBLE BY GUIDED TOUR ONLY. I pulled on it anyway, but the latch clanged against the lock.

Maybe I should have thought twice, but I didn't. I grabbed the top of the gate, braced a sneakered foot on the post, and hopped over the stone wall.

CHAPTER THREE

∂つくら

DROPPING ONTO A PACKED-DIRT PATH BETWEEN THE TERRACE wall and an outer one that marked the cliff's edge, I stumbled on the steep slope before gaining my footing. I headed down-hill but didn't get far before I ran into another metal gate, this one blocking the cave entrance. There was nowhere else the monk could have gone, but the gate was secured with a shiny modern lock like the one on the gate I'd just jumped. Not knowing what to expect, I grabbed the bar nearest the latch and gave it a hard yank, and the gate swung open.

I took it as a sign and went through. Almost immediately, the downward angle of the path turned into a jumble of stairs, cut into the sandstone and worn by time. Most of the light came through the opening behind me, but from the tunnel below there was a soft, artificial glow, and I saw a shadow move through it.

Down the ramshackle stairs I went, leaving sunlight and brisk Nottingham air for underground twilight and the tang of damp stone.

As I went, the work lights got farther apart, forcing me to pass through patches of dark, one hand against the wall to help me keep my balance on the uneven tunnel floor. The cold grew teeth sharp enough to bite through my sweater, and clammy fingers of mist touched my face and neck. Farther down the tunnel, the air thickened with an earthy aroma, the clean smell of dirt mixed with river and a whiff of barnyard.

I slipped on some loose rocks, one foot skidding out from under me, and stumbled into a patch of darkness so thick it seemed to push back. Now I understood why the caves were gated to keep people out. I fumbled for the handrail, but only scraped my knuckles against the wall.

The blackness became viscous, not just blinding me but stopping my ears and flooding my nose and mouth until there was nothing else, until I couldn't tell down from up. I grabbed at the wall with both hands, curling my fingers as if I could dig in and hold on. For a horrible, eternal instant, that gritty chill of sandstone seemed the only thing that anchored me to the earth.

The liquid dark tugged at me like a current, and I had to pick a direction and move, or be swept away and drowned. The wall had been on my right when I'd run into it, so I kept that hand on the stone and felt my way in the dark, edging my feet cautiously along the rough path.

I followed the tunnel blindly for what felt like an eon, but was probably more like an age. Finally, the tunnel angled upward. Ahead I saw a spot of less-black. Monk or no monk, I picked up my pace, incredibly relieved to see an exit. I had no idea where the tunnel would put me—back in the castle somewhere, or maybe outside the walls. I only knew I saw daylight.

The passageway widened and the floor became a ramp. I sprinted out of an opening framed by a brick arch and a wide open wood door. Inertia carried me about three more steps before I came up against a solid wall of *what the hell*.

I'd emerged into a stable yard. The horses plus the sweet and pungent mix of hay and manure were a dead giveaway. A stable wasn't totally weird, but the geography felt wrong, like I was in my house but someone had rearranged all the furniture while I slept.

I should be at the bottom of the cliff, but behind me was only a high stone wall. A wooden roof jutted out from it, sheltering a paddock full of short, sturdy horses. They gave me the side-eye but didn't stop munching the oats in their trough. Dogs ran free and a fat tomcat stalked mice in the straw that littered the ground. Nearby, a hammer banged on an anvil. That wasn't a sound I heard a lot in Indiana.

With relief, I realized where I was—the tunnel had led to another part of the castle and I was in the middle of a living history demonstration. What else could explain the sound of iron striking iron, the man in a peasant costume hauling buckets across the yard, and the woman feeding chickens with grain from her gathered apron? No sign of the white friar, but a historical re-creation would explain him, too.

Maybe.

The relief didn't stick. The longer I looked, the eerier the feeling that everything was just *too right*.

Where were the tourists? Where were the baby strollers and iPhones? Where was that one reenactor who wore blue jeans with his puffy shirt and knee boots because he thought no one would notice? I'd been to enough Ye Olde Medieval Faires with Mom to know there was *always* that one guy.

Across the yard, the woman had disappeared and the chickens were now feasting on the pile of grain she'd dropped. I heard the jingle of metal and the thud of heavy feet. I swung around and saw a group of men dressed in roughly woven tunics under jerkins of padded leather, with coifs of mail covering their heads. They carried pikes and wore conical helmets with nosepieces. This operation must have a huge costume budget.

"Halt!" shouted the one with the fanciest tunic, which clearly made him the guy in charge. His troops halted all right, and lowered their pikes toward me.

"I'm sorry," I said, as if it made perfect sense for me to be apologizing to a group of overenthusiastic cosplayers accosting tourists with their deadly-looking weapons and way-too-authentic smell.

"How came you to trespass in the caverns of the castle?" The squad's leader—I didn't know what he'd be called in MedievLand, but I was going to call him the sergeant—was burly and jowly like a pit bull, and he held his pack of soldiers in check with a raised hand. For a re-creation, the sergeant

26

had the worst accent I'd ever heard. It hardly sounded like he was speaking English.

"There was a monk?" It came out like a question, because I was sure about the monk but absolutely nothing else. The man stared at me without any change in expression. "He must have been one of your reenactors?" Another question and still nothing. I adjusted my satchel across my chest and began inching back toward the tunnel. "You know what? I just realized I didn't pay for this part of the tour, so I'll return to the gift shop and . . ."

I turned quickly back the way I came, but the way I came wasn't there anymore. The tunnel was there, but it was wider and lined with casks and crates. It didn't lead to the bottomed-out darkness through which I'd stumbled. There was a cross-breeze and a light at the end of the tunnel, but not in a good way. More in a that-wasn't-there-when-I-came-in way.

I froze, not just because there were two men with pikes and padding and helmets blocking the passage. How had they gotten behind me? And more important—where was the way back? I mean, it had to be there, right? A side tunnel I hadn't noticed that merged into this one. That was logical—not like this weird feeling of a one-way door whooshing closed with me on the wrong side.

"Answer the question, knave," barked the sergeant, and I whirled around to face him.

What? I didn't even know what a knave was, and I couldn't remember the question anyway. I just knew I couldn't stand there like a nitwit. And apparently, I couldn't go back. I couldn't go left, and to my right was the horse stall. The sergeant saw me eyeing the only open path and gestured for his men to close it off. "Stand where you are!"

I did what any sensible person would do when confronted with a wall of armor, muscle, and pointy metal telling her to stand still.

I ran like hell.

Maybe no one expected me to actually make a break for it, or maybe no one expected me to ruin my shoes by going through the horse manure. But instinct said I was already in deep shit, so what did a little more of it matter?

I vaulted over the feeding trough, startling several ponies, and jumped into the bed of a wagon on the other side. The tongue of the wagon—where the horses would be hitched—was flipped up for storage, and as the closest guards came for me, I kicked the hinged timber down. It hit their helmets with a satisfying double clang.

Ordered and calculating Ellie said it was so rude to crash this reenactment party and start a brawl. The deeper part of me, the part that didn't aim, the part that just *felt* . . . that part said *run, run, run.*

I jumped over the side of the wagon and landed in a crouch. My only advantage was agility and surprise. The heavily padded men moved to block me, but I changed direction. I wasn't sure where I was headed other than away from their pointy sticks.

"Stop that boy!" shouted the sergeant, meaning me, I guessed. "Stop him or answer to the reeve!"

More men poured from a low building. A barracks.

Memory helpfully supplied the right words, even if some had dust on them. I was in the bailey, the walled courtyard surrounding a medieval keep that has a tower in its middle. The encircling wall was the parapet, where the archers would be, which meant the way out should be downhill.

I sprinted toward the only thing that looked familiar—the two round towers flanking the gate. Except when I came in, there'd been a turnstile instead of an iron portcullis, and no giant oak capstan where the museum shop had been.

But that was unquestionably the same stone gate tower, unblemished by weather or time. I was *in* Nottingham Castle. That parapet wall marked the drop of the cliff, and beyond that was the same Midlands countryside, only without the soccer stadium or the train tracks or water towers. Without any of the landmarks I recognized.

Without any landmarks at all.

Just land.

I was dreaming. I'd fallen asleep under the Robin Hood statue and was having a nightmare. Or I'd tripped in the tunnel and hit my head and this was an incredibly detailed hallucination full of ponies pulling carts, women with muddy clogs and tied-up skirts, and people staring and—

"Shut the gate, you imbeciles!" bellowed someone with authority. "Stop that boy or take his place in the dungeon!"

The groan of rope and wood torqued fresh knots of panic inside me. The iron gate was coming down, and whether I was lost or dreaming or quite possibly delusional, every instinct said escape now and figure it out later.

The stones were muddy and wet. I threw myself onto

them and rolled under the portcullis like Indiana Jones escaping the Temple of Doom, except that my satchel tried to strangle me. I sprawled there for a second, stunned that I had not gotten skewered by the spikes on the bottom of the gate as they crashed down next to me.

The courtyard through which I'd entered was gone. I was crouched on a bridge that spanned a river that hadn't been there on my walk from the inn. I could hear shouting coming from behind me, and the creak of wood and rope as the men in the guard tower reversed the capstan to reopen the gate.

I scrambled away but hadn't even gained my feet when an arrow whistled by to my right. I yelped and dove left, and another shot clattered to the stones beside me.

Like hell was I going to be killed by an arrow, dammit. That was more irony than I could handle.

I grabbed the loose arrow—I felt better with it in my hand—and fell back until I was too close to the tower for the archers to shoot down at me. But the portcullis was climbing and the guards were like big angry dogs barking behind a chain-link fence. I got my feet under me, ready to take my chances with the archers, when I made the mistake of looking over my shoulder.

Above the gate was a series of spikes, and on one of the spikes was a head.

A *head*. On a spike.

I screamed. There was no pretending I didn't. I stumbled over my own feet to get away from the awful thing, and then I saw there was more and it was worse. On the other side of the gate, two corpses hung by their necks and I yelped again, as if they might pull themselves free and come after me. The whole place smelled awful, but now all I could smell was death. All I could see was the slack skin and open mouth and sightless eyes of the head, the rotting flesh of the hanged men.

A noise behind me jolted me out of my paralyzing horror. I whirled to see a man on horseback blocking the other end of the bridge.

"Hold!" he ordered, and everyone froze. The riders behind him, the archers, the guards at my back. For all I know the river stopped running under the bridge. It was that kind of voice.

He didn't wear a helmet or any kind of uniform. He had dark hair, tanned skin, an aquiline nose, and an angled jaw covered by a close-cropped beard. He was all hard lines and slashes, this guy. And his horse . . . if the ponies in the stable were Hondas, this beast was a freaking Porsche.

"What is happening here?" the man demanded.

I wasn't sure what I *meant* to say. But what came out was "There is a *head* on a *spike*."

The horseman looked up at the thing without any visible change in expression, and then back at me. "*That* was there when I left. *You* were not."

I jumped as a guard grabbed the strap of my messenger bag where it crossed my back, his knuckles grinding into my spine as he tightened his grip. The sergeant had pushed his way through the guards blocking the gate and shot me a look like I'd gotten him in trouble on purpose. "We found this lad mucking about in the caverns under the castle, Sir Henry."

"I was lost!" I protested to the guy on the horse. It was the truth, but the way I said it sounded like a lie, so I blathered on and made it worse. "There was a man. A friar. I was looking for him."

Sir Henry raised one brow, questioning my story, then glanced over my shoulder. "Did you lose something, Your Honor?" he asked in a wry tone that only a guy with a horse and an accent and the ability to lift one eyebrow could pull off.

As I turned to see whom he was talking to, the guards fell away to let another man pass. He was older than the horseman, and his knee-length tunic was belted with leather and silver and trimmed in velvet. A fur-lined cloak made his shoulders look broad, but his calves were skinny. His face would have been unremarkable, except for the expression of clear and cold disdain on it.

The robed man drew himself up to his full height and dignity. "Excellent, Captain Guilbert," he said, as if things had gone totally according to plan. "You've caught our trespasser."

I recognized his voice as the one yelling for my capture. I swung my gaze back to Sir Henry–slash–Captain Guilbert. It was clear from the tension vibrating between the two men that they were at odds. For a moment, I had a hope that the guy on horseback would take my side just to piss off Tunic Man. But he just flicked a finger in my direction, and gave orders to the men behind him. "Take this intruder to the dungeon."

Well, crap.

I had kept my grip on the shaft of the arrow, just under the barbed tip, but the guard still held me by the strap on my bag, and men from both sides of the bridge were about to converge on me like fifty medieval linemen in chain mail.

The only way out was by river. Iron Ellie, international archery champion, calculated the distance down to the water, the swiftness of the flow as an indicator of depth, the windage, and the air temperature—all in a heartbeat.

But the other Ellie? The one who loosed her arrows when it *felt* right?

She just jumped. I jerked free of the guard and left the soldiers, the overdressed civil servant, and Captain Sir Whoever tracking my arc into the muddy river below.

CHAPTER FOUR

IN THAT INSTANT BEFORE I JUMPED, I'D DONE A LOT OF CALCU-
lations, but I'd forgotten one very important thing: There was
no waste disposal service in the Middle Ages. There was only
the river.

The smell was awful. It was also offal and rotted vegetables
and I didn't know what else, nor did I want to.

The river was high and running fast, and it carried me
quickly out of range of the castle's archers. When I dove from
the bridge, I'd felt the strap of my satchel tighten across my
chest and then jerk free, and now I didn't feel it at all—no
strap, no bag, no passport, no phone. Before I could do more
than panic about it, the current gave me a hard yank, dragging
me under. I was a good swimmer, but the flow snagged my

sodden clothes and pulled me to the rocky bottom. I banged along the shallows like a sneaker in a washing machine, smacking my head hard enough to turn up into down.

Then a hand grabbed the back of my sweater and hoisted me out of the log-flume ride from hell. I coughed and choked and opened my eyes, despite the filthy water running down my face. All I could make out were the flanks of a horse and the boot and stirrup belonging to the rider who had hauled me up like a kitten by the scruff of its neck.

I'd lost track of what was the frying pan and what was the fire. This rider might drag me right back up to the castle, or into some new attraction in this Dante's *Inferno* theme park, but at least I wasn't going to drown in three feet of water. Especially three feet of *that* water.

The horse waded to shore and climbed the riverbank, where the rider set me on my feet. Or at least tried to. My legs gave out and I dropped to my hands and knees, spewing up any river water the horse hadn't already jostled out.

My fingers were cramped around something familiar. I'd kept hold of the arrow but lost my satchel on the bridge. *Nice priorities, Ellie.* They were welcome to the Moleskine and Lärabars and travel umbrella. But my passport and iPhone were in there, too.

That was a problem, but was it my most immediate one? I needed to look up, get my bearings, see what dangers surrounded me, but breathing and not puking were the best I could manage for a long moment. Maybe more than a few long moments.

Something nudged me—the horse. It snuffled my hair, then snorted in disgust. I didn't blame it.

The rider swung out of the saddle in a motion as fluid as a gymnast's dismount but somehow even more badass. "Can you stand?" he asked, in an accent so thick I wanted subtitles. When I didn't respond immediately, he repeated, in French, *"Pouvez-vous vous lever?"*

"Donnez-moi une minute," I managed.

The language wasn't the problem. The problem was that I'd finally gotten a look at who had pulled me out of River Le Pew.

A knight. Not a figurative one, a *literal* knight in armor looking like an illustration out of a book on chivalry, while I dripped water and sewage into a foul-smelling puddle at his feet.

His horse was the color of polished oak, big enough to carry a man draped in a hundred pounds or more of chain mail. The knight looked like he came from the Crusades, gauging not only by his outfit and weapons but mostly from the crimson cross emblazoned on his whitish surcoat.

I didn't have to be a history nerd—or the daughter of one—to recognize that. I'd watched *The Da Vinci Code*. I knew a Knight Templar when I saw one.

That was the reason I couldn't speak.

Well, that on top of everything else.

Frowning, the knight dropped to a crouch in front of me. I still didn't know whose side he was on, the frying pan's or the fire's, but there was concern mixed with his impatience.

36

"Nous n'avons pas beaucoup de temps. Êtes-vous gravement bles-sée?"

We don't have much time. Are you badly injured? His gaze went to my temple, which throbbed almost worse than it stung. I reached under my dripping hair and found a big lump and an impressive trickle of blood.

I *had* hit my head. That would explain everything. I was lying in the tunnel under Nottingham Castle and any minute now a tour group was going to stumble over my unconscious body.

Except I'd hit my head *after* I jumped into the hell river, not before.

What if I really had slipped my gears? What if I'd run out of Nottingham Castle in the middle of a psychotic break, and the guards were really the paramedics or something and I'd escaped them by jumping into the river?

Except the river wasn't there in the twenty-first century.

What if I wasn't *in* the twenty-first century?

I stared numbly at the blood on my fingers. My head didn't hurt anymore because it was floating away from my body.

What if I really was in the Middle Ages?

"Oh. My. God," I wheezed. "I'm going to die of some horrible medieval disease."

The knight blinked in confusion. *"Qu'est-ce que c'est que ça?"*

"The bubonic plague. Oh, wait. That's from fleas." Random bits of history slipped uselessly through my brain.

His concern was turning into a grim sort of alarm. "*Êtes-vous folle? Ou êtes-vous désorientée de votre chute?*"

Was I mad? One thing I did know—I should not appear crazy in the Middle Ages. Whether delusional or sane, the safest thing was to stay calm and go with it. Eventually I'd wake up . . . or die of the Black Death.

I took a steadying breath and told him, "*Je vais bien.* And I speak English."

He gave me a doubtful look that needed no translation. "You speak something vaguely *like* English."

I gave him as tart a look as my pained head could manage and began an unsteady climb to my feet. "Your accent isn't exactly BBC standard."

He may not have understood the reference, but he got my point. He rose from his crouch, and good Lord, there was a lot of him. I thought that people were smaller in the Middle Ages, before vitamin-enriched breakfast cereals and whatever. The knight was a head taller than me, broad-shouldered and *fit.* Then there was all the chain armor and the leather and the way he took my hands and pulled me up as if I weighed nothing at all.

"We don't have time for nonsense," he said. "If you can banter, you can answer my questions."

"I doubt that." I couldn't even answer my own questions.

He frowned—he had a face that looked good frowning, all strong angles and steely eyes—but before he could reply, the sound of a large animal moving through the trees stopped me, and I grabbed the knight's arm.

"What's that?" It sounded like a bear. Or a wild boar. Hell, it could have been a dragon, the way my day was going.

The knight tactfully peeled my fingers from his biceps. "That is an ally, which is fortunate, since you've attached yourself to my sword arm."

I let go. Weaving through the trees was a sturdy pony. Astride it was a skinny boy with a wild thatch of hair and eyebrows like caterpillars. Not exactly the kind of ally I was expecting.

"Sir James! You caught him!" The knight's name was the only useful thing I got from the barely intelligible gush of words that came next. I grasped about a third of it—as opposed to the half I got from everyone else—and filled in the rest from context. "I've never seen anything like that dive from the castle bridge. We saw you from the road, and I thought for sure you'd dashed your brains out on the river bottom."

Sir James gestured to the boy. "This is Much . . . who told me he could move through these woods without so much as disturbing a deer."

"That was the pony making noise, not me. And I was in a hurry. The reeve's soldiers are riding out from Nottingham."

"How many?" asked the knight, in a grimly tactical kind of way.

"All of them, I think." The boy gazed at me with a mix of awe and . . . awe, mostly. "What did you *do*?"

"Nothing." I'd protested my innocence so often, even I was starting not to believe it.

Sir James, all business, asked the boy, "How far away?"

"They just left the town gate and are staying on the road. But the rangers are cutting through the woods."

The knight exhaled the way most people would curse. "You should have started with that, Much."

The kid finally looked chastened. "I'm sorry. I'm just a miller's son. I'm new to this. Well, not new to evading the reeve's men, but—"

I had a billion questions, but I broke in with "What's a reeve?" just to have a place to start.

"The worst thing that ever happened to this shire," said Much, so vehemently that a thatch of his hair flopped into his eyes and sprang back up again.

Sir James gave a more textbook answer. "The shire reeve administrates for the crown—collects taxes, enforces common law, oversees trial by combat or ordeal . . ."

Shire reeve. I ran it together like he'd said it—*shirreve*—a few times and then *bam*—I got it. "You mean, the *sheriff*? Of *Nottingham*?"

"That's what I said," said the boy, in his barely interpretable accent.

I laughed, slightly hysterical, and gestured to the woods around the river and the clearing where we stood. "Then I suppose this is Sherwood Forest."

Much gave me a suspicious side-eye. "Where else would we be?"

I rubbed my forehead. The pain cleared some of the fog. Nottingham and Sherwood Forest were real places. The shire reeve, or *sheriff,* was a real job. Mom had said so . . . maybe an hour ago, maybe hundreds of years from now.

The thought brought on a twist of fear and loss, like homesickness. Whatever was happening to me, my subconscious had recognized that I was, one way or another, far, far from home.

The knight's horse looked up suddenly, ears pricked, nostrils flaring. Sir James and Much exchanged a look.

God. The ride wasn't over. The roller coaster had only leveled out before the next drop. Every instinct said to bail. *Adieu. Godspeed. It's been surreal.*

Sir James must have read my mind, because he caught my arm when I would have taken off blindly. "Don't run. They'll have dogs."

His matter-of-fact tone made the image of rabid teeth tearing my flesh even more coldly vivid. Plus, where would I go? All I had on me was a tube of lip gloss and my BritRail pass.

"I'll jump back in the river if I have to," I swore. I would take my chances in the water over what passed for justice in Head-on-a-Spike-Land.

Sir James swept a tactical glance over me. Whatever factors he was weighing, he quickly came to a decision. "Much, keep a lookout." The boy didn't hesitate, but rode to the edge of the clearing and tied his pony to a low tree branch, then scrabbled up into the boughs. To me, Sir James said, "Adjust your garments. And don't speak if you can help it."

"Why?" Indignation rallied me a bit. "Because I'm a girl?"

"Because your speech is deranged." With that, he turned to his horse and started unbuckling saddle things.

He had a point. I quickly wrung the foul water out of my soaked sweater, stretching the knit so that it hung loose and covered my hips as well. Good thing I was more a Diana than an Aphrodite. My hair was short, and I was so covered in muck my own mother wouldn't recognize me.

When the knight turned back, he ran another quick eye over me and nodded as if it would have to do.

Much's face appeared in the foliage above the riverside clearing where we stood. "It's Guilbert and his men, coming from the northeast. They're not even trying to be quiet."

I could hear the sound of dogs and horses, but the trees dispersed the noise so it seemed to be coming from every direction, like my panic.

Sir James stepped into my line of sight. A pair of gauntlets were folded over and tucked into his belt, which rode low on his hips, pulled down by the weight of his sword.

A freaking broadsword. The scabbard and the leather-wrapped grip were dark both with use and careful maintenance. The weighty-looking pommel was stamped with the same equal-armed cross that he wore on his chest.

I didn't know why that was the pivot point. Maybe it was the weapon, and the way it seemed so natural to him, like how I carried a bow. Maybe it was my options: bad and worse. Maybe it was because, looking upriver, the way I'd come, I could see the castle atop its sheer rock face, surrounded by woods and hills instead of Victorian town houses and modern football stadiums. Above it was a gray-blue sky without a power line, cell tower, or vapor trail in sight.

Suddenly, I was shaking. My soaking-cold clothes had triumphed over body heat and adrenaline. Shock crept numbing fingers between my ribs, making it hard to breathe. I focused on the man in front of me, staring at the intricately linked chains of his mail shirt. The tidily mended hole in his linen surcoat was more vivid than the memory of what I'd eaten for breakfast that morning.

"Is this real?" I whispered, not sure who I was asking.

The knight answered, hands bracing my shoulders, "You are in very real trouble. Let me help you. We will sort all else out later."

"Okay," I said, and then, with more conviction, "okay." This was happening—however it was happening—so I'd better pull myself together and deal with it.

I picked up the arrow I'd left on the ground. The fletching was caked with mud, but it didn't need to fly straight, it just needed to remind me who I was on the competition line.

Six riders dressed all in brown and green and black came out of the trees. It looked for a moment like the woods were closing in around us, trapping us with our backs to the river.

CHAPTER FIVE

THE RIDERS WERE EXPECTING ME, BUT NOT THE KNIGHT. Before they had even arranged their horses—and their three pony-sized dogs—to loosely pen us in, every one of them had eyeballed Sir James from the top of his close-cropped hair to the spurs on his boots, and none of them missed his hand resting nonchalantly—but not accidentally—on the hilt of his sword.

Leading them was the captain from the bridge on his performance sports car of a horse. He was dressed for business—sword at his side, leather jerkin with a padded tunic beneath it, and suede breeches to guard against branches as he rode. His men were outfitted the same way, except most carried bows and had knives on their belts. They looked keenly formidable, much more so than the lumbering castle guards.

My game face was totally wasted on them. The captain's sharp-eyed gaze checked me off his roll call and noted Much's riderless pony, but his attention was focused on Sir James. I was the one-point circle. The knight was the bull's-eye. I tried not to be offended.

Sir James smiled, which nobody, including me, expected. "Henry Guilbert," he said, with a note of discovery. He used the French pronunciation—*Geel-BEAR*—and continued in French, or close enough to it that I could follow. "I'd heard that a Guilbert was chief forester, but I didn't know it was you."

I sensed a weird undertone, like Sir James wasn't as surprised as he let on, and Henry Guilbert ... Well, the guards had addressed him as *Sir* at the castle, when they weren't calling him *Captain,* but *Sir* James hadn't used either title. Guilbert took in the emblem on the knight's chest, then his deeply tanned face. Abruptly his confusion cleared, and he shifted back in his saddle. "James? I had no idea you were back from the Holy Land."

"Just barely. I haven't even seen my family yet." Sir James glanced at the riders surrounding us. "Has the sheriff got you and your rangers chasing down waifs and strays?"

Guilbert didn't like that. He had a game face, too, but it didn't go deep. "Only when they trespass on a royal castle and attack Nottingham's soldiers. I should thank you that we didn't have to pull this half-drowned cat out of the sewer." He finally gave me his attention—me and the arrow in my white-knuckled fist. "What are you planning to do with that?" he asked.

"I'm going to put the point through anyone who tries to put my head on a spike."

One of the rangers—my translation was slippery, but that's the word I was going with—turned a laugh into a cough. The captain arched that brow. "You mean you're going to try."

"Give me one of those bows and I'll put the point through anything I want."

It was a statement, not a boast, though the riders took it as one and dismissed the threat. Guilbert, on the other hand, didn't look so sure.

Sir James clapped a hand on my shoulder. His manner was composed, but there was a warning in his tightening grip. "You must forgive my friend," he said, nodding to me. "He was kicked in the head by a horse."

I pressed my lips together to keep in any more ravings, and touched the warm trickle on the side of my head, producing a very real wince. Then I held up my bloody fingers and wiggled them. "Nasty horse."

Captain Guilbert gave me a narrow-eyed look that transcended eras. "So you know this . . . person, James?"

"We met recently on the road," the knight said smoothly. "I'm sure you noticed his foreign speech. He went ahead of me to Nottingham town and became lost. Isn't that right, er . . . lad?"

"Yes." "Lost" was the understatement of whichever century I was in.

Guilbert's expression turned drily doubtful. "So lost that you ended up in the cellars of the castle?"

I had no idea how I ended up in the cellars of the castle,

but that didn't stop me from coming up with an answer. "Well, I *did* say that I was looking for a friar."

"A friar?" Captain Guilbert laughed. "Are you trading your Templar shield for a monk's habit, James?"

Sir James acknowledged the jab with a wry half smile. "I am weighing every option, now that I'm home from the Crusade." It sounded like an honest admission. "All you and I wanted as boys was to become knights, but the sword grows heavy after it's tasted too much blood."

The bleakness beneath his calm kept him from sounding melodramatic. These guys said nothing without silent layers beneath; I was having to translate twice, once from French, and once from subtext. It was exhausting, and made my head pound even harder.

Guilbert's mood shifted at James's words, becoming stiff and prickly. "We all have difficult duties to perform." His horse sidled restlessly, conveying his tension. His men felt it, too. Saddle leather creaked as they awaited orders. The captain raised his voice and spoke in English. "You can start by telling your friend to come out of hiding or my men will shoot him out of that tree."

I immediately looked toward where Much was hiding because I have no game except on the sporting field. One of the archers nocked an arrow. It was a short bow, easier to ride with, but it would put a shot into the tree well enough. When the knight didn't speak fast enough, I grabbed his arm. "Don't call his bluff."

Sir James gave me a look like I'd just told him not to put beans in his ears. I dropped my hand, feeling stupid, and he called up into the tree, "All right, Much. You heard Sir Henry."

After a lot of rustling, the boy emerged and dropped into the crook of the tree trunk, looking very puckish with twigs sticking out of his hair. Guilbert looked from him to James. "It seems you're the one collecting waifs."

"Perhaps because Nottingham seems to have become a dangerous place for them." His tone was unmistakably critical.

Guilbert didn't deny it. "A lot has changed since you've been gone, James." He sounded cynical and resigned, or maybe just bored. "Strays don't just wander in and out of Nottingham Castle without answering for it. I've orders to seize the trespasser so he may supply those answers to the sheriff."

"But I don't *have* any answers," I protested.

Guilbert switched back to French and spoke directly to me. "That's not my concern. My men are saddle-weary and hungry, so I am motivated to keep you in one piece so that the sheriff can ask his questions and be done with it. If you'd rather wait for Nottingham's soldiers to find you, they won't care whether you're in any condition to respond to interrogation."

His tone conjured images of racks and thumbscrews, of the tattered flesh of the bodies hanging outside the castle. I stopped worrying whether this was reality or a delusion. The smell and nausea and fear were real. The *pain* was real. The rest was just existential nitpicking.

I hadn't realized I'd taken a step toward the river's edge until Sir James caught my wrist, gently but firmly pulled me to his side, and didn't let go. "He's already in no condition for an interrogation. Let me attend to his injury and then I will bring the boy to Nottingham."

Wait, what?

A soft and wordless protest squeezed through betrayal's choke hold on my throat. I felt like I'd plummeted from the bridge all over again.

Guilbert's scoff was almost a laugh. "My orders are to bring the accused to the shire hall with all due haste."

The rangers and Much were watching the conversation avidly, even though it was in French. Maybe because I was trying to decide which Sir I was going to stab with my arrow first. That needed no translation.

Sir James still had hold of my wrist, and I almost missed the subtle tightening of his fingers, like he was trying to tell me something. "You wouldn't want the boy to succumb to a brain fever and die before he can answer the sheriff's questions, would you?"

Oh. The *boy*. I see what you did there.

Guilbert gave him a long, measuring stare. Then he gave me the same. Finally, tight-jawed, he held out one hand with an imperious flick of his fingers. At the motion, his riders all came alert, and I heard the resettling of their weapons. Sir James let go of my wrist, freeing his sword hand. The captain was the only one at ease. He raised that brow, expectant, and I realized I was supposed to turn over the arrow in my hand.

I painfully uncurled my cramped fingers, stiff with cold and tension, and offered my surrender.

Guilbert nudged his horse forward and took the arrow. I stayed still somehow as he reached down with a gloved hand to lift the sodden flop of hair from my forehead and look at the knot on my skull.

"Kicked by a horse, was it?"

"Something like that." I tried to look like I might expire from a brain fever, but without being too obvious about it. It wasn't hard to look faint, though. The horse was big and restless, the captain was armed and . . . intense. So was his inspection.

With a swipe of his thumb, he wiped a track clean on my cheek, frowned, then flicked the river muck away with distaste. "There is the winning argument. I wouldn't inflict your smell on anyone in my command."

What an asshole.

He spoke in English then so the rangers could understand. "On your honor, Sir James, I release this prisoner into your charge, where the boy will appear at the shire hall in Nottingham by dusk today to answer for the charges of trespassing." His tone turned almost droll. "Barring death by horse hoof, of course."

"See you then." Sir James nodded, as unruffled as if he were dismissing the captain instead of the other way around. Guilbert shot him a look, gathered his men with another gesture, and led them away at a canter.

I exhaled fully for the first time in ages, feeling like I'd dodged a bullet. Or maybe . . . I slid a glance toward Sir James . . . like someone had yanked me out of its path.

Then Much crowed in victory and I nearly jumped out of

50

my skin. "That was amazing!" he said. "No one but the sheriff ever tells Sir Henry Guilbert what to do."

That raised a good question. "What is it the sheriff tells him to do?" I asked. "Because I doubt anyone has to tell him to be a jackass."

Much's mouth dropped open, and his eyes popped almost as wide. Then he laughed so hard he nearly fell out of the crook of the tree.

"Much," chided Sir James. Then to me, in the same tone, "Try not to corrupt him, if you please."

I wasn't sure he was joking, so I shut up. Much got serious—sort of—and answered my question. "He's the deputy sheriff, and chief forester of Sherwood. Take anything from the king's forest, and you better stay clear of the captain and his rangers, or it'll be your peril. Can you really put an arrow anywhere you want?"

"What?" He'd asked the question without a bit of transition, and I still had *Sherwood freaking Forest* and *OMG sheriff of Nottingham* reverberating in my skull. Now that I was coming off the adrenaline high, a pulse throbbed in the knot on my head. "Yes. I can."

So I wasn't totally unequipped for the—what, twelfth century?

God. I looked around and found a rock I could sit on before I fell down.

I was on the cusp of believing something unbelievable. All this time, the infinitesimal details had been filling up my subconscious like an underground spring until denial seemed more foolish than acceptance.

Just because something isn't proven doesn't mean it's not possible.

Okay, Dad. *I accept the premise that I'm in the past, or maybe some parallel or pocket universe.* So, what did that mean? If I wasn't lying unconscious in the caves under the castle, had I physically disappeared in my own time? Traveled here through some dark portal? How would I get back?

Oh my God. *"Can* I get back?"

"Back where?"

I looked up, surprised I'd spoken out loud, and found the knight watching me with concern, and more than a little bit of curiosity.

"Home." I stood up, relieved to find my legs steady, more or less. "I'm, um, not from here."

"You don't say." He went to his horse and pulled a bundle of cloth from his saddlebag, as well as the leather canteen from his saddle. On his way back to me, he handed the bigger bundle to Much and wet a smaller cloth from the canteen. "You aren't French, with that accent." I winced as he dabbed the blood from my forehead. Before I could protest, he took my chin, wiped the mud from my face, then turned my head for inspection. "You're not from the east, despite the flecks of caramel the sun has left on your cheeks."

The color of my cheeks was now actually bright pink. I was only human and he was a *knight in freaking armor* who had *literally* ridden to my rescue. I should be allowed a blush without turning in my feminist card.

"I'm from west of here," I said.

He looked dubious. "I suppose if you were Welsh, that would explain your terrible accent."

"Farther west than that."

Much gawped like I'd grown another head. "Never say you're *Irish*."

Sir James laughed. He sounded a little rusty at it, but genuine.

Finally he said, "Let's start from the beginning. I am James Hathaway, knight of the temple, defender of Jerusalem, son of the baron of Huntingdon, recently returned from the Holy Land." He rattled all that off very casually, and didn't seem to expect me to comment or curtsy or anything. He gestured to the boy and said, "Of course, you've met Much."

The boy touched his forehead as if tugging an invisible cap, and grinned.

"Much what?" I asked. A lame joke, but I'd had a rough day.

"Much the miller's son," he answered, missing the humor entirely. Or maybe it wasn't a pun in his version of English.

"And you?" the knight prompted. "What do we call you?"

"Eleanor." The sun had shifted from over the clearing, and the full shade, combined with my wet clothes, sapped my body heat. I folded my arms to keep the rest of it in. "Eleanor Hudson, but people call me Ellie."

"Fitting," said James, with a too-straight face. "Famously, the lady of Aquitaine is *also* not fond of doing as she's told."

"I'm named after her." Which was true. Mom had won the coin toss. Eleanor of Aquitaine was married to the English king Henry the ... Second, I think. Besides being the wife of two kings—not at the same time, obviously—and the mother of several more, she also ruled her own land in France,

53

went on a Crusade, and spent a lot of time under house arrest because she wouldn't do whatever her husband said. Basically, she was a pistol, and not a bad person to be named after.

Much's caterpillar brows wrinkled in confusion. "But . . . Eleanor is a girl's name."

"Well spotted," James congratulated him, taking the cloth bundle.

The mental cogs slowly turned, and Much's face lit up with realization. "So there *is* no boy to take to the sheriff in Nottingham. That's brilliant, um, Mistress Hudson."

"Ellie, please," I said.

"That's brilliant, Mistress Ellie!"

James didn't point out that it was his idea. "The question is, what do we do with you now?"

I had no idea, but as grateful as I was for his help, I wasn't sure I wanted him to answer the question for me. "Who says *you* have to do anything with me?"

"*I* said it," he answered, shaking the bundle loose. "In front of God, Guilbert, and everyone." The cloth turned out to be a worn and faded black cloak, which he draped around my shoulders.

"I'm filthy," I protested, because accepting the cloak seemed to be accepting too much—his help, his protection, or maybe just the fact that I needed it.

"This has seen worse." James wrapped the cloak around me with practiced efficiency, arranging the folds so my arms were free. The fabric was soft and warm and smelled of leather and damp wool and, faintly, of incense and desert spices, as if the man's recent history was woven into its threads. "There. I was chilled just looking at you."

"Thanks." I glanced up and offered the best smile I could muster. It was more of an apologetic grimace. He'd been beyond helpful, and I hadn't been overwhelming with my gratitude. "For everything."

"You are welcome." James gave the fabric a final adjustment and stepped back. The air seemed a little cooler when he did, and I was glad for the cloak. "Well, Mistress Hudson?" he asked. "Do you become a lady again and allow the sheriff's trespasser to vanish from the world?"

Good question. What next? The logical thing would be to retrace my steps, which meant going back to the castle, then *under* it. But after all his trouble to keep me out of the dungeon, it seemed ungrateful to turn around and go straight there. Also, as much as I wasn't really a planner, under the circumstances I could use to regroup and assess my position.

"I have no women's clothes." It wasn't my biggest obstacle, but I was starting small.

"I have sisters!" Much exclaimed. He had two settings— silent and observant, or bursting with enthusiasm. "They have clothes."

This seemed like as good a place to start as any. A bath, clean clothes, a new identity, and I'd be able to sort out what was happening and how to fix it.

James rubbed his jaw. I wasn't sure when I'd mentally dropped the "sir." Probably about the time he was inspecting my face for freckles. "Better we stay out of Nottingham town until Master Hudson is back to being a mistress."

"Helena lives in Mapperley," Much said, undeterred. "We can go through the greenwood to get there."

"I thought you said the greenwood was full of cutthroats and thieves?" said James.

"Usually," said Much, not sounding worried.

"Wait, cutthroats?" I interjected, worried enough for both of us.

Much went on like he hadn't heard me. "But the sheriff hanged some, and that always makes them lie low for a bit. And you have your sword. I have my slingshot. And the mistress has . . ."

He trailed off and they both looked at me. "And I have no bow," I complained to the universe.

Much inhaled loudly, the way he did before his exclamations, but James spoke first. "If you *did* have one you would be in worse trouble with Guilbert than you are now. It's illegal to carry a bow and arrow into the king's forest." He anticipated my question. "Because the only thing you'd have call to shoot is one of the king's deer."

"What about a cutthroat?" I asked. "What if I wanted to shoot one of them?"

I'd probably short-circuit before I could override my safety conditioning. It was a rhetorical question, and James treated it like one.

"A good reason not to linger." He stepped to his horse and collected the reins. As Much went after his pony—which had wandered a bit in search of clover—the knight swung smoothly into the saddle, then rode over to me and offered

56

me his hand. It was a long, long way up to the back of the horse.

Well, here goes nothing. I grabbed his hand and he pulled me up behind him. I couldn't believe how effortlessly he lifted me, or how gracelessly I sprawled across the horse's butt. It sidled under us as I tried to get a leg over to the other side. The whole thing was like straddling a sofa made of muscle, six feet off the ground.

Finally I got upright and gingerly took hold of the back of the knight's belt. He grabbed both my hands and put them around his waist, pulling me forward into the space between the back of the saddle and the widest part of the horse's rump. It was more secure, more comfortable, and more awkward. It made me wonder—strictly as a matter of curiosity, him being a knight, and social customs and all—if he'd had other women ride with him this way. It didn't really matter, except I couldn't help thinking they probably smelled a lot better, even in the Middle Ages.

"Hold on," said James, which I was already doing. He was really solid, even allowing for padding and armor, which I guess was why he could pull me up so easily. I tightened my grip, and he sort of wheezed. "I mean, hold on to the horse with your legs."

"Oh." I knew that. I didn't slack my arms, though, and was glad I hadn't when he kicked the horse into a canter. Much trotted behind on his pony and the three of us were off to Mapperley, and God knew where—or when—that was, or whether we would get there with our throats intact.

CHAPTER SIX

THE PATH THROUGH THE GREENWOOD WAS ABOUT ONE HORSE across, though it widened and narrowed with the terrain. There were some hills and gullies, and at least one outcropping that would make a good place for an ambush, but nothing happened except for a fox bursting out of the underbrush, startling me so much I nearly fell off the horse.

"Don't worry," Much assured me. "The bandits are much worse north on the highway, where it goes through Thieves' Wood."

I couldn't imagine how *that* got its name. "Do cutthroats really ..." I drew my finger across my neck in the universal sign for dead-as-a-doornail.

"As often as not," chattered Much. "The men, anyway. The women, they—"

"Much." James snapped off that branch of unpleasantness. The boy didn't seem to take it personally.

I wondered if the hanged men outside the castle gate were the thieves Much had said were caught and executed. Even so, leaving them there seemed . . . well, medieval.

"Whose head was on the spike?" I asked.

Much didn't have to ask which head. I took that as a good thing. "Sir Aethelstan, baron of Leas."

I had loosened my hold on James as the ride got smoother, but I still felt him tense up, though he didn't turn around.

"What did he do?" I asked, since James didn't. Maybe he already knew. He'd said that he was newly back in the area, but he seemed pretty savvy about the general situation.

Much was happy to gossip about poor Sir Aethelstan. "Well, he was *executed* for treason," he said. "But mostly it was because he was Anglo-Saxon."

"Is that important?"

"Not now that he's dead."

I twisted more fully around so I could see if Much was being sarcastic. He was not.

James spoke without turning. "You certainly ask a lot of questions."

That was because I *had* a lot of questions. "I don't want to break any more laws I don't know about."

My answer must have satisfied him, because he filled me in on the baron. "It's important that he was convicted of treason, because his family loses the title and the land."

"Let me guess." After all, I'd seen this movie—and all the other ones like it. "Now the sheriff of Nottingham gets it."

"No, it goes back to the crown. But the sheriff can appoint a loyal Norman to manage it and collect the taxes."

"Convenient."

Much piped up with "That's why Sir James is—"

What Sir James was would remain a mystery, because the knight interrupted, pointing out, "There's Mapperley."

I knew he was changing the subject, but I didn't care because I was so ready to be off the horse. Summer-camp trail rides had not prepared me for staying on the back of a freaking warhorse on a rutted track through the woods with nothing but my thighs to keep me from sliding off like a pat of butter on a hot ear of corn.

Well, there was James, but I had to let him breathe occasionally.

I had a loose grip on him as the track emerged from the woods at the bottom of sloping open fields. I could see a cluster of thatch-roofed cottages and the stone tower of a Norman-era church about midway up. Slightly uphill from that was a larger house made of timber. The high-rent district, I guessed.

"How many people live here?" I asked.

Much counted on his fingers and came up with "About threescore, I'll bet." About sixty people, I translated. "My sister married the baker. She always makes the best pies. It's not market day, but maybe she'll have some anyway."

He kicked his pony into a trot and went around us, heading up the track that ran between the divided fields. I tried not to groan as James spurred his horse to follow. I was aching in areas I didn't even know could ache.

I distracted myself by taking in the lay of the land. I didn't know much about agriculture, other than what I had picked up by osmosis, growing up in Indiana. It was obviously spring—like it had been when I'd woken up that morning—but there were far fewer rows of tender green sprouts than empty stretches of umber soil, when it should be the reverse.

The grassy meadow to the west was sparsely dotted with sheep, and the livestock pens weren't exactly bustling, either. There were people in the fields, doing ... field things. As we rode by, some stopped work to lean on a hoe or a rake, but all of them watched with curiosity and suspicion. Mostly suspicion.

That feeling of fallowness continued into the village. The only children playing were toddlers too young to work at planting. A few skinny chickens scratched for bugs in the lane. Housewives hung out their wash, and quickly called their kids in when they saw us at the edge of town. Mapperley was not a place full of pies and happiness.

James looked at me over his shoulder. "Put up the hood on that cloak, and *don't* speak. This is not the welcoming Mapperley that I remember."

Much and I exchanged a look at James's expense. I wasn't the one with the performance SUV of a horse, armed and emblazoned with God's insignia. The knight really had no idea how conspicuous he was.

On the other hand, I was a wanted, um, man. I pulled the hood up to cover my filthy hair and shadow my face, which probably only looked sketchier.

"Is this normal?" I asked Much. "The empty livestock

pens and barns?" The village itself wasn't shabby, but I'd expected more . . . bucolic bounty, I guess.

"Those that can't pay their taxes in money have to pay in kind," he said. "Wool or goats or chickens. Grain and herbs." Much wrinkled his nose. "The king is welcome to my beets."

James reined in where the lane split off at a large oak tree. "Much, perhaps you'd better go ahead of us and warn your sister of company. Come find us here, if she's agreeable to helping."

"She will be," Much answered with certainty.

"Do it anyway," said the knight. "Better not to surprise a village so wary of strangers."

"Yes, sir," said Much. He slapped the reins over his pony's rump and headed toward the other side of the village green.

The "here" where we would wait was the village church. Following the turnoff took us down a grassy path that ran in front of an oak-shaded churchyard. In the middle of the yard was a stone chapel—the nave with its tiny arched windows and pitched slate roof abutting the square tower I'd seen while riding in. On the far side was a graveyard set off by a low stone wall and dotted with daffodils lit up by the slant of the afternoon sun.

Someday they would sell picture postcards of whatever was left of the chapel and people would make charcoal rubbings of the gravestones' inscriptions. Today the headstones were pale and straight, and the dark patina of age had barely begun to touch the church walls. There was also a pig snoring under the oak tree.

"What's the matter?" asked James, sounding genuinely

concerned. He was waiting for me to get off the horse, but I hadn't moved.

"Nothing," I not quite lied. "I just keep forgetting how far from home I am."

He gave me a quick, studying look, and then swung me down from the horse. That sounds way more graceful than it was. My legs were rubbery and numb, and I felt like I was walking like a cartoon cowboy.

James's descent was better managed. One thing I hadn't appreciated the first time I saw him dismount was how hard it was to maneuver around all the stuff buckled and tied to the saddle—scabbard, saddlebags . . . some long, wrapped bundle that was too small for a lance. I hadn't investigated during the ride because I'd needed both hands to hold on, but I poked at it curiously while James was turned around. The horse was more attentive and swatted me with its tail.

James straightened his surcoat and his sword belt, then turned back to me. "I intend to talk to the village priest and hopefully draw out how things in Mapperley got to this state. You—"

"I know, I know." I raised my hands in surrender. "Don't speak."

One corner of his mouth turned up in what passed for a smile. "I was going to say, you can find the rain barrel and wash your face and hands if you want." He held out a lump of something he'd taken from one of the saddlebags. I accepted it warily. "Don't waste it. I brought that all the way from Constantinople, and once it's gone, it's soft soap from then on."

The fist-sized chunk was hard like modern soap and

smelled of herbs and sandalwood. Like James's neck, actually. I might have gotten close enough to catch the scent while we were on the horse. Not on purpose. Well, not on purpose the first time.

That's what I was thinking about when a short, skinny priest came from behind the chapel, with a rake in one hand and a spade in the other. He wore a brown habit and sandals, his shiny bald head ringed by gray hair. He stopped suddenly when he saw us.

"What are you doing here?" he demanded, dropping the rake and brandishing the spade like a weapon. "Go away! There's nothing for you here. Our tithe has gone to the cathedral in York and the sheriff has taken everything else."

"I haven't asked for anything," James said, sounding more bewildered than upset. The horse, though, gave a snort and a stamp, and James startled me by handing me the reins so he could intercept the red-faced man advancing on us with his garden implement. "What's this all about?"

"I know your kind." The priest stopped with the point of the spade at the Templar cross on James's chest. "Always ready to take and take for your holy war. Glory for the Church, glory for England, empty pockets for the people."

"Careful, Father," said James. I thought for a moment he was objecting to the tirade, but then he reached out to steady the man, whose anger had left him gasping and shaking. "Come sit over here."

He led the priest toward a wooden bench under the oak tree and near the pig. As he went, he told me over his shoulder, "Right saddlebag."

I untied the flap and rifled around until I found the only thing he could mean—a leather bottle, carefully stoppered.

The horse followed me over to the bench, where I handed the bottle to James, who then offered it to the old priest. "Take some of this. It will help."

The priest took a swig, coughed, and wiped his eyes. "That would bring Lazarus back to his feet." The color returned to his cheeks, and he sat up straighter. In fact, he looked a little embarrassed at his outburst. "I beg your pardon, my lord. I was overwrought and spoke without thinking."

"You needn't apologize," said James.

"I've just this morning buried a woman whose blood was too thin to survive childbed. Her husband turned to poaching to provide hearty meals for her, but the chief forester found him out and now the man is outlawed until he can pay his fine." The priest took a smaller sip from the bottle, then gave James and me both a rueful look. "When I saw your sword and armor I simply . . ."

"Snapped," I provided, when he faltered for a word. Snap was what I wanted to do to Captain Guilbert's neck right now. Practically taking food out of a pregnant woman's mouth *and* taking her husband away?

"Indeed," agreed the priest. He handed the bottle back to James and, for the first time, seemed to actually see us, curiosity sharpening his expression. "I am Father Anselm," he said, half information, half broad hint.

James began the introductions with himself, Sir James et cetera, et cetera, and then gestured to me. "And this is—"

"Robert," I said, cutting him off. "Robert Hudson."

James gave me a questioning look, and I shrugged. I just didn't feel like going through the whole dressed-like-a-boy, farther-west-than-Wales thing again. I wanted to stay on point, and I gestured to the priest with my eyes to indicate James should get on with it. Which he did. "I remember Mapperley being a much happier place," he said, putting the stopper back in the bottle.

"Our lord is away at the Crusade." The priest sighed and set the spade on the bench beside him. I glanced at the manor house on the hill over the village. It wasn't just larger but also more substantial: timber and plaster, wider lintel, bigger beams, two stories. There was a yard and outbuildings, too. "Without his protection, Mapperley suffers the worst of the sheriff's tax-collecting zeal. It seems they've taken every hen from the henhouse." Sounding old and tired, the man nodded to the snoring pig. "That's the only sow in the village now. They're going to have to send her out for breeding or there won't be any suckling pigs for the sheriff's men to take next time."

"What about—" James began, and then cut off his own question. "Never mind. You must be tired."

With his hands on his knees, the priest pushed himself up. "But I'm not dead yet, though it may seem so to young men like the two of you. Come inside and allow me to make up for my poor welcome with some refreshment."

My stomach growled. Both James and the priest politely ignored it. "Let me tie up the horse," James said, and the priest nodded and went around the other side of the church, picking up the rake along the way.

James turned to me immediately with a question. "Robert?"

"My brother's name." It was the first boy's name to come to mind, and I was used to turning when I heard it. And using Rob's name invoked my brother somehow, like wearing his team jacket to tournaments. But that wasn't what James was really asking. "I didn't feel like explaining . . . everything."

His laugh startled me. It was genuine, but so was his disbelief. "You haven't explained anything, Mistress Eleanor Hudson of West-of-Here. You dropped quite literally out of the sky, you barely speak French *or* English, and what you do say is nonsense. You are either the most helpless creature in England, or the most adept fabulist I've ever met."

A burst of anger burned off the fog that had settled when the adrenaline of my escape wore off. "I am not helpless," I blurted. James's amusement deepened, and I hurried to add, "I'm not a liar, either."

"I believe you." He loosened but didn't drop his folded arms. "But that doesn't say what you actually are."

An anachronism. A fish out of water. *An archer without a bow.*

I sighed the last one aloud, feeling so sorry for myself I almost missed the reflexive flick of James's gaze to his saddle. I didn't turn around, but I pictured that mysterious bundle that was too short for a spear or a lance, too thin for a sword . . .

I gasped. "You have a bow." I was an idiot. I'd ridden all the way here with it jabbing me in the hip and not realized.

I spun and started poking around the wrappings. "Is it a

longbow? Can I see it? What's it made of? Oh my God, I've never seen anything but reproductions—"

James's hand landed on top of mine, stilling my efforts to unknot the cords that bound the weapon tight.

"That belonged to a fallen comrade." He stood behind me, not touching anything except for my hand, but I could feel the vibration of his voice from the back of my neck to the crook of my knees. "He carried that all the way from his native Wales, and I brought it home because I couldn't bring him."

I spread my fingers over the cords like an apology. "I'm sorry," I said, without turning around. I'd crossed a line, and it made a heavy lump in my throat. "That was rude of me."

James let that sink in silently. Satisfied I wasn't going to rip into the binding like a wrapped present, he stepped back. "You were carried away by enthusiasm. All is forgiven."

The comment was wry, but the forgiveness was genuine. I turned to face him, explaining, "I just thought you were keeping it a secret because I'm a girl."

I was starting to get awfully familiar with his "be serious" look. Before he could say anything, though, the sounds of an escalating ruckus reached us from farther into the village.

Father Anselm marched out from the chapel door. "Do I hear soldiers in the village or have I gone completely mad?"

That was it—horses stamping and gruff voices shouting. I couldn't understand a word; I just knew it sounded like trouble. There was a crash—something being overturned or a door being kicked in—and then the wail of a frightened child.

James moved fast, taking me by the shoulders and lifting me away from his horse so he could swing into the saddle without kicking me. I was staring up at him before I knew what had happened. "Stay here," he ordered, in a voice that was used to obedience.

Had the past few hours taught him nothing about me?

The priest pulled me farther out of the way as James spurred his horse toward the muddy lane we rode in on. Father Anselm pointed across the graveyard. "We can cut through this way." After about twenty feet, he waved me on. "Don't wait for me, boy."

I took him at his word and ran between the headstones and wooden crosses. There was a low stone wall on the other side, easily hurdled, and then another side lane. On foot I could make a straight line behind the huts and houses that faced the village green.

The villagers were mostly clustered around their front doors, trying to stay out of the way of Nottingham's soldiers. No one noticed me, but I easily recognized the colors of the tunics from the castle. These weren't Guilbert's rangers. The men on horseback pulled on the reins and turned clumsily, while those on the ground hulked around, shouting and shoving. This was the chorus I'd come in on.

I found Much standing between a mounted soldier and the open door of what I guessed was his sister's house. There was a girl my age in the doorway, with a toddler clutching her skirts. It looked like the soldier was going to have to go through the scrawny miller's son to get to his sister and niece.

In the middle of all this, James cantered into the village green. "Stand down," he ordered. "Harm anyone here and you will answer for it." The way he said it, I totally believed that the hand of the Almighty would come down and smite any offenders on the spot, and some of the soldiers looked really nervous, like they were thinking the same thing. But James was one and they were a dozen.

The soldier in front of Much yanked his horse around to face the knight. "We are charged with the pursuit of a knave wanted for trespassing, vandalism, and unprovoked assault on the castle guards."

Those lying bastards.

"We have the full authority of the reeve of Nottingham to search all dwellings and outbuildings." The soldier turned his attention back to Much. "So move aside, boy, or we'll run you over."

All this just for being somewhere I shouldn't have? That was insane.

Much didn't budge. His little niece was wailing. The village looked like a tornado had gone through it. All the clean linens hung to bleach in the sun had been trampled into the mud. A horse's ass had knocked over a vegetable cart full of what little the villagers had to eat.

The sergeant posted horsemen in front of James, and his foot soldiers rushed at Much, picking him up and moving him out of the way. Another reached for his sister in the doorway. I didn't wait to see what would happen next.

"Stop!" I shouted, pushing out from behind two female villagers. It would have been much more impressive if I hadn't gotten tangled up in the cloak I still wore. I flailed my hands free and said again, "Wait. I'm the one you want. Leave these people alone."

Everything came to a screeching halt. I think even the baby stopped crying. No one had expected surrender. Least of all me.

CHAPTER SEVEN

A<small>LL THAT, AND</small> I'<small>D ENDED UP BACK WHERE</small> I <small>STARTED, ONLY FAR</small> worse off.

The guard at the city gate waved the soldiers through. Nottingham town wasn't walled, but the only bridges over the hell river were guarded, and the castle was protected on one side by the drop of the cliff. The legitimate approach involved a steady uphill course through the streets of the town, toward the gate towers I recognized.

The townspeople mostly stopped what they were doing to watch us go by, although some fell in behind, following us. As we neared the castle bridge, Much turned his head to tell me, "Don't worry. Sir James will be there to stand up for us."

"I'm not worried," I lied as we passed under the hanged

men and the iron portcullis. Sir Aethelstan stared sightlessly through milky, dead eyes.

I told myself I'd be okay. No one could prove I'd done anything wrong because I hadn't. I would remain free, and I would figure out how to get home, and then I would go to the tournament and shoot the best medal round of my life and come out of this whole experience with a medal and story I could never, ever tell anyone.

In the castle bailey, the soldiers stopped in front of the timber steps that led up to the central keep. I let them drag me off the pony, and didn't protest until they led Much away in a different direction. "Hey!" I yelled, craning my neck to see where they were taking him. "Where are you—"

A soldier's big hand shoved me between the shoulder blades. I stumbled and, with my hands tied, I braced for impact with the ground, but someone caught me easily and set me back on my feet. I opened one of my squeezed-shut eyes and looked up into the inscrutable face of Captain Sir Henry Guilbert.

"I did warn you the soldiers would be rough," he said.

Jackass. "Is this torture in Nottingham? Having to listen to Captain Guilbert say 'I told you so'?" My body ached, I had new bruises on my arms and shoulders, and my wrists were rubbed raw. But all I could think was that this guy's job was basically to take food out of the mouths of mothers and babies, and I let contempt curl my lip. "I thought you were supposed to be eating dinner."

He raised his brows. "And I thought you were supposed to be dying of a brain fever."

Before I could say anything stupid—or stupider—James shouldered through the guards to my side, stopping when he saw Guilbert. They looked at each other over my head and the captain tsked. "I thought better of you, James."

He was not having it. "And I thought better of you. This is not the Nottingham I remember."

Everything droll vanished from the captain's face. "You've been gone a long time." His gaze flicked to me. "And I *did* tell you so, *boy*. Don't blame me that you didn't listen."

He turned away and I inhaled to get the last word, but James stopped me with one steely-eyed glance. I pressed my lips together. He gave me a "that's better" look and settled his sword. "The sheriff has blood in his eye. If you won't allow me to speak for you, then at least say as little as possible," he said.

I shivered and looked around the muddy courtyard. The townspeople who'd followed us to the castle jockeyed with each other for a good view of me and the knight. There were guards behind me, and Guilbert stood a little in front, all facing the raised stone ... well, I'd have called it a terrace if it had been a fancy house and not a big stone tower, so instead I went with "dais." On it was a backless chair ... and some disturbingly dark stains. I'd seen this movie, too, and it usually ended with some lord from the north with his head cut off.

"This is crazy," I said. "All *this* for a ... a trespasser?"

"It isn't that you got in. It's that you got out." James stood to my immediate left, speaking low for my ears only—like he was a lawyer, except one wearing armor and a sword. "The castle belongs to Prince John. The sheriff keeps it for him, and you made him look foolish and unprepared. Your ballad-worthy escape will not reflect well on him."

The noise from the crowd shifted as two guards came onto the platform, and then the man I remembered from my arrival, the one with the fancy velvet tunic trimmed in fur. He was the only person in the courtyard not muddy to the knees. Medium brown hair, medium height, medium build, neither really young nor really old—he was distinct because of the meanness in the pinch of his thin lips and the calculating look in his narrowed eyes.

A herald in front of the dais said, "Attend the reeve of Nottingham!"

The sheriff swept over to the backless chair and sat on it like a judge's bench . . . or a throne. The guy had a sense of his own importance and a sense of drama, too. He gestured to the herald who swiftly ordered, "Boy, give your name."

It took me a second to realize he meant me. God, my mouth was dry. "Robert Hudson."

"Robert, son of Hood," the herald intoned, "you are here to answer to the charges of trespassing, espionage, and attack on a soldier of the crown."

"*Espionage?*" The charges had escalated to absurd. I wanted to ask what kind of medieval crack he was smoking, but James murmured, "Careful, Eleanor," in my ear. With superhuman effort, I reeled myself back in. "I wasn't . . . Just let me explain."

"Your Honor," James prompted.

75

"Your Honor, let me explain," I repeated, then started my refrain. "I was confused and lost . . ."

His Honor the sheriff waved me silent. "I will save time, since the day grows long," he said. "The only explanation for your actions is that you are a spy."

My mouth opened but only a strangled sound came out. James straightened, and a wave of excitement rose from the attentive townsfolk, but the sheriff spoke over it. "You were discovered coming from the understructure of the castle. Then, rather than be caught, you attempted to commit suicide by casting yourself from the castle bridge."

"What?" I caught myself before I laughed, because it wasn't funny. It just became worse and worse as the accusation rolled around in my head, gaining momentum. How did you disprove a complete logical fallacy? "Where is the evidence? You can't just *say* I'm a traitor."

The sheriff tsked. "Babbling madness again. A trial by ordeal will prove your guilt."

A hot-cold wave of nausea swept over me. "What is that?" I whispered, looking up at James. He didn't look at me, which meant it was bad.

"Your Honor," James said, sounding like he'd just been biding his time until now and was ready to unroll that long list of titles I couldn't remember. "I question the call for any trial beyond this hearing. As Sir Henry will attest, my companion voluntarily agreed to present himself to answer to the charges. Hardly the act of a guilty person."

Guilbert shot James a suspicious look as soon as he used his title, and his expression didn't lighten after being put on

76

the spot. But he turned to the sheriff and said, "That is true, my lord."

The sheriff, however, had reddened at the word "question," and he snapped at the soldier on the dais with him, "And where was he apprehended?"

"Evading arrest in a village on the road to York, my lord," said the guy, like I had done something to him personally.

"Hardly the act of an innocent man," said the sheriff, complacent again. "Captain Guilbert, you will secure the accused in the dungeon until all is ready for the ordeal by water."

"What does that mean?" I grabbed James's arm, just to stop the feeling that I was being swept downriver and tumbled over the rocks all over again. "Is it like waterboarding?"

James kept his outward calm, but he was pissed. No, outraged. He had to unclench his jaw before speaking. "It means the accused is weighted and lowered into a pond, where God will judge his innocence."

"You mean if I drown, I'm guilty?" For half a second I could breathe again, until the full sentence assembled itself in my brain. "Hang on. *Weighted?* Like, with weights on?"

James put up a quieting hand. "Calm down. Let me just—"

I didn't let him finish. Guilbert had come up on my other side like he was actually going to escort me to the dungeon. "*You've* done this," I said.

He remained cold, but his jaw shifted like he wanted to say more than "It's the law."

"What is wrong with you people?" I couldn't wrap my head around how much trouble I was in, which somehow made it easier to reject this decidedly no-win scenario. "What about a trial by jury?" I asked James.

"Only if the sheriff grants it," he said, then glanced at Guilbert before lowering his voice. "There's only one way to avoid this. You need to ask His Honor—*respectfully*—for a trial by combat."

"Trial by combat?" I hissed. "Are you nuts?"

"Were my instructions somehow unclear, Captain Guilbert?" asked the sheriff. He looked at the sergeant, who looked at his soldiers, but before he could order them forward, Guilbert gestured for two of his rangers to back him up, and I looked covetously at their bows. Not that I could shoot my way out of the castle, but when you have one particular skill—

Like a magician's rope trick, the snarl of my panicked thoughts pulled straight. Suddenly I had the clarity of the firing line and something almost like a plan.

"Your Honor," I said, "if I can't have a trial by jury, I want a trial by combat."

There was a collective sort of inhale, and then the courtyard was full of sound—laughter from the soldiers, exclamations from the townsfolk. Guilbert let out a curse, and the sheriff pursed his lips and narrowed his eyes. Beside me, all business, James took his gloves from where they were tucked into his belt and started to put them on.

"Now, listen," he said in that low, quick voice. "I have not seen Guilbert fight in years. I'm not absolutely sure I can best him. If I can't . . ."

"What are you talking about?" I figured it out before I finished the question. "You think I want you to fight for me?"

His look didn't allow for argument. "Regardless of what you want, this is what has to happen."

That was not my plan, and when I glanced at the sheriff, I could see from his sulky scowl that it wasn't his, either. Only my ignominious end would save face as far as he was concerned.

Guilbert wasn't nuts about James's idea, either. "Are you certain you want to take this course, James?"

James raised a brow in a good parody of Guilbert's favorite expression. "Are you saying you'd rather cross swords with this . . ." I thought he was going to say *fille,* but he went with ". . . fledgling?"

Guilbert's answer was spoken through his teeth and exceeded my vocabulary of French curse words. They were talking over my head, in voices not pitched for the public. Another glance at the sheriff showed him getting impatient as well as annoyed. My plan relied pretty heavily on his mood, so I took my chance. Raising my voice, as if I'd been part of the discussion all along, I called out, "Whoa. No. *Anything* but that."

James and Guilbert shut up, with weirdly similar expressions. James stared at me, baffled, and Guilbert looked worried I might be contagious. I stepped past both men and addressed the suddenly attentive sheriff. "Your Honor, please allow Sir James to stand champion for me. Don't make me do as the captain wants and compete with a bow and arrow against one of his men. I've heard how good the rangers of Sherwood Forest are."

"What's this?" asked the sheriff, sitting straighter as he noted the murmurs from the crowd.

"My lord," said Guilbert, his confusion sliding into suspicion, "I am not certain that this idea is—"

The sheriff snapped, "You don't have to be certain, Captain. You merely have to do what I command." He eyed me, calculating. "How do I know you would not be a challenge against even Guilbert's best shot?"

"It's just that . . . that . . ." I looked around desperately for a clue how to finish the sentence. I landed on James, and prayed he really would be my champion and come up with some divine inspiration right about now.

"It's just that . . . ," James began, looking at me like he was still fitting puzzle pieces together. "Sir Henry insists that Rob here shoot the bow that . . ."

He threw the lifeline and I grabbed it. "That Sir James brought back from the Holy Land!" I said, a little too excited. I tried to turn it to indignation. "Have you seen that thing? It's massive."

"Much too big for someone his size," said James, gesturing to me.

Guilbert stared at us like James had caught my crazy, which was fair and true. "Your Honor," he said to the sheriff in a reasonable tone that was about to ruin everything. "I don't know what—"

"I won't do it," I said over him. "You can't make me."

Finally. I saw the flash in the sheriff's beady eye. "You

won't?" he echoed. "It's not for you to say what you will or won't do."

"Massive!" I repeated, holding my bound hands as far apart as I could to punctuate this fish story.

"Let me see this monster bow," His Honor commanded.

James gave me a dark look, but he whistled, his horse obediently ambled over, and he untied the bow from his saddle, unwrapping it as he took it to the sheriff and handed it up without comment.

I held my breath, scared I'd blow the whole con, worried it was totally obvious how much I wanted to get my hands on that instrument. The sheriff weighed the length of smooth yew in one gauntleted hand, but I could tell he didn't know what he was looking for. He handed it to the commander of his soldiers, who examined the bowstring attached to one end, then flexed the wood experimentally. The commander looked at me, sort of snorted, and said, "This is too much of a bow for him. It would be a contest just to string it."

"Set up a target!" ordered the sheriff, and half the courtyard sprang into motion.

Holy crap. That actually *worked*.

I wiped a cold sweat from my face with my cloaked arm, ready for James to lay into me because my plan was possibly as insane as diving off the castle bridge. When he closed the distance between us, though, all he said was "Are you unwell?"

"Of course I'm not *well*," I whispered. My thighs trembled like I'd run the stadium bleachers. Twice. "But at least I'm not tied to a rock and praying for a miracle at the bottom of a pond."

Taking hold of my wrists, James deftly cut me free with his knife. "I wouldn't have let that happen," he said, leaving out that he *had,* after all, volunteered to champion me.

I rubbed the circulation back into my hands and looked up apologetically. "We made a pretty good team, though," I offered.

He slanted me a look that might have been amused if it wasn't so disapproving. "I cannot decide if you are madly reckless or simply much craftier than I first thought."

Was that a compliment or a criticism? "I'm not crafty. I'm just ... desperate." And he didn't know the half of it. I was stuck in the Middle Ages, and I'd just taken my strategy from a cartoon rabbit. That gambit had been one part reading the sheriff correctly, and nine parts dumb luck.

Two soldiers came to herd me away from James. "You should find Much," I called before we were too far apart.

"You should worry about yourself," he answered before I lost track of him.

The soldiers led me to one end of the court, where the crowd had been cleared so I'd have a lane to shoot in. Captain Guilbert waited for me with the longbow and a cold black stare. "You are a lucky fool, Master Hudson. For your sake, I hope you are the archer that you say you are."

I gave him my Iron Ellie game face. "I seriously doubt you care one way or the other."

He didn't deny it, just handed me the bow. "If you can't string that thing, this is going to be a short trial."

Oh my God, *finally.* The longbow was a thing of beauty as well as function, a smoothly polished curve, the striations in the wood like artwork. The yew—the best wood for a longbow—had been cut so the sapwood was on the outside and the heartwood on the inner bend, giving it flexibility and strength. Unstrung, it came to my shoulder.

I ran the bowstring between my fingers, checking for any fray or wear, ensuring it was secure over one end of the bow. I placed that end on my foot and leaned my hip into the curve of the wood, using my weight rather than my arms to bend it. A six-foot longbow could have a hundred-pound draw weight, and though this bow wasn't nearly that heavy, I couldn't have strung it by brute force. An archer would know the trick of it, but the sheriff wasn't an archer.

I slipped the other loop of the bowstring into its notch, then grabbed the bow at the center, feeling the balance. The grip was wrapped in leather, dark from the oils of an archer's hand. The hand of James's friend.

One of Guilbert's rangers handed me a quiver with only three arrows. I assumed I'd be shooting against him, but he offered a surprisingly genuine "Good luck" and stepped back.

A straight-up target shoot? The sheriff wouldn't make it that easy, no matter how impossible I had made the longbow sound. I cast around and found him on the dais. He wore a smile, and I felt sick before I even knew why.

I looked for the target. At the far end of the court, I saw Much, his hands still tied in front of him like mine had been, with thin cord that cut into his wrists. It took me a moment to realize he wasn't just standing there—he was bound to a post directly down range from me.

A roar started in my head, and it wasn't the cheer of a

crowd. Everything had faded away but the sheriff, Much, and the solider who carefully placed a turnip on the boy's head.

"Are you *kidding me*?"

"The jest is over." The sheriff of Nottingham stood to pronounce his sentence. "Here is your trial: shoot the target, and you are free to go. Miss three times, and await a traitor's fate in the Nottingham dungeon. Shoot the boy . . ." He preened with his own cleverness. "Well then, I'll let you live, and the boy's body will hang over the castle gate as a warning of what happens when someone tries to make a fool of the law."

CHAPTER EIGHT

⮐⮐

THE GROUND SEEMED TO LIFT UNDER ME LIKE AN OCEAN SWELL. The only reason I stayed on my feet was Much and his expression—equal parts fear and trust. He shouldn't trust me. Look what I'd done to him.

I didn't have to find Much's family. I could hear a woman crying, and the commotion of contained protest. I wasn't surprised when James shouldered past the guards and into the firing lane. "Sheriff, I object. The miller's son isn't on trial."

"Ah, but he is," said the sheriff. "Inciting a disturbance in . . . it doesn't matter what village." He was really enjoying this, and it was getting on my nerves. "The accused had best get on with it or the sun will be setting in his eyes."

I hadn't missed that. Part of me was already noticing things like the angle of the sun and the thirty feet to the post,

85

with a downward angle of about five to eight degrees. The turnip—securely set in Much's wild thatch of hair like a golf ball on an overgrown green—was as big as my fist, bigger than the bull's-eye on a standard tournament target.

Without quite planning to, I took the three arrows from the quiver. Iron bodkin points, gray goose feather fletches, straight and well balanced, but heavier than I was used to. Figure in the unfamiliar bow and the fact that I would have to break a lifetime of safety conditioning.

"Can you do it?" asked James. I hadn't seen him come to my side. He searched my face for the answer, and his voice was level but taut, as if stretched between the choice of saving Much or saving me.

That was my question to answer.

I handed all my incapacitating emotions over to Iron Ellie, letting her hold them for me so they wouldn't get in the way. I stuck two of the arrows, point down, into the ground, within easy reach. "Relax. Easy as pie," I lied.

James stepped back, hands in a defensive "I was only asking" position.

The third arrow I laid across the bow and nocked as I checked downrange, my eye on a second wood post beside Much, with a ten-point-sized knot in the grain. Excellent.

The shaft of the arrow lay in the V formed by the bow and my knuckle. My competition bow had an arrow rest, stabilizers, vibration dampeners . . . everything short of a cup holder.

The unfamiliar weapon should have been awkward, but a funny sort of calm settled over me as I lifted the bow and drew it in one smooth motion, my left arm pushing out, the right pulling back, my core tight, keeping everything steady. The full draw came exactly to the corner of my mouth, as if the bow had been made for me. With my eye on the target, I savored the burn of effort between my shoulder blades, the pinch of the string on the pads of my fingers before I loosed the arrow. I finally felt a little bit at home.

The shaft flew true but slightly high, just above the knot I'd been aiming for. Much jumped, and the turnip rolled off his head. The spectators erupted into excited noise, but I only heard the roar in my head.

"The first arrow is a miss!" His Honor the sheriff announced. The nearest soldier put the turnip back on Much's head.

James accused me quietly. "That was no miss."

I grabbed the next arrow from where it was stuck in the ground. "That was a practice shot." The arrow had stuck a few finger widths above where I'd wanted it to go. And it stuck *deep*. If that had been someone's head, it would have impaled it like a melon.

Guilbert lurked in my peripheral vision. "If you wanted to simply lay your head on the executioner's block, you could have saved us all a lot of trouble," he said, sounding bored, or faking it well.

James asked suddenly, "How many practice shots do you plan to take?"

"As many as required." Three shots would free Much. I wasn't a martyr, I just couldn't think of a better idea. As I readied the next arrow, I whispered, "You better rescue me before my head comes off."

I drew and loosed. The point embedded itself directly below the knot; I'd adjusted my elevation a bit too far.

"By God!" shouted the sheriff, coming out of his chair, his face red with anger. "You will not make a mockery of the law. Guilbert, cut that archer's throat if he deliberately misses again."

The sound of steel on leather erupted all around me. James drew his sword in a swift move to defend me, but just as quickly the guards had weapons ready to skewer him, me, Much, and God knew who else. Then I could hear nothing but the drum of my heart in my chest as Guilbert's blade came to rest gently on my shoulder, the edge against the side of my neck, so sharp it felt more like ice than steel.

"You have no more road on which to run, archer," he said. "Aim and fire."

In that measured, word-by-word command, I didn't just hear a threat. I heard Dad saying, "Focus." I heard Mom chiding, "Don't stall, Eleanor." And, louder than them both, Rob telling me, "You've got this."

I made shots harder than this just for a warm-up. I knew the weapon now, had a feel for the arc of the wooden arrows and their iron tips, had tasted the weight of the draw in my muscles.

Guilbert lifted his sword off my shoulder as I bent and plucked the last arrow from the ground, and laid it across the bow shaft. My fingers brushed the fletching as I fit the nock to the string. No fiberglass or Kevlar, just wood and hemp and goose feather. But the familiar action struck like flint in my cold, tight chest, igniting a steadying warmth.

"Much?" I called across the forty paces between us.

"Yeah?" he called back, both scared and trusting.

"Don't move." I wiped the salt of sweat from my face onto my cloaked shoulder and put my eye on the target. Then I raised the bow.

Drew the string.

And loosed.

It split the turnip like a kebab and kept going. The crowd of villagers went wild. Much opened his eyes, realized it was over, and sagged against the ropes that bound him. Over it all I heard Guilbert shout, "Release the boy and retrieve that arrow!"

James put a hand on my shoulder and squeezed, then ran to Much, elbowing the sheriff's soldier aside to cut the boy free himself.

I stayed where I was. I didn't feel triumphant. I felt sick.

"Not celebrating?" asked Guilbert. His sword had already gone back in its scabbard.

"I made the shot. But I did what the sheriff wanted."

Guilbert folded his arms and looked implacable. "He *wanted* you to kill your friend. I suggest you take your victory and leave Nottingham while you can."

A soldier handed the arrow with the turnip on it to the sheriff, who gestured for me to come stand before the platform. I did, with the shadow of Guilbert beside me.

"Robert, son of Hood," announced His Honor as he held the turnip kebab up like he was going to knight me with it, "you are found innocent, and you are free to be on your way." With that, he dismissed me and tossed the spitted vegetable to a soldier. "Feed that to the pigs."

The sheriff stalked off, his cloak swinging a little less majestically behind him. I turned and found Guilbert frowning at my throat. I reached up, in case I had a horrible medieval spider on me or something. But no. Maybe he was just feeling homicidal.

"Keep out of the forest with that bow," he warned by way of goodbye. About fifty feet away, he stopped to address two of his men, gesturing to me, nodding toward the gatehouse, and looking back to make sure I got the message.

Right. Do not pass Go. Or, in this case, anywhere on the grounds of the castle.

Or, more to the point, under the castle.

From where I stood, despite the milling, gawking Nottingham folk and the castle people getting back to work, I could see from the terraced courtyard down into the stable yard. The arch I'd come through was visible, as was the heavy wooden door, propped open with a cask. I couldn't see deep into the passage, but I remembered how it had looked—dank, wide, lined with barrels and crates—and nothing contradicted that.

Not even my gut instinct. I was certain, in a way that was as inexplicable as traveling through time, that the way back, at least *that* way back, was closed.

My head was full of white noise that pulsed with the throb in my temples. I felt stretched tight and brittle, and when Much slammed into me and nearly squeezed out all the air in my lungs, I couldn't believe I didn't shatter.

"That was amazing!" he said when he let go. "That arrow nearly parted my hair. What a shot!"

My stomach turned, even though Much's wild hair clearly hadn't been parted for a while. "I'm sorry, I couldn't think of anything else to do."

"I know!"

"I could have *killed* you!"

"I know!" he crowed. "That was *amazing!*"

The closed door to home had opened another, to the place where I'd been shoving all my outrage and fear, all my catastrophic, apocalyptic freak-out. "Oh my God, Much, that's not okay! No one should be forced to do that."

The frayed cords holding me together began to snap, fiber by fiber, under the strain of not completely losing my shit. I was yelling, and people were staring, and they should, because I'd shot an arrow at a *kid* to save my own skin.

Suddenly James was there, wrapping me in one arm and whisking me away from the center of attention. He turned so that he and his big Templar cloak with its big Templar cross hid me from view. "Calm yourself," he said.

"Calm myself?" Now that I'd popped the top on my outrage, it just kept bubbling out like a shaken soda. "It's not okay that the sheriff can just say something is true and not have to prove it. It's not okay that you can drown someone in a pond, or raise taxes until people have no food to eat. What about jurisprudence? What about no taxation without representation? It's not okay that everyone thinks that's normal!"

James said nothing until I finished flailing against my helplessness, and then he waited a little longer, studying me while I wound down. "Are you wellborn?" he asked finally, as if nothing but curious. "You seem very educated, even if your ideas are . . . far-fetched."

"My parents are scholars," I confessed, subdued.

"Ah," he said, but he might as well have said *That explains a lot.*

Maybe it did. My dad the physicist could theorize how I had somehow looped backward on the string of my own space-time continuum and landed in the Middle Ages, or in some pocket parallel universe. Mom might have a clue about the who, what, and where of this flea-infested, tyrant-ruled, plague-ridden *pit* of the past. But it was up to me to figure out the *why* of it.

"Both of them?" James asked.

"What?" I'd forgotten what we were talking about.

"*Both* of your parents are scholars?"

Oh yeah. Women's lib was about a million years away. By now there didn't seem any point in lying, at least to him. Least of all about this. "Yes."

He gave me another one of those studying looks. "What an interesting place your land must be." Thankfully, he dropped the subject. "We should go. I believe we can make Northgate Priory by sundown. I did promise to see that your injuries were treated."

"Right." That seemed like a long time ago. "What *is* a priory, anyway?"

"A convent with a prioress instead of an abbess."

Well, of course. Silly me. I would have nodded except it hurt my head.

James continued. "Much and I are headed to Rufford Abbey, but we cannot reach it by nightfall. Northgate is close."

"I vote for close."

That amused him for some reason, and he turned, calling to Much to find his pony and join us. I got ready to unstring the longbow but couldn't resist drawing it one more time, now that life and death weren't at stake.

It was really too short for an authentic Ye Olde English Longbow, but it was perfect for me. I couldn't have chosen a better length. I glanced at James, who was a head taller than me, and long in the arm. "This is too short for you."

He got that slightly guarded look I'd noticed only happened when he talked about the Crusade. It was subtle, but consistent. War sucks on all sides in all centuries.

"David had no family, so his belongings were dispersed among his brothers-in-arms," he said after a pause. "I'm not sure why I kept it."

"Because he was your friend. What other reason do you need? Here." I held it out to him, biting back my reluctance.

He covered my hand with his and pushed the bow back to me. "Take it. You're right, it's too short for me, and I'm not an archer. Maybe it was meant for you."

Meant for me.

If that was true, then maybe this was not an accident. Maybe I was here for a reason.

In all my worry about what the past could do to me, it hadn't occurred to me that *I* might affect *it*. Maybe there was something that needed setting straight—that's what always happened to time travelers in fiction, right? Either that or they screwed something up and then had to fix it.

How did I know which it was? What if I'd already screwed something up?

"Eleanor?" said James, sounding worried. "What is it?"

Only the possible total annihilation of history.

I wanted to tell him. Maybe my gut said he would have advice, or maybe I just wanted to share the burden. But what if that was the thing that screwed stuff up? It was safer to just say, "It's nothing."

He surprised me by putting a hand on my cheek. It was cool, and callused from the reins and the sword. It felt good, no lie. "You don't look well. I think the sooner we get to the priory, the better."

I shook my head, and wouldn't admit even to myself how dizzy it made me. "You've been more than kind, Sir James, but I can't. Look at the danger and the trouble I've already caused."

James looked at me soberly. More soberly than usual. "Mistress Hudson . . . May I call you Eleanor?"

Was he serious? "You've been calling me that most of the day."

He actually blushed. He had a deep tan, but not so deep I couldn't tell. "My apologies. It's been an unusual circumstance."

"You mean it's not like this all the time?"

That got a smile out of him. "Perhaps it is. I've been away a long while." The smile didn't completely fade, despite his return to business. "Eleanor, when you threw yourself into that river, Providence threw you into our path. If you are determined to cast yourself on the goodwill of strangers, it might as well be us."

"When I say my situation is complicated . . . ," I ventured, in the biggest understatement of at least eight centuries, "I mean *really* complicated."

James raised a brow. "You do not tell me anything I haven't guessed already."

"Oh, I doubt that," I muttered.

He decided to play hardball. "Do you know anyone in Nottingham? Do you have any money? Where will you stay? Where will you go?"

I squirmed, because he was right. Everything I'd carried was at the bottom of Hell River. At least losing my iPhone meant one less thing to possibly alter the course of history.

James took the edge of my cloak that had fallen open and tucked it back around me. "Keep your secrets, then, but allow me to take you someplace safe."

"All right." I relented. I supposed there was no sense seizing the reins of a horse if I didn't know which way to steer it. "A priory is as good a place as any to figure out what I'm going to do next."

"Good," he said, shifting back to business. "Let's collect Much and be off, before the sheriff thinks of something new to charge you with." With that cheerful thought, James gathered the reins of his horse, swung into the saddle, and held out his hand to me. I timed my jump to his pulling me up, and got my leg over the horse's rump first try. The altitude shift, though, made everything spin, and I grabbed James, closing my eyes and pressing my face into his cloak until I was sure I wasn't going to fall over.

He didn't turn, but covered my hand at his waist with one of his own. "Are you settled?"

"Yeah. I'm just tired." Morning had been centuries ago.

His fingers tightened on mine as he turned the horse toward the gate. "You can rest at the priory."

I'd asked the universe for a lot today, but I sent up one more prayer: *Please don't let the place be too far.*

CHAPTER NINE

I WOKE UP KNOWING I WAS IN A HOSPITAL BUT WITH NO CLUE what I was doing there. Then I moved my head. God, I must have one hell of a concussion, because I'd had the weirdest dream about church bells and ministering angels.

When I pried open my gritty eyelids, a round and feminine face hovered in the haze of my fever and splitting headache. When the owner of the face saw my eyes focus, she smiled. "There you are. Welcome back."

"What day is it?" I croaked, my voice as unoiled as the Tin Woodsman. "Did I miss the competition final?"

The nurse—she was wearing some kind of white hat— reached for a cup on the bedside table. The contents smelled herbal and pungent; not pleasant, exactly, but reassuringly medicinal. "Don't worry about that now," she said. "Can you take a bit of drink, do you think?"

Could a drowning man use a breath of air? The nurse helped me lift my head and tipped a bare sip of something wet and sweet past my lips. Bliss.

"Do you know where you are?" she asked.

"Nottingham," I said, and fell back onto a mattress so thin that it scarcely merited the name. The National Health Service really needed to upgrade.

"What's your name?"

"Eleanor Hudson." I let my heavy eyelids close. I was shivering, but the nurse's hand on my cheek felt cool. "My driver's license and passport are in my satchel."

There was a brief, consulting murmur of two voices, then the first spoke again. "Very good, Eleanor. Now, who is on the throne of England?"

Why did they keep asking me things when I just wanted to sleep? "Elizabeth," I said. "The second."

A snort from the other side of my bed. *"La folie."*

"Shh, Clothilde. *Elle a de la fièvre délirante."*

I opened one eye and squinted the bedside nurse into view. Her headwear was not a white nurse's cap but rather a wimple and veil. Of course it was. My last clear memory was of agreeing to go with Sir James to the priory of . . . what was it again? Everything after that was a blur of muscle-wracking chills and sweat-drenched fever. When I shivered, someone piled on warm blankets, and when I sweated, they soothed my face and the back of my neck with something cool and wet.

"Try again, Eleanor," said the nun. Her cheeks were pink

and her blue eyes full of intelligence and humor. "And then you can tell me what a driver's license might be."

Who *was* the king? I wasn't sure that would be a fair question even if I didn't feel like I'd been dragged down five miles of bad road. "Is it Richard the Lionheart?"

The second nun stood at the end of the cot, arms folded. "The Lionheart," she scoffed. The room was dimly lit, but I think she rolled her eyes. "Not that his backside has graced the throne long enough to warm it."

"Sister Clothilde," chided the nice one. She leaned over and dabbed at my face with a cloth that smelled of rosemary. "All shall be well, Eleanor. You have a fever and must rest."

Like I had a choice. "I *told* Sir James that I was going to die of some horrible medieval disease."

She laughed. "You are not going to die. We will take good care of you."

"No bloodletting," I insisted, with my last bit of energy.

The older nun loomed over the cot. "We'll do what's best for you, and you'll be grateful."

The young nun covered my hands with hers. "Don't let her frighten you. We don't hold with bloodletting here."

"Or leeches," I said.

"Well, sometimes leeches."

Oh God. They were going to put leeches on me and I was sure I had fleas and the only way I knew back home was closed and though I'd had every inoculation in the world, I was going to die for lack of a tube of Neosporin.

I didn't fall unconscious so much as pass out from the awfulness of it all.

· · ·

When I woke again, I found myself in a tiny room lit by diffuse daylight, with the fading notes of a chapel bell drifting in the casement window. The first thing I did was check myself all over for leeches, then sighed in relief. I was alone, remarkably clearheaded, absolutely ravenous, and reassuringly free of bloodsuckers.

I was wearing a loose linen nightshirt. It was clean, and so was I, pretty much. The ache of fever was gone, but I had plenty of bruises from my adventures. Gingerly I reached up and felt around on my head. The lump was covered with a thick, stiff bandage; when I poked it, there was a sharp smell of sulfur and herbs.

I looked around the room. No clothes, and no place where they might be. Also, no bow. I felt around in the cot, but the bow wasn't there, either. The mattress was too thin to hide anything beneath it.

James probably had it with him for safekeeping. That was logical. I should not be panicking. I should not be nearly so attached to something that I'd owned for—what, less than twenty-four hours?

Except that as soon as I had the bow in my hands, I felt like the Ellie I'd been before all of this madness began. It was the only thing that home and *here* had in common—me and a bow. It was my anchor across eight hundred years.

I was working myself up into a state, as Mom would say. Dad would recommend—what else—to focus on my goal. I had to get home. I had no idea how I was going to do that, but you don't hit a bull's-eye without going through all the steps that come before you loose the arrow.

Purposefully, I swung my legs off the cot and stood up—

Then almost jumped back into bed again. The floor was *freezing*. The cold raced up my legs like the stone had flash-cooled my blood.

Hopping from foot to foot, I wrapped the blanket from the cot around myself. There was no fireplace, so I shivered my way to the little brazier nearby and stoked the coals. Then I went to the window to get my bearings.

The casement was more than a foot deep. In the distance, just a few miles away, was Nottingham castle, high on its cliff, with the town clustered around the base. The land between the priory and the castle was mostly wooded.

And basically everything around was Sherwood Forest. Much had made it sound like a cross between a national park and a royal game preserve. Also, I thought it would be all . . . forest. The highway, such as it was, appeared here and there, and I could see clearings in the trees that must have been villages like Mapperley. There were also larger cleared areas—for planting or pasture was my guess.

To see the convent grounds I had to lean on the casement and peer out the window. To my right was the chapel. That one was obvious. To my left was a collection of smaller buildings, mostly timber and plaster with thatched roofs. I could see a large garden, but not much beyond that without leaning out dangerously far. Circling the courtyard, the chapel, and the garden was a wall, tall enough to deter trespassers but not to stop anyone really determined. The gate was open, and at it stood a line of four or five families, some pulling small wagons, some carrying baskets.

The door swung open behind me, and I whirled around guiltily. Why I felt guilty, I didn't know. Maybe it was a conditioned response to an angry nun standing with one hand on the latch, the other balancing a tray on her hip, and a face like Nemesis herself.

"What are you doing out of bed?" demanded Sister Clothilde. I hadn't seen her clearly the night before, but I recognized her voice. "If you're so anxious to pop your clogs, I'll thank you to swim in the river of someone else's parish."

"Sorry," I said quickly, steadying myself with a hand on the wall. Apparently I wasn't quite up to whirling yet. "I just wanted to see where I was."

"And where are you?" she asked, with the same forbidding expression.

"Still a long way from home."

"Oh, poor wee lamb," she said, without any sympathy. "Now get back in that cot."

I hurried to do as she ordered, as if the speed of my obedience would lessen my sin. Sister Clothilde gave me a steely look as she came to the bedside and placed her tray down with a thump that rattled the pottery bowls and thick glass jars. I kept a wary eye out for leeches.

"Who are those people lined up at the gate?" I asked.

"Once a week we give alms to the poor." Sister Clothilde felt my cheeks and listened to my chest, harrumphing as she rearranged the blanket over me.

"Alms? You mean money?"

"Do we look like a treasury?" Back to poking and prodding, she elaborated, "We have little, but there are many in the shire with even less, thanks to His Honor the sheriff. We have grain for bread, goats for milk, and a garden for vegetables, which we can share. Some of the poor are sick, and are *properly* grateful for our care."

"I am grateful," I assured her.

"Hmph," she said, untying the linen dressing on my forehead and peeling off the dried poultice. For all her grumping, she turned my head gently toward the sunlight for inspection.

"How does it look?" I asked, scrubbing my fingers through my hair where the bandage had matted it.

Sister Clothilde raised an eyebrow. "Are you worried about a disfiguring scar?"

That wasn't my *first* concern. "I mean, is the infection gone?" Open wound plus open sewer meant open season on my immune system.

Her look had been acerbic before. Now it was practically caustic. "Do you wish to prescribe your own treatment? Perhaps my twoscore years of experience in the medicinal arts are insufficient for you?"

"No, ma'am," I said meekly.

"That's what I thought." She put the dressing in a basin, then wet another bandage with a potion from a glass bottle and daubed my forehead with it.

"What's that?" At my question, Sister Clothilde glared, and I quieted as she continued her work.

"The suppuration has greatly diminished," she told me, grudgingly. "I will put another poultice on it to ensure all the corruption has been drawn out. I trust this is acceptable to you?"

"Yes, ma'am." I was in favor of anything that prevented corruption or suppuration. I didn't even know what those were, exactly, but I knew I didn't want them.

I knew what I did want, though, and so did my stomach, which growled loudly. "So, I was wondering about my stuff. My clothes and my bow?"

She gave a snort. "Clothing? Is that what you call it? Breeches so tight we had to peel them off like skin from a rabbit?"

If that shocked her, I didn't want to know what she thought of my underwear. Even I considered an underwire bra to be an instrument of the devil.

"It was in no condition to wear," she concluded, and lifted her tray of potions to balance again on her hip. "Isabel will be in shortly with some barley tea for you. You may ask her about your *belongings.*"

My stomach was as unsatisfied by this answer as I was, and I sighed. "I don't suppose there's any chance of a nice English breakfast. Bacon and eggs? Grilled tomato? Beans on toast?"

She rolled her eyes. "This isn't a royal palace, your worship. And even if it were, it would still be gruel for breakfast until you've got your strength back."

I wanted to argue that I did have my strength back, but I realized how ungrateful I'd sounded. Especially I thought about the line of people at the priory gate.

"I really do appreciate all your help, Sister. You've taken excellent care of me when you'd no obligation to."

"We've the obligation of Christian charity and the example of our Lord," she said briskly. "And if we helped only those who could pay, we'd have nothing but an empty infirmary and a lot to answer for in the hereafter."

I found myself grinning without meaning to. Sister Clothilde glared. "What's so funny, girl?"

You. The way her wimple framed her face made her look like a grumpy Persian cat. But I couldn't say that.

"Nothing," I answered, with what I hoped was a straighter face.

"Hmph." Tray still hitched on her hip, she headed to the door. "We'll see about that."

As she went out, she met someone coming in. The room was so small, I had no trouble hearing what they said just outside the door.

"How is the patient?" I recognized the voice of the *nice* nun from the previous night.

"Stubborn," said Sister Clothilde. "And full of questions. I'll leave that for you to sort out."

"Sort out" was *sort of* ambiguous. Maybe even a little menacing, except that they were nuns. Or especially because they were nuns. It had been following a friar that had led me into this mess. Good grief, a lot had happened since then.

The pink-cheeked nun—Isabel, I assumed—came in right after that. In the daylight she looked barely older than me. "You seem to be feeling better," she observed with a friendly smile as she put a small tray of her own on the table next to the cot.

"I am." I sat up, cross-legged and facing sideways so I didn't feel like an invalid. "Especially since I woke up with no leeches."

"We're only a poor convent. We can't afford to call a surgeon for bleeding every fever. But Sister Clothilde has the gift of herbs and tinctures, and she's teaching me."

I did remember we'd been headed for a priory, aka convent, but that didn't exactly narrow things down. Mom said that in the Middle Ages you couldn't spit without hitting a monastery. "So, where am I, exactly?"

"The priory of Saint Mary," she said. "Though usually people call us Northgate Priory because we're the first one on the road north from Nottingham." She placed the palm of her hand over her heart and made a tiny, graceful bow, just a dip of her head and one shoulder, the formality offset by a friendly smile. "I am Isabel." Then she handed me a pottery mug. "And this is for you, Eleanor. Drink up."

I took the cup from her, but eyed the cloudy liquid with suspicion. "What is it?"

"A tincture of willow bark in barley water."

That didn't sound like anything that would kill me, but the cautiousness of my first sip made the nun laugh.

"You leapt into the river, evaded the chief forester and his rangers, dared the sheriff to give you a trial by combat, yet take barley water as if it might be poisoned?"

The drink was slightly lemony and sweet, but the memory was sour. "You heard about that?"

"Everyone in Nottinghamshire has heard about the hooded knave who escaped the sheriff's best men." There was subversive amusement in her eyes. "Much the miller's son relayed the tale to us all. He's half besotted with you, which makes the telling all the more amusing."

I winced. "Everyone in Nottingham?"

She let her grin out. "'The Tale of the Turnip' is halfway to Huntingdon by now."

The Tale of the Turnip. Very droll. Less funny was how pissed the sheriff was going to be with most of the shire laughing at him. And notoriety wasn't going to make it easier to stay inconspicuous while I found my way home.

Isabel watched my expressions with what seemed like benign curiosity. "James told us very little about you, Eleanor, other than that we should maintain the ruse that you are a young man, if you wish."

"Thank you." My conscience pinched me again. "I'm grateful for your care. Especially since helping me isn't going to make you friends with the sheriff or the chief deputy park ranger."

She waved a hand. "The priory has its own problems with the sheriff. And as for his deputy, the chief forester ..." She corrected his title, but then gave a dismissive little shrug. "Henry, I don't worry about."

Time-out. She'd just called Captain Sir Henry Guilbert by his first name. And, I realized, she had *also* called James by his Christian name. I knew the guys had known each other growing up. It didn't take a genius to guess that Isabel probably had, too, especially since she seemed about the same age.

I gave her a closer look as she alit on the stool by the cot. Though her habit was made of simple brown wool, her posture was graceful and her hands lay lightly clasped in her lap; she looked like a figure in a tapestry.

"So, what's your deal, Sister Isabel?"

"My what?" she asked with a surprised laugh.

I had *not* meant to say that aloud, but since it was out there, I decided to satisfy my curiosity. "How did you come to be a nun?"

Her sigh fluttered the edges of her veil. "It's not an unusual story. All my close male relatives are dead or gone to fight the Crusade, so I am a ward of Prince John. He said I had the choice to marry one of his fawning courtiers or go to a nunnery. I picked the nunnery."

Isabel was smart and pretty, and not just by medieval standards. She also had great skin and straight teeth, and her figure was softly rounded and, um, womanly. It sounded like her family had money or land, too.

"That's absurd," I said. "You should be able to marry whoever you want."

I meant it in the sense that she should have her pick of suitors, not in a feminist way. Though, also I meant that.

She just laughed. "*You* think a woman could rule England."

"Well, one *could*." She would have certainly heard of my namesake. "What about Eleanor of Aquitaine?"

Isabel looked surprised, then chagrined, and then intrigued. "What do *you* know of the duchess of Aquitaine?"

Now what? I couldn't say that she was one of the wealthiest and most powerful women in Western Europe at the end of the twelfth century, because that sounded like a history book. And I didn't know what would be general knowledge in whatever year I was in. No CNN in the eleven hundreds.

Something broad and obvious, then. "She rules a duchy in France." Isabel raised her brows in a silent "go on." "She's the mother of King Richard. And Prince John, who is running things here while Richard is off fighting in the Crusade and what all."

Those two offspring were safe to mention, because they were English kings. Richard had a legend of his own built up about him, like the Lionheart thing that didn't fly with Clothilde last night. And Prince John became King John who signed the Magna Carta, which was the first document that laid out rules for what the government can and cannot make you do. Apparently, John was the kind of ruler who made people want to get limits in writing.

But that was enough of that. I didn't want to know too much, and I certainly didn't want to tell Isabel too much. So, I changed the subject. "Do you like living in a convent?"

She blinked at the sudden turn, but she rolled with it. "I like being apprenticed to Sister Clothilde, which gives me freedom, and I enjoy being useful." Then she sighed. "If it weren't for getting up in the middle of the night to pray at matins, I would probably like it very well. Alas, God did not make me suited to a life of piety and poverty."

We shared a smile over that. I liked her, and nothing in her curiosity seemed malicious. If she knew James well enough to call him James, then he must know her well enough to trust her. Or he had before he left for the Holy Land.

"Where *is* James?" I asked, as the question occurred to me.

She didn't question my train of thought. "The prioress sent him on to conduct his business at Rufford Abbey." She pressed her lips together over a smile. "He was distracting the novices."

I pictured a trail of nuns-in-training following a clueless Sir James around like baby ducks. Isabel went on, "We sent word as soon as your fever broke. He'll come around soon."

Wait . . . allowing for travel times, and time at each end . . . "How long have I been here?"

"Two nights and a day," Isabel answered, collecting the tray. "Sister Clothilde is pleased you're recovering so well."

I'd been out of it for *thirty-six hours*? Plus the day of the trial? I'd been here—this century—two full days and then some. This was bad.

"I need my clothes," I said, flinging back the scratchy wool blanket and jumping out of the cot. The floor had not gotten any warmer since I'd last stood on it. "Oh my *God*, that is like *ice!*"

Isabel's brows climbed almost to her wimple, and then came back down. "It will feel a lot colder if you faint on it. You should be in bed," she scolded.

I should be a lot of things. I should be dominating the medal round of the international archery championships. I should be driving Mom and Dad crazy making Snottingham and "it's not rocket science" jokes. I should be hanging in the

Trip to Old Jerusalem with Rob, telling him about the weird-est dream there ever was.

I meant to ask "Where are my clothes?" but what came out was "Where's my bow?" My subconscious knew what I needed to feel better, at least. Isabel blinked in surprise or confusion. "The longbow I had with me when I got here. Did James take it with him? I need it."

"Why?" she asked, alarmed.

So I didn't feel so powerless. What a stupid question. What I was going to *do* with it . . . that was *not* a stupid question, and probably what she actually meant.

Iron Ellie must still have been down for the count, be-cause I couldn't find any grace under pressure as I cast about for an answer. My stomach growled and gave me one.

"I know about that whole 'don't hunt the king's deer' law. But I could hunt some, um, partridges or something to help out." I gestured to the window, indicating the line of families at the gate for alms. "Help with feeding the poor and all."

Isabel didn't balk at the suggestion except to say, "Par-tridges are also against the law." She tapped her chin with a finger. "But some pigeons, maybe some rabbit, would not go to waste."

I wasn't sure I could shoot a bunny, but I glossed over that. "It would make me feel like I was paying you back for taking care of me for—" Suddenly, incredibly, I yawned. "Two nights and a day."

Isabel put her hands on my shoulders and steered me back to the cot. "You owe us nothing. And in any case, that can wait until you've rested some more."

"I've rested too much already," I protested. Then I yawned again, and because I wasn't totally stupid, I shot her a look of betrayal. "You drugged me."

"I did nothing," she said, too innocently.

"Clothilde," I accused. "I *knew* not to trust that tea. And you taunted me into drinking it."

"It wasn't difficult." Isabel gently pushed me horizontal and threw the blanket over my bare legs. She didn't say anything about my red-white-and-blue pedicure. "Now, sleep."

I had no intention of sleeping, but I pretended to while she went to the door. I had plans. Okay, well, I had plans to make plans, as soon as she left. . . . Then I would get up. . . .

A loud noise startled me awake.

I coughed on my dry throat and realized I'd woken myself with my own snoring—and hours later, at that, judging by the movement of the square of light from the window. That . . . *Clothilde.*

Someone had brought more wood for the brazier, and another cup of barley tea. Like I would fall for that again. What I didn't see were shoes, clothes, or a longbow.

If Clothilde or Isabel thought that keeping my clothes would keep me in bed, they had grossly overestimated my modesty. I'd walk through Nottingham naked if it would get me home.

CHAPTER TEN

THE CHAPEL BELL BEGAN TO TOLL. FROM OUTSIDE MY ROOM came the sound of a door opening and closing, and then another. I got out of the cot and went to investigate. I could easily spy through the large gap between my door and the frame. At first I saw nothing but the opposite wall. Then a nun went by. And then another. When I didn't hear any more footsteps, I pulled open my door and peered into the hall.

Apparently this was the dormitory, or whatever they called it in a convent. I was at the end of a hallway with eight doors evenly spaced on each side—my room included. I remembered what Isabel had said about having to go to prayers around the clock and figured the chapel bell had summoned the sisters to do just that.

I trotted the couple of steps to the window and lay on the

casement, wriggling on my belly until my head was past the wall and I could see below and to the side. I was right—the nuns, in their brown habits and linen veils, were headed at a brisk but decorous pace to the chapel.

Any nuns who weren't coming from the dormitory came from the gardens or the outbuildings. I took notice of two women in particular—they were dressed the same as everyone else, but I recognized Isabel's ladylike movements and Clothilde's purposeful way of walking. They'd come from the direction of the fenced garden and were headed to afternoon prayers with their sisters.

Ask and ye shall receive. Everyone would be in the chapel for the next . . . I had no idea how long. But long enough for a quick search for my belongings. I was betting Clothilde or Isabel had my clothes—unless they'd been thrown out or burned, in which case, well, I would deal with that if it came to it. But the longbow I had to find.

I went back to the door of my room, peeked out again, and then headed down the hallway looking for Isabel's quarters.

I checked out tiny room after tiny room. All of them were exactly the same as mine—one narrow bed, one table for a candle and a Bible or prayer book. There were pegs for hanging up a change of habit, and in each room a lone crucifix adorned one whitewashed wall. Maybe one of these rooms was Isabel's, but I didn't think so. She'd said she wasn't suited for a life of piety and poverty.

The last door paid off. Most of the room appeared to be the same as the others—bare walls, pegs for clothing, one plain, sturdy cot. There were two nonstandard items, though—a large wooden chest pushed up against the wall, and a table by the window. No sign of a longbow—it would be hard to miss in the unremarkable room. I lifted the mattress but only discovered that it was stuffed with feathers, not straw. Very sneaky, Isabel. I was pretty sure that was cheating. Underneath the mattress was nothing but crisscrossed rope that supported the bedding. No longbow, no skinny jeans, no sneakers.

The chest was locked, so I went to the table. On it was a box of rolled parchments and a wax tablet for writing notes. A pretty hardwood box with a hinged lid held a stylus and some pens and ink . . . and a small iron key.

I picked the key up and turned to the chest. It was too small to hold my bow, but it might have my clothes. There wasn't any time to debate with my conscience, so I unlocked the trunk and raised the lid on a lady's wardrobe. It was a tidy tumble of color—warm rose and pale blue and leaf green—embroidered in gold thread and bright silk on the softest wool and finest linen and velvet. There was a headpiece made of gold wire and pearls, and a silver circlet for holding a veil.

It all gave me insight into what Isabel's life might have been like before her guardian's ultimatum. Did she take these things out and wish she'd made a different choice, or were they just too nice to get rid of?

Focus, Ellie. Jeez.

I respectfully neatened everything up and closed the chest. Now what?

I could convalesce until Clothilde thought I was recovered enough to be trusted with clothes, let alone a bow. Or I could see where she and Isabel had been coming from when the midafternoon bell rang. Isabel had said she was apprenticed to the older nun in the apothecary. Apothecary meant herbal stuff, so maybe the hut in the center of the garden was more than just a toolshed.

I left Isabel's quarters, closing the door behind me, and headed down the stairs at the end of the corridor. They were fairly narrow, with one turn, and they opened into a largish hall with tables and benches for dining and working. A cross-breeze came through two open doors, and I might have appreciated it if I'd been wearing more than a nightgown. One door led to the courtyard, the front gate, and the chapel, so I took the other one.

It led outside, straight into a yard full of chickens. Well, maybe not *full* of chickens, but a few can seem like a lot when you charge in and ruffle their feathers. I followed a well-beaten path that led past a pen of nanny goats and their frolicking kids. I could see the vegetable garden, and the landscape beyond was green with the fragile foliage of spring.

I ignored the adorable baby goats and turned into the herb garden gate, startling a cat that was stalking something in the long grass by the low split-rail fence. The cat ran off, and I picked my way between planting beds, mindful of splinters and rocks and whatever the cat had been hunting. The air was rich with scent released by the herbs as I brushed by them.

Now that I wasn't leaning out a window, I could see that the hut was more of a cottage. Its door was open, and I quickly slipped inside. Bunches of drying plants hung from the timber beams, something was being distilled over a low fire in a stone oven, and in the middle of the table was a giant mortar and pestle with a partially mashed paste. There were pottery jars and a few brass and copper boxes. This was either the apothecary or a wizard's workshop.

Through a large unshuttered window I could see into the back garden, where my sweater and jeans hung on a clothesline. Score. The window was big enough that I could climb out easily, so I did, and grabbed my clothes from the line. The sweater was even more shapeless than before, its green more olive than hunter. But it was clean, and when I pulled it on over the linen shift all I smelled was a whiff of garden herbs. I pulled on my jeans next. They had turned gray, but they hadn't shrunk. No sign of my underwear, though, so no choice but to go commando.

There was no sign of my sneakers, either. I had just gone back to the window, to look inside, when the front door of the apothecary opened. Without thinking, I dropped flat in the planting bed under the window. Then I spat out a mouthful of mint and realized hiding would just make it harder to explain what I was doing. But before I could get up, a familiar voice said a familiar name. "Isabel, I only just arrived," said James. "I haven't even stabled my horse. Can't this wait?"

"No. I'm too angry with you." She didn't sound angry, just annoyed, the way friends can make you. "You arrive home after how many years away, leave a strange young woman like an orphan baby on the church steps, and ride away without telling me *anything*. About *anything*!"

Orphan on the church steps? Ouch.

"If you mean the matter of which you wrote to me," James said, "I'd just arrived from York and been a little busy."

What other matter? Isabel wrote to him about some problem in Nottingham? Now I couldn't announce myself, or I wouldn't find out what it was.

Wait. What if it was personal? Did I want to find that out? Did I want to find that out like this?

Isabel went on. "You could have told me what the bishop said. Did you discuss the rumors here with him?"

"I did." There was a bearer-of-bad-news pause. "He considers them just that—rumors. And it does seem unbelievably bold that the sheriff would take from the Church's tithe as part of his taxes, no matter how badly he wanted to curry favor with Prince John."

"And what do *you* think?" asked Isabel.

"I think the bishop of York has no wish to interrupt Prince John's revenue, no matter how it's gotten. So I am here to see for myself." There was a pause. James had a habit of collecting his words before he spoke. "You were right. Things are much changed here. All of England is heavily taxed to pay for King Richard's wars, but Nottingham seems to suffer more than most."

It was also taxing to follow this conversation, because they were speaking fast, in unfamiliar French. But the gist seemed to be the sheriff wanted to suck up to Prince John by collecting more taxes than he maybe should, and the bishop also wanted to suck up to the prince by not complaining.

"And your business at Rufford Abbey?"

118

There was a longer pause before James answered. "I discussed a number of things with the prior." And that was clearly all he was going to say about that.

"How does Eleanor fit into all this?" Isabel asked.

Boy, wouldn't I like to ask that question—of the universe, or God, or *whatever* cosmic lightning strike had put me here.

"I don't know how Mistress Hudson fits into things," said James. "I had hoped you might learn something."

"So you didn't take her up because you suspected her of being an agent of France or . . . Stop laughing, James!" It took all my willpower not to peek over the bottom of the window. Isabel lowered her voice. "She might even have been John's spy."

James's silent laughter colored his voice. "Even John wouldn't choose someone so inept at espionage."

My skin grew so hot, the bed of mint beneath me should have crisped. How dare he say I was inept at espionage? I was espionaging that very minute and doing a fine job of it, if I did say so myself.

"Well," said Isabel, "I hope that's true, because I like her."

"You'd like anyone who took the sheriff down a peg."

"True. But she says the most extraordinary things. And look—" I heard rummaging, then Isabel spoke again. "Did you see these? Have you ever seen anything like this before?"

I froze. She'd better not be showing James my bra.

"This is some ingenious footwear," James said, and I relaxed. "These lacings must keep it very secure. And the material is hard but flexible. If you could put foot soldiers in such shoes—"

Dammit. I had only *two* goals besides getting home:

One, don't get killed.

Two, don't change history.

I didn't want this to turn out like some science-fiction story where Victorian London is terrorized by steampunk cyborg clones of Jack the Ripper all because someone had reverse engineered my Converse sneaker in the 1190s.

Time to move. I stood up, framed by the window. I must have looked like I'd appeared from nowhere, judging by their faces. "That's my shoe," I announced with dignity.

"Eleanor!" Isabel blushed, and I could see her trying to remember what she'd said about me.

James, on the other hand, took the second shoe from Isabel's slack fingers without a bit of chagrin and then held both sneakers out to me. "Your slippers, m'lady."

I glared at him. "Is sarcasm a knightly virtue?"

Isabel smothered a laugh. James merely raised his eyebrows, still waiting for me to claim my shoes. I climbed over the window ledge and grabbed them. Only then did I realize what he was wearing. Gone were the armor and surcoat and all that knightly stuff. He was dressed in a brown robe, a cowl over his shoulders, the folds of the hood thrown back. He still wore his boots, but without his knight's spurs. I guessed he was supposed to be a lowly cleric, but nothing had changed about the way he stood or moved, so there was a little bit of a Jedi Knight thing going on.

"Are you in disguise?" I asked, baffled by why he was dressed the way he was, and by how he still looked sort of badass.

"Not precisely." His tone said I wasn't going to get any more explanation than that. He looked me over, and I was sure it wasn't because *I* looked surprisingly badass. "How fares your head?" he asked.

The question spun Isabel's dial from lady to nurse. "What are you *doing* out here?" She came over to the window, took my face in her hands, and pulled my head down so she could check the completely unnecessary bandage. "If you relapse into the fever, Sister Clothilde will kill us both."

"I'm fine." I wriggled from her grasp and glared at her. "And I was fine this morning, before you drugged me."

"Perhaps you were more tired than you thought," she said, with a sassy toss of her wimple and veil.

It occurred to me that both James and Isabel were good at not answering questions. I looked from one to the other. "You two aren't related, are you?"

"No," said James, puzzled. Isabel, though, blushed sunburn-red. I logged that reaction and changed the subject.

"I'm looking for my longbow," I said, making it into an accusation.

"Now?" asked Isabel in disbelief. "Have you a sudden craving for pigeon pie?"

I was so hungry that actually sounded not entirely awful. I mean, it probably tasted like chicken, right?

"Maybe," I said.

Isabel looked at James. Before I could protest that he was not the boss of me, he raised his hands, palms up, and said, "It's hers. If you ever see her shoot, Isabel, you'll know it was meant for her."

"Very well." She went to an overhead shelf and reached up to retrieve the bow. "We weren't hiding it from you, Eleanor. But you're not supposed to be out of bed yet."

She held the bow out to me. It was unstrung, with the bowstring wrapped around the smooth wood so it wouldn't get tangled. My hand closed around the leather grip and a knot inside me loosened. I gave her a heartfelt "Thank you."

"I don't know what you will do for arrows," she said.

I thought about it, then turned to James. "Where is Much? He must know a fletcher."

James actually laughed. "He's probably related to one. He is to everyone else."

"Are you staying in Nottingham, or . . ." I trailed off, leaving room for an answer. When James didn't take the hint, I gestured to his outfit. "I mean, you must be dressed that way for a reason."

"Ah." He seemed surprisingly uncomfortable, and ran one hand over the back of his neck. "I will be nearby. There's a hermitage just at the edge of Mapperley. Much and I will be staying there."

"You're going to be a *hermit?*" I asked. "Sir James the *hermit?* How does that work?"

Isabel's eyebrows had climbed as well. "Yes, Sir James. How does that work? Aren't there lands your father is expecting you to come home and manage?"

James reddened a bit but remained calm and evasive. "I need some time and seclusion to reflect and pray for guidance about my next step, now that I'm home. Father Anselm could use some assistance with repairs on the church. So for the moment I will be Brother James"—he gestured to his robe and cowl—"humble friar."

"Oh." Steepling my fingers, I said melodramatically, "A clever ruse."

James raised one hand in a gesture of innocence. "I said nothing that wasn't true. The roof on the Mapperley chapel is in terrible shape."

"Fine, don't tell me," I said.

He had a knowing sort of half smile when he met my eye, admitting something and nothing at the same time. Fair was fair, said that look. I wasn't telling him my secrets either. "I'll see if Much wants to come over with some hunting blunts later this afternoon. He can show you what's fair game. I don't hold out much hope that he'll keep you out of trouble."

Isabel studied me with her hands on her hips. "If you're determined to be up and out of the sickroom like that," she said, gesturing to my clothes, "then two things you need to know."

"What are they?" I asked, warily.

"One, *you* have to persuade Sister Clothilde not to manacle you to the bed."

I winced. It wasn't the nun's fault she didn't understand my resilient twenty-first-century constitution. But it *was* her fault she was so mean about it. "What's the other thing?"

"You may wish to make a few adjustments to your attire."

I looked down. The shift I was wearing reached my knees, too long for an undershirt. That wasn't what she meant, but it gave me an idea. "Do you have a pair of shears?"

"Here." James pulled a knife from his boot and I indicated

where I wanted to cut, just below the hem of my sweater, about mid-thigh. Rather than giving me the knife, he started the tear himself, then ripped the even-weave fabric in a neat, straight edge.

"Um, thanks." That was efficient. I shouldn't be blushing. I stepped out of the remnant and tore off a six-inch-wide strip long enough to wrap tightly around my chest several times. Isabel watched with one hand covering her mouth, her eyes laughing.

"What is that for?" asked James, and I was glad he didn't know everything.

"Mind your own business." One thing Sir—no, Brother James, humble friar, did not need to know was the details of my medieval sports bra.

CHAPTER ELEVEN

"How can you be such a good archer," asked Much, genuinely baffled, "and such a bad hunter?"

I'd just missed my third shot in a row. It was tough to endure the scorn of a ten-year-old, especially one who'd thought you were the bee's knees a few hours ago. But try to explain in Old English that the yips are a real thing.

I went after the blunt-tipped arrow that had come close enough to ruffle the fluff of a rabbit's tail. Simulated hunting with a feather-covered lure had given me the skills I needed, but not the constitution.

Much had shown up at the priory just as the sisters were finishing Morning Prayer. He had a sister who was a sister—as he put it, with his gap-toothed grin—and their father sent flour from the mill when he could spare it, so Much came and went from the priory regularly enough to be unremarkable. I'd kept to myself, and whatever story Clothilde had told the nuns must have satisfied their curiosity.

Much and I had hiked out into the pasture where the sisters grazed their sheep, when they had sheep. First bird, first shot, I'd brought down a big, fat grouse with an arrow through its neck. The bird dropped from the sky, and by the time Much and I reached it, it had almost stopped flopping around. I couldn't watch as Much finished it off with a merciful wringing of its neck.

"Well done, Ellie!" he'd crowed, and handed me the bloody arrow he'd wrenched from the dead bird's throat.

That had also been the last thing I'd managed to hit all morning. The sack slung over Much's back held the grouse and two rabbits he'd taken out with his slingshot. It was worse than embarrassing.

We took a break to snack on the bread and goat cheese Much had brought with him, and I silently berated myself while Much chattered on about his family. He seemed to be related to all of greater Nottingham and was happy to tell me all about each one of them.

How is this getting you home? The question came in Dad's voice, but no suggestions came with it.

How is it hurting? said the Rob that lived in my head. *These people need food. You can provide it.*

God, he was such a freaking Goody Two-shoes.

Nobody needs *a gold medal.*

Shut up, Mental Rob.

My parents had already lost one child to uncertainty. I had a vision of them sitting in a police station, cardboard cups of tea pressed into their hands by a constable with pitying eyes. Or waiting for days in their hotel room for word about their vanished daughter while the news ran my picture next to Rob's: *Double tragedy strikes American family.*

"What's the matter?"

It took me a moment to realize that a real voice had asked the question. Much watched me with concern.

"Nothing," I lied. He didn't look convinced, so it must have been a really bad attempt. "I'm just missing my family."

He nodded his understanding. "Are they waiting for you at your home?"

"Yes." I pictured Rob there with our parents. "But I don't know how to get there."

Much's laugh rang out like the noon chapel bell echoing over the hill. "How do you not know how to get home?"

I didn't try to explain, just lightened my tone and re-routed the conversation. "I'm hopeless, I guess. I can't even shoot a rabbit."

"You could if you was hungry enough," he pointed out, very pragmatically.

Target panic was not that simple, but Much had a good point. Maybe I just wasn't hungry enough to shoot anything that cute. "All right," I grumbled. I stood and dusted the bread crumbs off my front and the grass off my backside. "Let's try something else. I did better with the bird."

"Okay." Much had adopted my word, and it suited his

agreeable personality. He jumped to his feet and put the sack over his shoulder. "I'll go ahead and see if I can flush some out."

While I nocked arrow number umpteen, Much picked up a stick and high-stepped through the long grass, sweeping the branch through it to scare any birds into flight.

I stood ready, two arrows in hand. When I heard the rustle and coo of a startled covey, I lifted and drew the bow. A small cloud of pigeons broke cover, and I shot like I had something to prove. The first shaft was low, but the second, let off a heartbeat later, took down a plump wood pigeon in a clean hit. The bird dropped fast and hit heavy. It was decidedly dead, thank God.

"Ha!" cried Much, running to where the bird had landed. "What a shot!"

Not really. If I'd hit it with the first arrow, maybe. A miss counted for nothing.

"Is the blunt nearby?" I called, heading toward Much. A hunting blunt is an impact weapon, so the bird and the arrow hadn't necessarily fallen together. Much looked around, and I saw him pick up one arrow. "Did you see where the other went?" I shouted.

He pointed to the trees. "Into the woods."

Nuts. I'd shot the first shaft at nearly a full draw, so until it hit a tree, it was going to keep going a good ways. There was no question of just leaving it. I wouldn't have left behind a cheap arrow, and what Much had handed me that morning—bright-red fletching, straight shafts, and well-balanced tips—were nice. Like, really nice. I slung my longbow over my shoulder and into the woods I went.

"Be careful!" Much shouted, when he saw me set off. "There's robbers in the woods. And the foresters won't be happy to see you either."

I didn't thank him for the reminder.

Stepping into the dappled shadow of Sherwood Forest was like stepping through a curtain to another world. The meadow smelled of warm grass and fresh clover, with the occasional whiff of sheep shit. The woods were cooler, the scent both sweeter and darker—green and woodsy and rich with damp earth and decaying leaves.

The trees weren't so close together here, and I could move purposefully, pretending the woods weren't a little eerie. I caught a glimpse of scarlet, in line with the arrow's flight, so I hurried along a deer path in that direction until I got to a gully—a streambed that, by nature or design, was deep enough to keep sheep in and men out, if not for it being bridged by a thick fallen log.

On the other side stood a giant, twirling my arrow between his fingers as if it were a pencil.

"Lose something, boy?"

I was glad for the gully between us, log bridge or not. He was as broad as an oak and seemed about that tall, and he had a wicked-looking walking staff planted next to him, held with his free hand. Standing slightly behind the giant was another man. He was smaller and younger, and he carried a quiver and a hunting bow. A brace of rabbits was thrown over his shoulder. He was wiry and handsome in a rakish way that suited the jaunty green cap he wore. There was even a red feather stuck into it—the only color the pair wore that didn't blend in with the woods.

So ... they were poachers, then. It didn't totally rule out my throat getting cut, but more likely I'd get shot, or bashed with that staff of the giant's.

"I, um, see you found my arrow," I said, brazening it out. "Thank you."

"You're welcome, m'lord." The man held the arrow out to me with a flourish, inviting—or daring—me to cross the fallen log to get it.

I sensed sarcasm ... and a trap, because I'm an intuitive genius that way. A glance behind me showed no sign of Much. His faith in my self-reliance was both flattering and inconvenient.

Across the bridge, the mismatched pair smiled too-innocent smiles. I had my bow and two hunting blunts. Not much of a prize, or a threat.

"Why don't you just shoot the arrow over?" I suggested.

"What if it stuck in a tree?" said Green Cap. "Or if it went into the stream? Or if I were to accidentally shoot you?"

That was ridiculous, since we were less than twenty feet apart, but I continued the line of reasoning. "You're a good enough shot to poach those rabbits."

Green Cap grinned. "Those coneys? We didn't shoot them. They just dropped dead all on their own."

I didn't even try to sound persuaded. "I'll bet they got a look at your giant friend and died of fright."

"Ha!" said the big man, shaking the branches above him. "I like you, lad." He stuck the arrow into the ground at the end of the log bridge. "There you are, boy. All yours."

He backed off, a grin splitting his dark-red beard. I looked from him to the rakish young man, who doffed his cap and swept one arm forward, inviting me to claim my property.

Well, I had to do something. I needed that arrow back. My gut said the pair were more tricksters than thugs. I had nothing to steal, and I was on my guard. I called it a calculated risk and stepped onto the sturdy tree trunk.

It remained steady and so did I, as long as I didn't look down. The stream running through the gully was shallow and wouldn't do much to break my fall. I turned my feet toes-out, like a tightrope walker, and leaned slightly to the right, since I held the bow on my left.

The red-bearded Gigantor stepped forward and onto the other end of the log, the wood creaking and bowing under his weight. He brought his staff up, slapping it into his left palm so he held it horizontally. I groaned at the flashback to pugil sticks in PE class.

"You said I could get my arrow," I protested indignantly, like that would make him play fair.

His smile widened. "The arrow is free for the taking." He tossed his staff, then caught it. "But the toll for the bridge is that very fine bow you're carrying."

Great. A comedian. I glanced at Green Cap, who just

stood by, bow held across his shoulders, grinning like a fox. "I don't need the arrow that badly," I bluffed.

"I think you do," said the big guy. He spun his staff in front of him, meaning to intimidate me and succeeding. "I think you need to come and take it. And we'll take your bow."

"Here's the thing." I really hoped to talk my way out of this, not least because I didn't want my ass kicked. "The bow was a gift, and I can't give it away."

"You don't say." He didn't look surprised, just gave a horizontal swing of his staff, so I had to jump back and pinwheel my arms to stay upright.

Over on the other bank, Green Cap bestirred himself to speak. "You see, my lad, we've heard tell of you and that bow. Such as how you could split a silver coin at forty paces."

"I could," I said, wondering who *hadn't* heard the Tale of the Turnip. "But that's not what happened. You should get your story straight."

Green Cap said lazily, "The point being, I'm sure you could make a fool of the sheriff with any bow, so why do you need that one?"

"Because it's *mine*," I snapped. Green Cap had his own bow; he only wanted mine to be an ass. I couldn't stand that kind of baloney.

"Why not walk away, then?" the giant taunted, with another swing of his staff.

Now I was just pissed off. "Because I know better than to turn my back on a bully."

"You're smarter than you look, laddie." The giant lunged, his great weight shaking the log. I deflected the thrust of his staff with my bow, gritting my teeth at the clash of wood.

"Knock it off!" I demanded.

"That's what I'm trying to do," he said, with that big grin of his. Then he swept his staff low, trying to knock my feet out from under me. I jumped just in time and stuck the landing by pure luck.

"Hey, jackass," I snapped, when I'd regained my balance. "What did I ever do to you?"

"You bested the sheriff and the chief forester," said Green Cap, his arms looped over his bow where it lay across his shoulders, the fingers of one hand ticking off my offenses. "You consort with Templars. You poach game from the Marian Sisters . . ."

"The who?" I asked, startled by the name.

The giant gave his staff another spin. "The Sisters of Saint Mary at Northgate Priory. Don't you know whose pheasants you're taking, boy?"

"Okay, first of all," I said, keeping a wary eye on him, "I'm hunting pigeons, not pheasants. Second, I'm hunting on their land with their permission, for their kitchen. Not that it's any of your business."

"Anything that makes the lord sheriff wroth *is* our business," said Green Cap.

"Sorry I made your life of crime more difficult," I retorted. "What with the extortion and poaching rabbits in Sherwood Forest and all."

Gigantor gave a pissed-off kind of roar—I barely managed to duck as the big man swung his staff at my head. The unyielding wood came close enough to part my hair.

I popped back up. Dammit, what would Douglas Fairbanks do? The giant jabbed his weapon straight at my middle. Wincing at the thought of damaging my baby, I parried with the bow and knocked the staff to the side. Before I could recover, Gigantor delivered a stinging smack on my thigh. The pain rushed up my leg, my vision went blurry, and, worst of all, I lost my balance and toppled off the log bridge. I was airborne for a split second, then landed in the shallow stream that ran through the gully.

I made a ridiculously huge splash as I hit the shockingly cold water and mud. All the air exploded out of my lungs and I couldn't force any back in, but I held the bow tightly while I tried.

"See if he's still alive," said Green Cap. "And grab the bow."

What kind of asshole steals a person's only weapon while she is flat on her back, soaking wet, and in the middle of a forest known to harbor bandits and cutthroats?

Over the ringing in my ears and my beached-fish gasps I heard great big splashing footsteps wading my way. Gigantor planted the end of his staff beside me and leaned down to take the bow.

I kicked the staff out from under him, then rolled away as he crashed into the stream where I'd just been. The huge man flailed in the foot of icy water, bellowing curses in what I assumed was fluent Anglo-Saxon. I got to my feet, grabbed the quarterstaff from where it had fallen, and, when Gigantor tried to get up, I jabbed him in his barrel chest with the staff, hard enough to knock the air out of him. Payback's a bitch.

Out of the corner of my eye, I saw Green Cap run to the edge of the gully. I spun, trying to sweep his legs out from under him with the staff like some kind of ninja, but I only managed to bang him across the shins. It was enough to make him stumble, and I reached up, grabbed his cowl, and yanked him into the stream along with his pal. He made a significantly smaller splash and knew fewer curses.

I grabbed the arrow and scrambled up the bank. Only then did I turn back, lean my hands on my knees, and wheeze, "You should be kinder to strangers. Here endeth the lesson."

Then I slung the bow over my shoulder and hurried back out of the forest and into the meadow, where Much waited anxiously. "Are you all right?" he asked. "I was getting so worried."

"I'm fine," I said as I squelched past and started the hike back to the priory.

Much had strung the sack of game from the end of the stick he'd used for driving the birds, and when he fell in beside me, it dangled over his shoulder like Huck Finn's handkerchief bundle. "Are you wet *again*?" he asked, wide-eyed.

"Yep."

"What happened?"

The farther I got from the forest, the more I began to enjoy my little moment of victory. I laughed, and it felt as good as a stretch after a long cramped sleep. "I think I just kicked Little John's ass."

CHAPTER TWELVE

NEWS SPREAD THROUGH NOTTINGHAM LIKE SOMETHING SUPER-
natural. That night, the sisters put full pots over the coals to
stew; the following morning, there was an orderly queue of
alms seekers at the priory gate by the time the bell tolled for
Morning Prayer.

I watched from the door of the apothecary as the sisters came from their individual chores, met in the courtyard,
and went into the chapel together. It was very familial, and
made me homesick. I had been away from my folks for ninety
hours, MRT.

"Medieval Relative Time," I explained to the empty
apothecary, but there was no one there to appreciate my cleverness. Much was with James, Isabel was at prayers, and not even
Mental Rob weighed in on it.

Of those ninety hours, I'd been running, shooting, or un-conscious for most of them. And what did I have to show for it? Zilch.

Okay, I had a really nice longbow. But as far as progress toward getting home? Nada, and it wasn't going to come and get me while I was hiding out here.

I went back to the worktable and picked up the leather strips I'd sewn into finger guards last night when I couldn't sleep. The longbow's rough string was murder on the calluses on my right hand, and stitching the leather was a lot more productive than trying to stitch together a return-home plan out of absolutely nothing.

Where to begin? Nottingham Castle was the obvious place, despite Captain Guilbert's dire warning. I had to start somewhere, because in addition to having no clue how to get home, if Hudson Standard Time ran the same as Medieval Relative Time, then I had two parents worried out of their heads and, incidentally, no international championship medal.

No one needs *a gold medal.*

"Dammit, Rob!"

I stalked to the back window, where my poor hoodie had been hung to air out, grabbed the sweater, and yanked it on over my shift. I didn't need to play this game of What Would Rob Do? *He* had chucked a sure shot at an Olympic medal to go off and save the world in a place maybe just as medieval as where I was now. If he were here, he wouldn't start looking for a way back until he'd filled the priory larder, dug wells for all the villages, and maybe constructed a proper sewer system too. The difference was, he'd already done that once, and I couldn't disappear on our parents a second time.

Except this is time travel. You don't know that you won't get back at the moment you left.

"Oh, right." I grabbed my sneakers from where they'd also been airing out on the windowsill. "Because nothing ever goes wrong with *that* plan." It was like Mental Rob had never watched an episode of *Doctor Who,* which made it even more obvious he wasn't Real Rob. "Or I could show up ten years older—or worse, middle-aged. Which is not to mention all the things I could die from here. Plague and pestilence and no running water. And did I mention plague? And that's if the sheriff of freaking Nottingham doesn't hang me."

"Who on earth are you talking to?"

Isabel's question nearly startled the life out of me. I hadn't realized prayers were over. "I was just thinking aloud."

She put on the apron that had been hanging by the unlit fire. "What are you thinking about?"

I spun the stock-answer roulette wheel. "Ending world hunger."

"Starting with Nottingham?" she asked, sounding amused. "There are twice as many poor at our gate today as usual. If this keeps up, you may well have to get over your fear of rabbits."

Dammit, Much, you have a big mouth.

"I'm not *afraid* of rabbits," I grumbled, and sat to put on my shoes. "People are awfully excited about the pigeon pie. I don't know how anyone heard about it so soon."

"How did the Tale of the Turnip reach Dorchester in a day?"

Seriously, it was like Nottingham had a Middle Ages social media network. I think it was called Much the Miller's Son.

I went to the door again, leaning against the jamb to peer out. The sisters had set up a long table—what looked to be planks across sawhorses—and they had big pots and baskets of dark bread. Besides those seeking alms, some people appeared to have brought goods to trade for the sisters' goat cheese and milk. Clothilde was at the dispensary, where I assumed Isabel would be taking the noxious potion she was spooning from a big jar into a smaller jar.

I slipped the leather guards onto the pads of my index and middle fingers, flexing to make sure they weren't too tight. "I have a question," I said.

Isabel faked a look of shock. "A question? From you, Ellie? *Quelle surprise.*"

"Funny. Okay, you grew up near here, right? Are there any, um, stories about places in the woods or the castle where people have, say, gone missing . . . ?"

Her amusement was obvious. "Fairy stories, you mean? How—?"

A new, unwelcome clamor interrupted her. We exchanged a glance. The sound of horses and raised voices and the metallic rattle of weapons could be nothing but bad news. I knew that from Mapperley.

Isabel wiped her hands on her apron and headed for the door. "Stay out of sight. Especially with *that.*" She pointed to the bow I'd picked up automatically. "No need to rub salt in the wound you dealt to Nottingham's pride."

"I'd say it was more of a slap," I said.

"Well, you'd be wrong." She was out the door like a little whirlwind, closing it hard behind her.

Like that would stop me. I hid the longbow, because there would be no blending in while carrying it. The rest of me should do. I'd been getting ready to leave the protection of the priory, so that morning I'd tightly bound my chest. My sweater was tunic-length by now, and I grabbed the leather belt Much had given me and settled it low on my hips, the way James wore his. No way was I giving up my jeans, because pockets hadn't been invented yet. Neither had sneakers. Luckily, mine were well camouflaged with dirt. The last thing I did was tie back the front of my bobbed hair so that it looked short at my ears and neck.

This was more than I ever primped in my normal life.

I climbed out the workshop window and over the back fence of the herb garden. That put me on the path that led to the main hall, past the goats and chickens. A nun, younger than me, was coming out of the goat pen after washing up in the pail by the gate. Another nun met her by the chicken coop, and neither noticed when I fell in behind them, becoming just another body hurrying to see what was going on.

The pair came to an abrupt stop at the corner of the priory hall. I had to make a clumsy sidestep to keep from running them over. At the scene in the yard, my heart did a clumsy stutter step too.

The folks who had come for alms scurried out of the way

of the horsemen riding through the gate, led by Captain Sir Henry Guilbert himself. The chief forester reined in, bringing his smoke-black horse to a prancing stop. I had to admit, the guy could rock a leather jerkin and a don't-dick-with-me attitude. Two of his rangers forced the crowd to draw back to the outer limits of the space, making room for Nottingham's soldiers.

I stepped back with the rest of the villagers. I was between Goat Girl, who was wringing her hands, and a mother with her wide-eyed son held tight in front of her. Arms folded, I watched as Guilbert ran a tactical eye along the line. His gaze passed right over me, stopped, and jumped back to lock with mine. There didn't seem any point in pretending, so I gave him a wave and got the stink eye in return.

Then the sheriff of freaking Nottingham rode into the yard, and took center stage, dressed in rich silks and his fur-trimmed mantle, despite the warm morning. His weaselly face looked way too pleased, and I knew from experience the sheriff's good mood meant the people's bad news.

As the newcomers dismounted, I concentrated on staying still so I wouldn't attract any further attention. The sisters of the priory had all stayed at their posts. Sister Clothilde planted herself in front of the dispensary, as if daring anyone to try to get past her. I recognized the prioress, standing on the chapel steps, staying there so she had the height advantage once the sheriff got down from his horse.

"How can we assist you today, Your Honor?" Her tone was meticulously polite.

The sheriff adopted the same tone, but on him it was oily.

"My deputy tells me there have been reports of poachers and thieves in the greenwood."

She raised her brows coolly. "There are *always* poachers and thieves in the greenwood, Your Honor."

"Just so," the sheriff acknowledged, missing the point. "But so close to your priory lands? One might worry for the safety of your flock."

The prioress folded her hands into her sleeves and looked down her long, thin nose at the sheriff. "We have very little flock, m'lord. They've all gone to tithe or taxes."

His Honor's smile got tighter. "I mean your figurative flock, Reverend Mother."

She raised her eyes toward heaven with exaggerated piety. "The good Lord protects his humble servants."

As fencing matches went, it was hard to beat a God parry. But the sheriff went with the barely veiled threat.

"I would hate to see anyone take advantage of your charity," said the sheriff. "The penalty for aiding an outlaw is severe."

The look the prioress gave the sheriff said she was done sparring. "We share our gifts with anyone in need, Your Honor, and do not ask questions."

The sheriff turned in a slow circle to look at the table full of stew, roasted game birds, and pigeon pie. His gloved fists rested on his hips so his mantle swept out over his elbows, making his silhouette appear larger as he turned back to the nun on the steps. "And who has been sharing gifts with you, madam?"

Isabel, who stood near the prioress, smoothly took over,

addressing the sheriff in respectful tones. "Your Honor, one of our recovered convalescents was kind enough to rid our meadow of some excess wildlife." Her smile was the perfect politic mix of demure and rueful. "We've been overrun by rabbits."

"What a shame," said the sheriff, his tone turning much darker. "My deputy will just make sure you have not been overrun with venison as well. Captain, have your men search the kitchens and cellar."

Guilbert looked at the prioress for permission first, a token gesture, then sent his men to the priory kitchens with two sisters to show them the way. Indignation simmered inside me, but I held myself in check, feeling a precarious balance in the courtyard, one that any motion on my part would topple into disaster.

Then the sheriff gestured to his soldiers and jerked his pointed chin toward the table of food. "Sergeant, search that, too."

Two soldiers dismounted and would have barreled right through the nuns if they hadn't moved first. I squeezed my fists until my joints burned as the soldiers searched the provisions with viciously excessive thoroughness, tearing apart loaves of bread and digging filthy fingers into the soft cheeses.

"Your Honor!" exclaimed the prioress, horrified. "All that food! The waste ..."

"Have you something to hide?" the sheriff demanded, but he didn't wait for an answer. He addressed Guilbert exactly the same way as he did his other lackeys. "Search that rabble for illegal game or weapons."

The captain set his jaw and grimly moved down the line of alms seekers, who were largely old people or young mothers with terrified kids. They obediently lifted any baskets or bundles, which Guilbert gave a close but quick inspection. He rested his free hand on his sword looking all . . . swordsmanlike. I don't know. It was a look. Like *Lord of the Rings,* but better groomed.

Guilbert reached me and stopped. I folded my arms and stared back at him. He raised a brow; I raised my chin, determined I wasn't going to break the standoff.

I lasted longer than I thought I would. "Your boss is a rat bastard," I said when I couldn't stand it any longer.

"How can that possibly be a surprise to you?" He looked me up and down. "No bow today?"

"Where would I hide a longbow?" I flung out one arm, gesturing to the assembled folk. "Where would any of these people hide a—"

Guilbert caught my wrist, turned my hand over, and examined my finger guards. "What have you been shooting, then?"

I yanked my hand from his grasp. "Vermin."

He tipped his head, mockingly curious. "How fares your fever madness? Is it gone? I cannot tell."

I flushed, but before I could answer, one of Nottingham's brute squad called to the sheriff, "There's naught here but game birds, m'lord."

"Then look more thoroughly," snapped the sheriff.

The soldiers each grabbed a corner of the table and

toppled the whole thing. Bread and hard cheeses spilled off and rolled under horse hooves. Pitchers of goat's milk shattered, pots of soft cheese cracked and splattered, and the entire kettle of rabbit stew was upended, filling the air with the smell of meat and herbs before the broth soaked into the dirt.

The sisters rushed to salvage what they could, risking the soldiers' feet and the horses' hooves. The prioress choked on her outrage. "My lord. You . . . those starving children . . ."

I was the tip of a sparkler on the Fourth of July, a lit fuse burning down to blastoff. I knew the sheriff was taking revenge on the nuns for sheltering me, and I shook with the need to *do something.*

Something that matters. Rob's wish was a warning. What would Rob do? He wouldn't fizzle—he would focus and not waste his shot on a pointless target.

The sheriff turned to the prioress and Isabel, both of whom were frozen in shock. "Since the Marian Sisters can afford to be so generous to the poor, Northgate Priory can surely afford to help Nottingham prepare for the coming royal visit. Prince John travels with a large entourage, and we will need to host them in grand style."

Isabel collected herself first. "My lord sheriff, this is a tiny priory. We have little money."

"That is no worry, Lady Isabel. We can take it in kind." The sheriff looked for Guilbert, who stood stone-faced in the middle of the mess. "Captain, look to the livestock. Whatever they have most of, take half of that."

There was an outcry, not just from the prioress and Isabel,

though they were the most vehement. Even Guilbert objected, for his own reasons. "Your Honor," he said, "my men are foresters, not goatherds."

"An excellent idea." The sheriff waved a hand toward the pens behind the kitchen. "Take the goats."

"Oh *no!*" whispered the novice beside me, then more loudly, "Your Honor, please—we'll have nothing to sell, no milk for the little ones." She rushed forward, and a burly guard put out a hand and shoved her roughly away from the sheriff, sending her sprawling.

That was the limit. I sprang forward—and ran smack into Sister Clothilde, who came out of nowhere. She turned me around with a punishing grip on my arm. "Don't be a fool."

Her grip hurt, but it cleared my head. Over my shoulder I saw Isabel rush to the sobbing novice. "This is all happening because of me," I said through a tight throat.

"Yes." Sister Clothilde didn't spare my feelings. "But I didn't cure your fever just to let the sheriff provoke you to run onto one of those soldiers' pikes."

Guilbert, his jaw set and his shoulders stiff, gestured for two of his rangers to follow him to the livestock pens. They marched right past me. Clothilde turned to help Isabel, correctly guessing she'd talked me out of attracting the sheriff's attention. Since Guilbert already knew I was there, I chased after him.

"Captain!" I ducked around the surprised rangers and dogged his footsteps. He didn't even break stride. "You can't do this."

"Yet here is the pen, and here are the goats." He stopped in front of the goat enclosure and faced me. "And here are my rangers to take them away."

I jumped in front of the gate, arms spread. Like that would stop him. "The sisters need these goats for their milk. They basically live on cheese and curds and whey."

Again with that damned eyebrow. "Curds and whey?"

"I don't know what it's called." The rangers were watching our exchange with interest. "What about the baby goats? They'll die without their moms to nurse them."

"It is a harsh world," said Guilbert.

One of the rangers suggested, "We could take the kids, too, sir."

"No!" I cried, while Guilbert demanded, "Do you jest? We have over a mile to go."

"I know you can be reasonable," I said to Guilbert, even though I knew no such thing. Call it a positive affirmation.

"Move," he ordered. "Or I will move you."

"If you do this," I said, because clichés were all I had left in my quiver, "then you're just as bad as the sheriff."

A total miss. Guilbert grabbed me under the arms, lifted me with hardly a grunt of effort, and set me out of the way. Without his telling them to, the two rangers opened the gate and started rounding up goats.

"If I were really like the sheriff," said Guilbert in a dangerous voice, "you would be in irons by now."

He had let go of me and turned away before I allowed myself to take a rattled breath. I hadn't expected him to actually touch me. The rangers paused in their goat wrangling to smirk at my gobsmacked expression. I hoped all three of them got head-butted in the nuts.

I stalked away from the courtyard because I had to fix this, and if I went near the sheriff or Guilbert, I would do something reckless. Which ... okay, happened a lot, but I tried not to be a total idiot unless I absolutely couldn't help it.

Jumping the back fence of the apothecary garden, I climbed in the window and then up on a stool to get my bow. The sound of cursing men and bleating goats announced the sheriff's departure. A few moments later, Isabel came in, an arm around the weeping novice.

"How many did they take?" I asked.

The girl sobbed even harder. "Sassy and Polly and Su-su-suuuuue!" She flung herself against Isabel's chest, soaking her surplice with tears. "She was my favorite!"

Dammit. They had names. I couldn't let them be dinner for lousy Prince John. "Are the soldiers returning straight to Nottingham?"

Isabel watched me warily. "The sheriff is going north with some of his men. He has a half-day still to vent his spleen by making misery. The rest are leading the herd south to town."

"Good." Some was better than all.

"What are you going to do?" she asked, narrow-eyed.

"What does it look like?" I pulled up the hood of my tunic and settled the quiver with its three measly arrows into place on my back. "I'm going to get back Sassy and Polly and Sue."

CHAPTER THIRTEEN

RATHER THAN CATCH UP TO THE SOLDIERS VIA THE ROAD, I cut across the priory meadow and chose to go after them through the woods. It wasn't difficult to get a fix on them. Goats and guards alike were complaining loudly enough to wake the dead. The racket covered any noise I made as I paralleled their progress, keeping the trees between us.

I counted six men making their way down the wagon trail they called a road. Two had dismounted and, trailing the other soldiers, were herding the goats with their pikes. The goats didn't like being marched in a line, let alone being tethered to a length of rope like beads on a string.

Okay, if I could figure out what to do about the soldiers, I could handle three tethered goats. I jogged ahead to scout a good spot for an ambush. There was no end of trees I could climb and then drop down from, onto the soldiers . . . and get skewered by a pike.

A little farther, I finally found an optimal place, where the road looped around a rocky outcropping. It offered high ground and a blind curve, and limited room for the ambushee to maneuver. On the downside, I'd be completely exposed while shooting. The fact that I had only three blunt arrows and no desire to actually kill anyone was also a hindrance.

I stood for a moment, my thumb absently strumming the bowstring like a one-note guitar. The woods were quiet, but not silent. The wind in the trees was a gentle constant, and a rustle in the grass said there was a small animal burrowing nearby, stirring up the scent of loamy earth.

There was another sound, a high, steady hum. Curious, I followed the noise over the hill, where the hum thickened into a visible cloud around a huge oak tree. One of the branches had succumbed to age and gravity and split from the trunk. The wood had rotted out at the scar, and a nest of hornets had moved in.

Holy crap. I had a plan.

Giving the tree a wide berth, I checked out the other side of the road from the hornets' nest. I was looking for a spot with both cover and a clear shot when a voice whispered, "Girl."

I froze, wondering stupidly what other girl was out in the woods and where I should hide. Then the voice came again, less whispery, more mocking. "Hey, girl. Be careful you don't get stung."

The voice came from above me. I spun and saw two men sprawled on separate limbs of a tree, like high-rise construction workers on a break. Once I got over the shock, the men's identities were not a surprise. One was the handsome man in the jaunty green cap, and the other was his giant friend.

Green Cap grinned. "What are you doing out of the nunnery? Might it have something to do with the barnyard parade headed this way?"

"What barnyard parade?" I played clueless, just to gauge their motives.

He gave me a look that said "Seriously?" in any language. "The one screeching like the devil's own musicians."

"Right," said the giant, who, unlike the last time we met, was not grinning. "What's that to do with you?"

I debated telling a lie, but figured I might as well cut to the chase. "I'm reclaiming the priory's goats."

"What a coincidence," said Green Cap. "So are *we*."

"No," I said, drawing the word out. "*That's* called stealing."

He shrugged, still perched on the tree limb, legs dangling. "We're outlaws. Stealing is what we do."

That was a hard point to argue, so I changed tactics. "If you help me, I will give you one of the goats."

"Why should we help you when we could just take all of the goats?" asked the giant.

"Because I have a plan." At least, I had most of a plan, which should count. "*You* have muscles and sticks against armor and horses."

"Oh, we have a plan," said Green Cap, leaning back against the tree trunk. "We plan to watch you try to draw that great huge bow that's as big as you are. I haven't had a really good laugh since John here got knocked on his arse by a *girl*."

The giant scowled. It was fiercely effective, what with his bushy brows and thick, reddish beard. "I didn't know she was one, did I? I've daughters of my own, and know better than to cross one."

I finally caught up to the fact that he had called me "girl" earlier. They were talking about me.

"How could you tell?" I asked, trying to sound casual.

Green Cap gave me a droll and roguish look. "That's a fair disguise, m'lady Longbow. But you don't wear boots, and the day I don't appreciate a delicate feminine ankle is the day I'll meet my maker."

Well. That had not been on my list of things that might give me away.

I almost didn't blush. "Got a good look when I knocked you flat, I guess." From his grin, that was a yes.

I'd kept my Robert Hudson identity so that I could go where I wanted without attracting attention or harassment. With these two I wasn't worried about my secret so much as I was their interference in my goat reclamation mission. But their reaction brought up a good point—how much angrier would the sheriff be if he found out the lad who got away was actually a *lass*?

"Are you going to tell anyone?" I felt stupid talking up into the tree like Alice politely addressing the Cheshire Cat.

"Not likely," grumbled the giant. He jerked his thumb at his pal, who doffed his cap with a flourish. "Will doesn't want it spread about that he accosted a young lady any more than I do."

Okay, there were probably fifteen Williams in spitting distance, and fifty Johns. But *seriously*. "Let me guess," I said drily. "Will Scarlet?"

"Will Scarlet?" He laughed, then said it again, trying it out. "Well, I like that better than the name my father left me."

"What's that?" I asked.

"Fitzhugh." He said it like it was significant, and when I didn't react, he explained, "The 'Fitz' is the Norman way of saying 'bastard of.'"

I gave him a narrow-eyed look. "Really? What's the Norman way of saying 'condescending bastard'?"

John laughed until he nearly fell out of the tree. "She has you there, Will."

"So what's *his* name, then?" Will asked, nodding to his large friend.

"He's Little John, *obviously*." When they were *both* done laughing, I shifted my bow and said impatiently, "Do you want to help me steal some goats, or what?"

The pair exchanged a look, and then John swung down from the branch. "We've nothing better to do today."

Will jumped down. "Well then?" he asked as he adjusted his cap to the perfect angle. "What do we call you?"

I'd been avoiding naming myself because the obvious alias was so . . . obvious. But it also seemed inevitable. "Just call me Robin Hood."

The name was clearly meaningless to them. I sighed and got back to business. "They'll be coming down that road in a minute or so. Once they get to that big tree with the hornets' nest, I'll cause a distraction so the soldiers let the livestock go. You stand clear, and when the goats run, herd them back around the bend and keep going. I saw a little cave between the two hills. . . ."

"I know it," said Will, amused for some reason. Maybe because I was telling him his outlaw business.

John squinted at the tree. "You're going to hit that nest? And not get stung? Or spotted by the soldiers?"

I pointed to the spot I'd scouted. "I'll be over there."

"You'll never make that shot," said Little John. "It's too far."

With an evaluating eye on the flight path, Will agreed. "All those trees? It'll be like threading a needle."

He was right, but I knew what would make it easier. "Do you have sharp arrows in that quiver?" I asked.

He put a protective hand around the fletched shafts. "Do you know how much of other people's money these cost me?"

"Do you know how much I want to get the priory's goats back?" I asked, giving him my game face.

"Give her the arrows, Will," growled John. "It's for the nuns."

"Fine." He gave me a handful, which would have been extremely generous if he'd paid for them himself. He'd probably paid a good bit of other people's money for his clothes, too.

"How do you sneak up on anyone in an outfit like that?" I asked, eyeing the red tipping on his cowl, and his royal-blue leggings. This was apparently an old subject between the two friends, because John laughed again and Will looked disgruntled.

I shushed them as I heard the riders approaching the bend. The goats made it impossible for them to be stealthy, so at least that was one thing going right. Leaving the outlaw pair behind, I ran for the spot I'd selected, across from the hornets' tree. I had to stay pretty far back if I wanted cover from the spring brambles.

My clothes were the gray and green of the forest and the dark brown of just-turned earth, and I raised the hood to cover my blond hair and break up my outline. With one arrow nocked, I sighted the target, shifting right and left to find the best path. Fifty meters away, downhill ten to fifteen degrees. Making the shot through the trees ... would be tough. Arrows don't fly straight. They wobble, just a little bit, just enough to worry me—especially with an angle that tight.

I stuck the other two arrows in the ground where I could grab them fast, and dropped behind the low thicket, holding the image of the target in my mind. The hum of the hive seemed incredibly loud, but the rush of my blood was even louder. I had to focus past it so that I could hear the soft clop of the horses' hooves on the packed-dirt road, the small shift in sound as something passed between me and the buzzing hornets.

Time to rock and roll. I visualized the path to the hive, the arrow finding space between the trees. Everything happened in rehearsed and precise order, like a dance with my pulse beating the time. Up, nock, sight, draw, loose.

The arrow made a clear flight. The shaft hit true and stuck deep. Will's fletching was white as a swan, and as easy to spot against the tree trunk, but I couldn't savor the moment. I dropped flat again, out of sight, and listened as the lazy afternoon hum of the hornets revved up to a wrathful roar. It buzzed like a chain saw until the shouts and screams of men and horses—I did feel bad about the horses—drowned it out.

Guilbert shouted orders at the chaos like King Lear shouting at the storm. "Stop flailing about! You're only making it worse!"

Poor Captain Guilbert. My French wasn't up to interpreting all his curses. Not through all the screaming and yelling. I risked a peek to make sure the goats were getting away. All I saw of them was their white tails disappearing around the bend, and Little John beckoning them along.

Guilbert finally put his heels to his Porsche horse, and he and his men galloped away from the hive, taking the opposite route from the goats. He'd figure out pretty quickly they were missing—and possibly why—so I had to move.

I jumped up, grabbed the extra arrows, and ran, staying out of sight of the road. I'd spotted the cave as I was scouting. Useless for an ambush, but good for a quick hiding spot. I bet any outlaw would know that too. Will certainly had.

I'd expected him and John to be waiting, expected to be greeted by the grateful bleating of rescued goats. But the gap between the hills was quiet and the cave was empty.

No, not completely empty. There was a scarlet feather from someone's cap, and it had been used as a pen to write in the dirt. The script was so old-fashioned, it took me a minute to realize the message was French.

Merci pour les chèvres, mon amie. Bonne journée.

At least he was a literate bastard son of a Norman.

CHAPTER FOURTEEN

THERE WAS NO WAY I WAS GOING BACK TO THE PRIORY WITH-
out the goats, but I couldn't stay in the forest, so that left
the only other place I knew in the entire twelfth century. I
headed for the village of Mapperley.

From the north, I didn't have to go through the village
to get to the chapel. The priest—Father Anselm—was out in
the churchyard, and when he saw me, he pointed wordlessly
to a path through the trees. It led to a hut in a clearing. The
building was old, but the thatching on the roof was new. A
low rock wall circled the yard, like maybe the space once had
chickens or ducks running around in it. Now it just had a
very un-friarly horse in a new-looking pen, and Much, who
ran to meet me.

"What did you *do?*" Much asked, sliding to a stop. "Lady Isabel sent a message that you were going to get yourself killed or hanged. Sir James is putting on his *sword.*"

I grimaced, feeling even guiltier. From what I could tell, James's humble-friar ruse involved putting *down* the sword, so it was a big deal he'd picked it up. "I guess I'd better go tell him that I'm not in need of rescue."

The door to the hut was open, but I knocked on the lintel and waited rather than barging in. "Hey, Friar Tuck. I'm not dead."

James barreled out so quickly, he nearly knocked me down. He'd had to duck to clear the doorway, but he straightened when he saw me, and took an awkward step back. His expression was a mix of startled relief, a little bit of happiness at seeing me, and a lot of another-fine-mess-you've-gotten-into. "What did you call me?"

"Nothing." I waved it away. James was the complete opposite of the fat, jolly friar from the Robin Hood stories. He was tall and young and soldierly, even in the brown friar's robe. The neck was open—he'd ditched the cowl—and the sleeves were rolled back. His throat was tanned, and so were his forearms, except for a white scar running up the back of his right arm. Not that I was staring. I took it all in at a glance, as well as the fact that he carried his longsword, still in its scabbard, the belt wrapped tidily around it.

"Aren't friars supposed to be peaceful?" I asked.

He frowned and countered with, "Aren't you supposed to be shooting partridges and keeping out of trouble?"

"I *was* keeping out of trouble," I said. "Then trouble came to me and confiscated the priory's goats. So I took them back."

He searched behind me in an exaggerated way. "And where are they?"

"Someone took them from *me,*" I said, fuming.

James sighed, gesturing to the door. "You'd better come inside and tell me what happened."

I accepted the invitation, grudging as it seemed. The hut was cool and dim, and I leaned my bow against the wall. James offered me a drink in a wooden cup.

He'd laid his sword on top of a chest. Some tools had been dumped on the floor, as if the lid on the trunk had been opened quickly. "Did you build the horse pen yourself?" I asked.

"Of course." James pointed to a stool. After I sat, he hooked another stool with his booted toe and dragged it closer. There was one cot, and a rolled-up pallet that must have been Much's. For the moment, the boy sat on the dirt floor. James seemed to be making a thorough job of this friar disguise, vow of poverty and all.

"Speak," he ordered. "Start at the beginning."

I did, laying it out one outrage after another. Much thought the hornets were hilarious, and my description of the soldiers trying to herd the goats with their spears made even James smile a little. But at the end of my account, he rubbed his hands over his face in exasperation.

"Let me see if I understand," he said, in that way that meant "Let me make sure *you* understand how stupid this is."

The stool was too short for him, and he sat with his elbows on his knees. Good thing he was wearing trousers, because he was obviously not used to sitting in a poor friar's robe. "You attacked the chief forester and his men, which will enrage the sheriff when he hears of it. And you have nothing to show for your trouble."

"I'm working on that," I grumbled.

"The large man could be John the Smith," said Much. He said "the smith" like a last name. "He was outlawed early this year because he couldn't pay his taxes."

"Why isn't half of Nottingham outlawed, then?" I asked.

Much gave me a look I'd come to know well. "Half of Nottingham *is* outlawed."

"Oh." I'd thought an outlaw was the same thing as a bandit, like in the Wild West. But apparently being outlawed was like being in the penalty box, only instead of getting shut out of the game, you were shut out of the community. "The other man wasn't a villager, though. Nice clothes, dark hair, lean . . . kind of roguishly handsome."

James frowned. "Do you not have larger concerns than a handsome face?"

"I'm just trying to give you a visual," I explained, then saw Much grinning at me, then James, and then me again. I shot him a silent "What?" just as James caught the exchange and gave him a suspicious look. I changed the subject. "Can you track them or something, Much? Three goats and a guy the size of Little John . . . John the Smith, I mean . . . must make a trail."

Sensing adventure, Much answered eagerly, "John the

160

Smith is from up Barnsdale way. I have a cousin in Barnsdale." He jumped up from the ground and dusted off his backside. "I can learn a few likely spots they might be in the forest."

James held up a hand and tried to put the brakes on. "And when it gets back to the sheriff that you are asking after outlaw outposts?" The boy rolled his eyes, and the knight sighed in defeat. "Just be careful."

"Okay," said Much, and *pfft!* he was gone.

James frowned at the empty doorway. "You are a bad influence on him, Mistress Hudson."

I'd never been called a bad influence before. Or bad, even. Despite my *lack of focus,* I trained hard, got good grades, did volunteer work, and generally represented the Olympic spirit. But maybe that was all because of Rob's example. Look what happened when I was on my own. Total anarchy.

"Don't frown like that," said James, leaning forward to catch my downcast gaze. "Much doesn't need encouragement to cause mischief."

I flushed, a little embarrassed he'd read my mood so easily. "It's not that." I'd figured out already that Much didn't do anything he didn't want to do. "I was just thinking about my brother." I looked up with a rueful grimace. "This has all forced me to admit what a steadying influence he had—has . . ."

Will have. God, this was messed up.

Maybe it was the tense shift, or maybe just something in my tone, but James seemed to sense the underlying current of tangled loss and worry and hope. "Where is he?" he asked. "Back home in West-of-Here?"

I smiled slightly. "No. East."

His brows climbed. "In Jerusalem?"

I nodded. Rob was farther east than that, but it got the idea across. War. Desert. Suck. "He's part of an aid group. They dig wells in the desert, build irrigation systems, that kind of business. Helping refugees . . ."

"A Knight Hospitaller, then?" At my blank look, James explained, "They protect pilgrims in the Holy Land."

I could see Rob as a knight—in an idealistic, Sir Lancelot kind of way. "No, his group is made up of people from all different countries, with no religious affiliation. They provide medicine, food, shelter—whatever they can—to all people and faiths."

James turned that over in his head for a moment, his gaze distant. "Yes," he said. "There's a need for that." It was an iceberg of a statement—starkly economic on the surface, but haunted and wistfully deep underneath. "How long since you've had word of him?"

Communication here must count time-lag in months, if not years; I didn't know how Skype compared to that. "Long enough to be worried. Their camp was attacked, and there's been no word. The authorities think he and his friends are lost in the desert."

"I'm sorry," James said, his gaze intent on my face. The prayer he offered was just as genuine. "God grant that he is safe somewhere."

I nodded, swallowing a sudden thickness in my throat. I missed Rob every day, but it was easier to stay emotionally level when people didn't stir things up with their sincere concern and stuff. The roller coaster of my situation hadn't helped.

"What about you?" I asked, changing the subject. "Do you have brothers or sisters?"

He stood, taking my empty cup. "None with whom I'm close."

"Why not?"

"I went to Huntingdon as a squire when I was eight. That's how I met Henry and Isabel." James set his cup and mine by the jug of ale, straightening them as he spoke. "We three were good friends before I left with the Crusade, if you can believe it."

"I can believe it." It takes a certain level of familiarity for someone to be able to piss you off in a particular way. "I just can't believe you were a squire at eight."

He raised his brows. "How old were you when you picked up a bow?"

Family legend said I made one out of my crib mobile, but I didn't believe it. "That's different. A practice target doesn't try to shoot you back." I lifted his scabbarded sword from atop the trunk. I knew it would be heavy, but it still nearly tipped me off the stool. "Good God. How did you lift this thing?"

"Well, I didn't start with that, obviously." He watched me lay the weapon across my knees so I could examine the equal-armed cross on the pommel.

"But you've had this awhile," I said. There wasn't a single shabby thing about the scabbard, the silver hilt, or the sword belt, but I recognized the care that goes into a thing that suits you perfectly. I can shoot anything, but I don't have a *relationship* with every bow I pick up.

I squinted at the grip, flicking my nail over the join on the cross guard. "Is that some blood left there?"

"What?" Horrified, James bent over to see. I laughed, and he shot me a glare. "That's not funny."

"That's because you didn't see your face."

He took the sword from my lap and laid it back on the trunk. The hut was cool and smelled of ale and clean dirt and sawdust. It wasn't a bad smell at all. I caught James's hand, turning his forearm to look at the jagged white scar that cut across it. "How did you get this?"

"Point of a Saracen lance went up under my shield." He was matter-of-fact about it, and about pushing up his sleeve to show the straight red line of a newer scar across his triceps. "Sword cut here. An arrow broke this bone"—he pointed to his clavicle—"and to show you the rest would make us both blush."

I stood up to get a better look at his collarbone. There wasn't much to see. Scar-wise, I mean. I was looking for science. "Oh, wow. So the chain mail really does stop a . . . Was it a broadhead? A bodkin point should have pierced the armor, especially from a recurve—"

He took my shoulders and set me back a pace. "It was pointed and it hurt. Let it suffice that I dealt more than I received, or I wouldn't be here for you to prod at."

Now I was blushing, and I took another step back, toward the open door. "Sorry."

Suddenly I was looking at the Spartan hut in the light of new information. The place was plain as a monk's cell, with no attempt to trick things out for comfort. The horse's pen outside was the fanciest part. I wasn't even sure Much's bedroll wasn't cushier than the bedding on the cot.

"Are you doing penance?" I asked. My insight seemed to startle James, and he looked ruffled, like he was searching for a way to explain. I helped him out with a matter-of-fact "We have veterans in West-of-Here, too."

His hand dropped to rest on the hilt of a sword that wasn't there. He caught himself and made a rueful grimace. "When I returned to England, I made a vow." The banter was over, and the stillness of conviction settled back over him. "If called upon, I will use that sword to defend the innocent to my dying breath, and I will give my life for any godly cause, but I'm done killing for the Church or the crown."

"And the, uh, Knights Templar are okay with that?"

James didn't sigh or shrug, but both were in his voice. "It's under negotiation."

I was still working out what that meant when a ferocious pounding shook the entire hut, dislodging straw thatching and endangering the whole structure. I didn't know what I was thinking—earthquake, meteor shower, giant ogre—but I was closest to the door and stuck my head out to see what was happening. Someone—someone strong and furious— grabbed the back of my tunic and yanked me out of the hut like a cat yanking a gopher out of a hole.

I yelped, tripped over my own feet, rolled as I fell, and came to a sprawling stop, blinking in the sudden sunlight.

Sir Henry Guilbert, chief forester and goat confiscator, stood over me, thunderous, armed, and *covered* in hornet stings. "Robert Hudson, or whatever you are calling yourself, you are under arrest for theft, assault, and whatever else I can think of between here and the Nottingham dungeon."

CHAPTER FIFTEEN

I SCRAMBLED BACKWARD LIKE A CRAB, ONLY LESS EFFECTIVELY. I saw James run out of the hut, but mostly my vision was full of Guilbert, his face, throat, and hands covered with angry red welts the size of quarters. In my few, but memorable, dealings with Guilbert I'd seen him snide, stonily businesslike, and vaguely irate, but I'd figured him too much of a cold fish to get truly furious. I'd figured wrong. He was livid, literally and figuratively.

He was also alone. There was only his horse outside the stone wall, and even *it* looked mad at me.

James strode forward, his sword half drawn. He may have vowed not to kill anyone, but he looked ready to mess someone up. Guilbert gave him a glance; then his eyes were back on me, just waiting for me to offer an excuse. "Do you really wish to interfere with an agent of the crown in the midst of his duty, James? What does your knight's code say about abetting treason?"

James slammed his sword back into its scabbard and stopped where he was. "It says you need a better reason than anger to arrest a yeoman."

"Let's start with attacking the king's foresters," snapped Guilbert. "Then there is stealing from the sheriff of Nottingham."

"I didn't steal anything," I said truthfully. "Do you see any goats here?"

"I see this." Guilbert grabbed my ankle and lifted my sneakered foot. "No one else leaves tracks like this."

Curse you, Chuck Taylor.

Guilbert let my leg drop with a thud. "When I saw your direction, I remembered that Mapperley had a new friar, supposedly the son of an old Nottingham family." He finally widened his attention, taking in the hut, the yard, and James's plain woolen clothes with a mix of bemusement and contempt. "What does your father say about your humble status?"

"He says the barony will pass to my younger brother," James said, in his not-rising-to-the-bait voice. "Same as it would have if I'd never returned to England."

I took advantage of their sparring to slowly get to my feet. I wasn't above sneaking away. I hadn't taken more than a step, though, before Guilbert, without even looking, shot his hand out like he was going to grab me by the scruff of the neck. I reacted instinctively, jabbing my elbow in his undefended torso, nailing him in the diaphragm and knocking the air out of him. He doubled over and I was free.

"Chapel!" ordered James. "Go!" Without questioning, I ran for the church.

Leaping over the little stone wall of the friary, I raced down the trail to the churchyard, low tree limbs catching at my hood and my hair. When I burst into the lane, I didn't waste time with the gate but vaulted over the fence, which would have been much more impressive if I hadn't immediately tripped on a gravestone and hit the ground in a skid.

When I pushed myself to my feet, I heard someone coming down the trail, hoped it was James, and was wrong. How had Guilbert gotten his wind back so fast?

Father Anselm was tending his flowers, and it was a wonder I didn't give him a heart attack. The ancient priest closed his dropped jaw, looked me up and down—my jeans were torn at both knees, and blood dripped down my shins—assessed the situation, and said, "Into the chapel, young Robert. Get to the nave."

I figured it was some medieval tradition, like tagging home base, and I limped the way he pointed. Guilbert came over the fence like I had, with James on his heels, both looking like there had been a scuffle for the lead. My sneakers hit flagstone, and I blundered through the chapel door. In the sudden dimness, I nearly brained myself on a support column, then stumbled into the slanted beams of sunlight coming through the high, narrow windows of the sanctuary.

I stopped and propped my hands on my thighs, catching

my breath in the tiny nave of the tiny chapel. Guilbert burst in with James so close behind that when the captain spun and slammed the door shut, it sounded like it hit James in the face. Guilbert put his shoulder to the timber to hold the door closed, then shot home the thick bolt.

My hopes did a roller-coaster drop at the sound. That was not the sound of *safe on base*. Did I have to tag up? Yell "Not It"?

James shouted something I couldn't hear, but I bet it wasn't very friarly. Guilbert yelled back, "This doesn't concern you, James!"

Sweat had broken out as soon as I'd stopped running, and it stung my skinned elbows and knees. "It's going to concern him a lot if you kill me inside a church," I said.

Guilbert turned from the door. "I'm not going to kill you," he said, too dismissive to be reassuring.

I backed up a step. "Maim, then."

"I'm going to do what I should have done from the first," he said, still advancing. "See you behind bars in Nottingham's dungeon."

"You can't." I retreated to the altar, my stomach heaving at the thought of rats and chains and God knows what.

Guilbert took the first of the three shallow steps, his gaze relentlessly, coldly furious. "Give me one reason why I shouldn't."

"Your sheriff was in the wrong today." At the priory, I'd seen the tic in his jaw that said Guilbert disagreed with his boss's actions. "It wasn't even profitable for him. It was just petty, and you know it."

"What I know is this," he said from the second step, so icily our breath should have fogged the air. "I've one man who broke his arm when his horse threw him, and another swollen like a . . . a . . ."

"Turnip?"

I winced as soon as the word was out of my mouth. Guilbert's hornet stings disappeared into a furious flush. "Is this naught but a *game* to you?" he demanded.

I dashed to put the altar between us. "Okay, okay! That wasn't funny. I'm honestly sorry your men got hurt."

He braced his feet, poised impatiently for me to go one way around the altar or the other, and I realized I'd cornered myself. "I am through with warnings and second chances. Now, come out and face your charges like a man."

"Why?" I demanded. "So you can put my head on a spike like poor Lord Ethyl Stone?"

"Sir *Aethelstan* was a traitor," snapped Guilbert. "He was part of an Anglo-Saxon conspiracy against the king."

"Was his trial as big a joke as mine?" I asked.

His face hardened into cold inscrutability. "There was overwhelming evidence against him."

"From the sheriff? Pardon me while I laugh."

"From the monks of Rufford Abbey—" He brought himself up sharp. "Stop changing the subject."

Like hell I would. "What about the hanged men?"

"Those sentences I did oversee," Guilbert said. "Since I was the one who found their victims in the forest, an extra smile opened in each of their throats." I tried not to picture it, but how could I not? He saw my reaction and pressed on that nerve. "Would you like me to describe how they left the women?"

"Then you should be chasing men like them, instead of stealing from nuns. It just makes you as big a bully as your sheriff."

"What does that mean?" he demanded. "That word, 'bully'?"

"Someone who beats up on people weaker than him because he's too much of a coward—"

I had barely gotten the word out before Guilbert was over the top of the altar. I was so surprised that I froze, screwing my eyes closed, waiting to be skewered, or maybe I'd just be collateral damage to the wrathful bolt of lightning about to smite Captain Sir Henry Boots-on-the-Lord's-Table Guilbert. The flash didn't come, and the captain grabbed the shoulder of my tunic and pushed me against the stone wall.

"Call me a coward to my face, *thief.*"

Clearly I'd hit a nerve.

"You are kind of proving my point," I wheezed.

"I am not thrashing you." But he did let up a little on his grip. "I am taking you to Nottingham for judgment."

But I was in the chapel. Was he disobeying the rules, or was I missing the magic phrase? Not It? Ollie ollie oxen free?

Oh, wait. I knew this—

"Sanctuary," I blurted. "I want to claim sanctuary."

Guilbert cursed in French, and let me go. I sagged against the wall, knees shaking. I realized the loud banging I heard wasn't just my heart in my ears. It was James trying to break the door down.

"I am no *bully*," Guilbert said, drawing back his shoulders and reining in his temper. But it still simmered under the surface. "I may be bigger, but only a fool would think you are weak."

And only an idiot would forget his layer of cool was merely the ice cap on his temper.

"Thank you, I think."

"We're not done." His unchecked anger had been a swinging broadsword, easier to dodge. The focused intensity of his sharp gaze pinned me to the spot and made me squirm. "Forget about the thievery. This is between you and me. When your sanctuary is done, if you haven't disappeared into the wind, Master Hudson, we will meet over swords and see who is the coward."

He turned with finality and stalked toward the door. I peeled my tongue off the suddenly dry roof of my mouth and said, "You—"

I was going to say, again, "You can't," but over his shoulder he gave me a look that cut me off. "Why. Not?" he asked, very deliberate.

My brain was empty except for "I don't know how to sword fight."

Up went one hateful brow. "Then you have forty days to learn."

I slid down the wall, too exhausted to do more than that. My bloody knees poked through my jeans and my elbows hit the stone, but I didn't even feel it.

Relief, though . . . that I *did* feel when James appeared in front of me. "Eleanor, I'm sorry. He should never have taken me by surprise that way." He made an efficient battlefield examination for bruises where Guilbert had grabbed my shoulder, then the scrapes on my elbows and knees. "This is my fault."

"No, it's not. I wasn't paying attention, either." My aches and stings were minor. James was going to have his own. There was a red lump on his jaw about the size of a fist. "It takes a real gentleman to punch a friar."

"Or a woman," he said, in a deadly sort of voice.

Face your charges like a man, Guilbert had said. Chauvinist. "Not to defend him, but he doesn't know I'm a girl."

"Then he must be blinded by anger."

That might have been a compliment if he hadn't said it with a don't-be-stupid look. I dismissed both the comment and the look. People saw what they expected to see. "I hope you at least got a punch in," I said, starting to my feet.

James showed me his bruised knuckles. "I hit him first." He turned his hand and offered it to me. I took it and accepted his help up. "What happened?" he asked as I dusted myself off.

With a heavy sigh, I gave him the short version. "I sort of called Guilbert a coward and he challenged me to a duel."

We'd started toward the door, but at that, James stopped in a pool of sunlight in the middle of the chapel. "That is a poor jest, Eleanor."

"I hope it is." I faced him, wary that James wasn't laughing. "He's not serious about dueling, is he?"

In the diffuse light, his eyes were more gray than blue, and his manner matched. "If you called him a coward, I would say he's deadly serious."

"He called me a thief."

"You did intend to steal the animals from him," he pointed out.

"But I didn't *do* it."

James adopted a pulpit tone that resonated through the chapel. "But I say unto you that whosoever looks on a goat to steal her hath committed theft already in his heart."

I gave him a narrow-eyed stare. "Are you *seriously* misquoting the Bible at me right now?"

He gazed back, unintimidated. "If the sin fits . . ."

Grumbling, I started for the door. "No wonder I haven't been to church in ages."

"You'll make up for it over the next forty days," he said, almost conversationally.

That was worth stopping again. "What does that mean?"

James stopped, too. "You claimed sanctuary. But if you set foot out of the church grounds for the forty days it lasts, then that protection is forfeit."

"Wait. *Forty days?*" I stared at him, but he was not joking. "I'm stuck in here?"

"The grounds extend to the churchyard and the friary," he said. "And nothing prevents you from leaving. But then you will have to immediately answer Guilbert's charges."

"But I have things to do!"

James looked at me quizzically. "Like what?"

Well, I knew what I had to do *first*. "I have to get the sisters' goats back."

He folded his arms and stared down at me like I was being pointlessly stubborn. "Perhaps you should be more concerned about facing Guilbert over swords in forty days' time."

"I am." Definitely. I was, however, more concerned about finding a way home long before forty days were up. But just in case . . . "I should probably learn how to sword fight. You'll teach me, right?"

James rubbed a hand over his face in a frustrated but resigned way. "Yes, of course I will teach you the sword. As for the other matter . . ." He sighed. "Please keep me in the dark, so I won't have to lie about it if asked."

"That's fair." And smart, since he was such a bad liar.

I had never thought of myself as a rule breaker before. Maybe because in sports, that's called *cheating*. But this wasn't sports, and I regretted nothing. Okay, I felt bad the horses had gotten stung, and I was kind of worried about the forester with the broken arm. But I probably wouldn't have cared much if it had been one the sheriff's brutes. If it had been the one who'd pushed the goat-keeping novice, I might have even relished it.

Maybe I really was a bad influence on myself. The moment I'd grabbed my bow and gone after Guilbert and the confiscated livestock, I'd stopped asking myself What Would Rob Do, and only done What Ellie Would Do.

CHAPTER SIXTEEN

MY ARROW SPLIT THE BARK BESIDE WILL SCARLET'S EAR. BE-
fore he could do more than flinch, I put another shaft on his
other side so he'd know the first one hadn't been a miss.

"Stay put," I said from the other edge of the clearing. I
had a third arrow ready to fly. "You too, Little John, or I'll give
Will a new feather in his cap."

The big man had gotten halfway to his feet. Seeing me at
full draw, he considered his chances of jumping me without
my skewering his friend, then sank back to his seat against
the tree.

Will, irrepressible, just grinned. "Well done, Mistress
Hood. The last time we met in the woods, you sounded like
a boar hunt on two legs."

"You're lucky Captain Guilbert went after me and not

the livestock, because you left a trail of goat droppings like Hansel and Gretel."

"Like who?"

"It doesn't matter." It was hard to be intimidating when someone was openly laughing at you. "Where are my goats?"

"The better question," said Will, getting slowly to his feet, "is whether you're prepared to shoot me over a few farm animals."

"Do you want to risk it?" My arm was getting tired. Even a half-drawn bow is heavy.

"Fortune is a lady, and I've always been good with the ladies."

I hadn't forgotten about Little John, but I hadn't thought he could reach his stave—not until it hit my heels, sweeping my legs out from under me.

I hit the ground and my fingers let go. The shot went straight up, and it was going to come down sometime, which was one problem. The other was Little John, who jumped to his feet, swinging his stave. From the trees came a whir and a *ffft,* and a rock that smacked the big man between the eyes and felled him like a tree.

Will had his own bow in hand by then, and he aimed for the brush, where Much was reloading his sling. I grabbed a heavy-tipped blunt out of my quiver, nocked it, and loosed it at barely a quarter draw. The blunt hit Will in the ass, which had to hurt like hell. His shot went wild, and so did his language.

Rolling to my feet, I grabbed another shaft, a white-fletched sharp, and laid it across the bow. The outlaw limped in a circle, trying to walk off the sting. "*Merde!* That hurt! *And it's going to leave a bruise,*" he added, craning his neck to check for damage.

"You'll live." I was shaking with adrenaline, but I managed to keep my voice steady. I hadn't expected a fight. Well, I had a little bit. But there's *expecting* and there's *that just happened*.

Little John groaned on the ground as Much came into the clearing, still spinning his sling and eyeing Will with extreme dislike. "Meet Much," I said, regaining my poise. "The first of my merry men. He can hit a gnat at fifty paces with that thing."

Will raised his hands in surrender. "Put the sling away, lad. I call a truce."

Much looked at me, and I nodded. But he kept his sling loaded, and I had an arrow still in hand.

A bird called from the trees over the hill. Will wet his lips and answered with a similar trill. At my inquiring glance, he explained, "That's the all clear."

"To who?" I asked, watching him try to pull John to his feet.

"Some friends."

I gave up watching and went to help. Will and I each took one of Little John's big hands and leaned back, hoisting him up. The man pulled down his tunic, recovering his dignity despite the lump coming up on his forehead like a unicorn horn. "Thank you kindly."

"Um, Rob?" said Much. I turned and saw his nose twitching like a rabbit's. "I'm reckoning I know where the goats are."

I sniffed tentatively, wondering what he smelled that I didn't. All I got was wet mulch and sun-warmed wood ... and roasting meat. "Oh no. You *didn't*."

Will bowed and swept one arm toward a slight path through the trees. "Would you care for some luncheon?"

Dammit, Will Scarlet! Forgetting caution, I started down the trail, quickening to a trot as the smell got stronger. I glimpsed an almost invisible sentry, who let me through, so I figured Will must have been right behind me and given him some gesture.

On the other side of the hill was a sort of semipermanent camp made up of woven twig shelters. A few of the residents were hard-looking men, but the rest of the outlaws ranged from a boy as young as Much to a man who needed a walking stick. They all stood as I approached.

In the center of the camp was a fire pit with a small haunch roasting on a spit.

"You *ate* them?"

"Quiet, lad," warned one of the outlaws. "If you call the foresters down on us, we won't be thanking you."

"Those were the *nuns'* goats," I said, still outraged, but quieter about it. Will, I noticed absently, didn't correct anyone about my gender.

Little John folded his arms, gruffly shamefaced. "We didn't roast all of them."

"The others are in the stewpot," quipped some joker in the band.

I heard bleating coming from nearby, less a call for help and more of a complaint that help hadn't come quicker. None of the outlaws moved, but I kept my bow and two sharp arrows ready. "Much, would you reclaim the priory's property, please?"

Much jogged off. One of the scarier outlaws moved as though he would follow, but Little John stopped him with a raised hand. "Let them have it," he said. "It's for the nuns."

"*It?*" I echoed, horrified. "There's only one goat left?"

Will shrugged. "It takes a lot to feed a man John's size."

I glared at him. "You are a . . . a *wastrel*." His brows rose, but I moved on to Little John. "And *you* should be ashamed of yourself. Outlawed for taxes, and now you're stealing from the poor and pushing around people smaller than you. Which is everyone."

The big man's ears reddened. "We stole the goats from the sheriff."

"If you're going to steal from the sheriff, shoot his deer, don't take the sisters' milk goats." Much was headed back, leading a goat by a tether. I jerked my head toward the path and the boy made his way out of the camp. The goat trotted nimbly behind him, unaware how close she had come to being *cabrito*.

"If you follow us," I warned, "I will shoot you."

Will gave a disbelieving snort. "You'd kill a man over a goat?"

"You think I can't shoot you somewhere that won't kill you?" I backed toward the path, trying to look as brave as my words. I kept my eye on Will, with the rest of the outlaw outpost in my peripheral vision. "Don't make me do something that will get blood on your fancy clothes."

Will finally frowned, and Little John's laughter followed Much and me out of the camp. My knees stayed wobbly long after we cleared the sentry.

Much and I headed vaguely Nottingham-ward until we were sure we weren't being followed, then took a "thataway" heading back toward Mapperley and the priory. It made for a long walk through the woods, but it was a pretty day for it—the morning clouds had scattered, and the sun lit the canopy of leaves like a green glass awning. A lazy rustling underscored the melody of Much's buoyant chatter, punctuated by the soft footfalls of the priory's lone surviving goat.

"Why are you so downcast?" Much asked suddenly. "We pulled away the plan, didn't we?"

"Pulled off," I grumbled. I didn't want to harsh on his mood, but failure made me cranky. "We pulled off one-third of the plan."

"The sisters will have milk tomorrow where this morning they had none. Isn't that good enough?"

There's no such thing as good enough. There's ten points and there's try harder.

My mood sank even lower. "They had three goats before, and now they have one."

Much was silent for a second, then said simply, "One goat is still better than no goats."

He was right, and rationally I knew there was nothing I could have done differently. The time it took to find the camp was the time it took to find it. Much had come back last evening with several areas we could look; we'd prioritized based on our best information, and set out at first light, while James was still bunked in at the chapel with Father Anselm. Quick-Draw Ellie was just pissed at Iron Ellie for letting James persuade me—us—not to run willy-nilly into the night. But she—I, for God's sake—shouldn't have taken it out on Much.

"I'm sorry," I said.

"I know," he said, forgiving me as simple as that. "But if we'd brought that roast back, we'd be up to one and a half goats. I wish I'd thought of that."

"I wish I could just go into Nottingham and buy the sisters another goat."

"Except you'd get arrested. And you have no money."

"Don't trouble me with details, Much," I said, and he laughed. I was going to miss him a little when I went home.

"Serious question, though," I added, dropping back so that we walked side by side while the road allowed for it. "In the woods, is there any place that's known for people, um, sort of vanishing? Like they go in and don't come out?"

"Well, sure. Thieves' Wood." Much drew one finger across his neck with a graphic sound effect.

Grim, but not exactly what I meant. "No, I mean like a cave. Or a stone circle."

He knitted his caterpillar brows and chewed his lip. "I've got an aunt who says her husband was carried off by the fairies, but most of us think he ran off with the butcher's wife."

That wasn't really helpful either. Much was my best hope for mining the local lore or, even better, recent rumors. Ones that didn't involve butchers' wives.

Much stopped so suddenly that the goat butted right into him. I heard the sound too—the jingle and clop of a harnessed horse approaching. We were on a track between villages, not on the main road, which made it way too likely we were about to see a forester on patrol.

Without exchanging a glance, Much and I split. He swerved to the right and I dove into the brush on the left. As I went I slipped my bow from my shoulder so it wouldn't catch on the branches. I loved this longbow, but it was not a weapon for being stealthy in the woods.

I peered from under a shrub and saw that the goat was being as stubborn as a, well, goat. The more Much pulled on her lead rope, the more she screamed like she was being murdered. Much stopped and straightened, and I realized the rider must have come into view.

"Boy!" snapped a man's voice in French. Not a forester, then. "Quiet that animal immediately." The goat did shut up, I assumed because Much had stopped trying to pull her where she didn't want to go. "Where are you going with that goat?"

There was a pause, during which I pictured Much's blankest look, and then the rider repeated the question in impatient English.

Grateful for the soft spring leaves, I slipped an arrow from the quiver, holding it where I could nock it quickly if Much sounded like he was in trouble. But he answered in his most easygoing voice, "I'm bringing her back home, good sir."

"I'm bringing her back home, *my lord*," corrected the rider.

"You don't have to call me my lord," said Much, so perfectly disingenuous that I almost busted an eardrum holding in a laugh. "I'm only a villager."

"And I am a baron, you . . ." The description challenged my grasp on Old French, or Norman, or whatever, but was along the lines of "filthy, ignorant Saxon peasant," only with words they don't teach in French class.

I risked a peek—he had some kind of heraldic thing going on with his fancy tunic, and a gold ring on just about every finger. His horse was nice at first glance, too, but from where I lay on the ground I could see she was knock-kneed. "All show, no go," as Rob would say.

"Begging your pardon, my lord," Much said, when the baron took a breath. "We'll just be on our way, then."

"Stop there!" He switched back to a language Much could understand. "I am on my way from York to Notting-ham, and have heard tell of a bandit who stole a number of goats from the sheriff—livestock taken in the name of His Highness Prince John."

"Oh, you have got to be kidding me," I whispered. You'd think that goat had golden freaking fleece. Jason and the Argonauts were going to show up next, and I wasn't sure it would surprise me.

"That's not me, my lord," said Much, in the same equable voice. "See, in the next village, they have a ram, and we don't. So once a year we bring Nanny here over so they can—"

"I know what they do," snapped the baron. "But I have

only your word, so you'll surrender the animal to me, and the sheriff will decide who is guilty."

Blah blah blah habeas corpus. I didn't wait for the rest but instead sprang up. Before the lord could turn my way, I let off a half-drawn arrow and pinged his knock-kneed horse in the butt, meaning to send it bolting off. It did, but not before rearing and dumping the baron onto his back in the middle of the road.

Shit!

Much stared at me, slack-jawed and wide-eyed. "You just shot a lord!"

Shit. Shit. Shit.

The lord lay there, making beached-fish noises and flailing his arms, the hood of his cloak covering his face. "*Fils de putain!* I'm blind!"

"Don't move," I warned, pushing through the brush and onto the road while nocking another arrow. Wheezing profanity in two languages, Lord Curse-a-Lot reached to push the hood off his face, and I put a shot into the ground next to his leg. "What did I just say? Leave the hood."

"*Imbécile! Dégénéré!*"

"Shut up," I snapped, because I couldn't concentrate. If he described me to the sheriff, or worse, Guilbert, my sanctuary would be revoked, and good luck finding a way back home from Nottingham prison. I'd leapt without looking again and now was calculating like mad to control my fall. "Facedown on the ground."

His face was only visible from the chin down, but a red

tide of outrage spread up from his neck. "*Va en enfer!* You'll hang for this, *crétin*!"

"Yeah, yeah. I've heard that before." I managed to sound threatening, not at all like I was totally freaking out inside. Much hadn't moved, but was still staring at me in horror and awe. The nanny goat still didn't give a crap about my problems.

"Give me a length of that rope, boy," I ordered, meaning Much.

"Do you know who I am?" the baron spat when I stepped over him holding the bit of the goat's tether Much cut off for me. "I'm the baron of Leas. I am a member of the royal court. The sheriff of Nottingham is—"

With a note of realization, Much said, "You're the one who got Sir Aethelstan's land." He met my questioning look, and I saw the grim answers in his eyes. "I heard how you treated the old baron's tenants."

"Saxon peasants. Prince John charged me to clear away those as traitorous as their late lord and master—"

"Shut up," I said coldly. The baron let out an "oof" when I grabbed his wrist and twisted until he flipped over onto his stomach.

"Coward," spat the baron, wriggling on his belly like an eel. "Give me your name, you treacherous cur, so I can dig up the graves of your mother and father and piss on their bones."

"Good luck with that." I focused on the knots at his wrists, not the growing twist of anger and loathing in my chest.

"I will give their bones to my dogs to gnaw," he spat, "and

their skulls to the kitchen to serve my soup. And then I will find that goatherd in whatever poxy pigsty village—"

His threats became so filthy that even the few words I caught made me sick. I planted my knee on his backside, finished binding his hands tight, then took one of my arrows and stabbed the point through his hood into the soft ground so he wouldn't be able to easily lift his head. His squawk of alarm was more satisfying than I wanted to admit. He'd crossed a line I didn't know I had.

Outrage was my kryptonite, and I pushed it down. I was left with its cousin, moral high ground, but I abandoned that pretty quickly, too.

"You're good at threatening the dead and the young," I said in French, so he would take me more seriously than the peasants he didn't care about. "Why don't you lie here and have a think about helplessness." Unless he was completely inept, he'd be able to roll over and gain his feet and start walking toward Nottingham. "Eventually."

And then the same devil on my shoulder that had kicked moral high ground to the curb pointed to all the rings the baron wore. Just one would buy enough goats to keep the sisters in mohair and chèvre for a long time. And he had eight, one for each knobby finger.

I left him with seven. The large gold nugget on his index finger slipped smoothly over his knuckle and into my palm. Let him complain to his buddies, Prince John and the sheriff of Nottingham.

"*Voleur!*" howled the baron, trying to throw me off.

"This isn't a robbery." I tucked the ring into the pocket of my jeans, hidden by my tunic. "This is a profanity tax."

The moment was somehow unreal and reckless at the same time and yet also weirdly inevitable. As we left the scene of the crime, I felt a little sick and wobbly, like when you get off an airplane and have to get your legs back under you. Which I did quickly. Much hadn't caught on to the theft, and I was glad, because I had a vague idea of not corrupting him. Or maybe just not disillusioning him. I did feel guilty, but only about not feeling guilty.

Much and I split in opposite directions, him to the priory and me to the hermitage. I approached from the woods and climbed over the wall behind the chapel. That way no one would have to admit they'd seen me leaving or returning to the church grounds. Instead of going straight to the hermitage, I circled to the front of the chapel, drawn by a rhythmic sound, which turned out to be James tamping dirt around a new gatepost for the churchyard. Father Anselm was letting him know the post wasn't straight.

I remembered Rob telling me in a Skype call that putting in fence posts by hand was a job with no shortcuts. As I approached, James paused, wiping his face on the sleeve of his linen shirt. Sweat kept collecting in the hollow of his throat. "I see you and Much made yourselves scarce while there's work to be done," he said.

I held up my bow. "You didn't see me practicing in that empty stretch behind the chapel?"

"No."

"It's good you're here, my son," said Father Anselm. "Now you can help James, and I can rest these old bones." The priest gave an exaggerated stretch with his hands at the small of his back, then toddled toward the rectory.

"Hold this plumb, will you?" said James, nodding to the gatepost. Pushing the post vertical, I found a sort of level with a string and a weight attached. I kept it aligned while James went back to tamping the soil in tight around it so that it would stay that way.

"I take it the Marian Sisters will have fresh milk tomorrow?" he said.

"Hmm. How serious were you about not wanting to know anything you'd have to swear to under oath?"

"That answers my question."

I'd already decided to either give the ring directly to Isabel to use however was best for the maids Marian, or to send it to her in a package via Much. James, from everything I'd seen, liked to work within the rules. Isabel hid a feather bed on her monastic cot.

James put another shovelful of dirt in the posthole and began packing the layer down. I could see what Rob was talking about. It was all arm and shoulder work, and James's sweat-soaked shirt stuck to his skin. For a swordsman, he had lean, efficient musculature made for endurance, not the powerhouse bulk of a—

"Careful! Keep it straight."

"Sorry." I'd gotten distracted for a moment.

Be honest, Ellie. You've gotten distracted for a lot more than a moment.

I was letting way too much stuff come between me and the target. None of this was getting me any closer to home. If anything, it had gotten me further off track. What did I think I was doing? I was a college freshman from Indiana with one specific skill. This wasn't a Hunger Games movie. I couldn't even shoot a rabbit.

The sound of the shovel had stopped, and James was saying "Eleanor" like he'd said it a couple of times before. "What's troubling you?" he asked, when I finally focused on him.

"Maybe it's that I have thirty-nine days to figure something out before Captain Guilbert skewers me with a freaking broadsword, and I'm standing here *literally* holding up this post."

"That's true," he said, with his maddening composure.

"And you're not going to get much spying done while digging holes, either," I said, just to shake him up.

He looked at me a bit longer, then stuck the blade of the shovel in the dirt and left it there. "Let's sit for a moment."

I left the gatepost and flopped onto the bench next to the churchyard's big oak tree. James picked up a leather canteen from the ground and took a couple of long swallows of whatever was in it. He offered it to me, but I shook my head.

"I wondered how much you'd pieced together from what you heard the other day." He dropped onto the other end of the bench, setting the canteen between us. "You're right. I met the prior of my order at Rufford Abbey, and he suggested my sabbatical here."

"I knew it!" Being right always cheered me up.

"There's no need to boast." James leaned with his elbows

191

comfortably set on his knees, and for a long moment he let the quiet of the afternoon sink in. If he was trying to torture me, he was doing a pretty good job of it. "I told you a truth," he said. "Now it's your turn to tell me one."

"I just want to go home," I said, which was honest, even if it wasn't complete.

He nodded. "And I take it you can't go back the way you came?"

"Right." I fidgeted with the hem of my tunic. The temptation to unburden myself was huge. The problem was, I couldn't remember if they were burning witches this year or hanging them. "The thing is . . . I'm not really from Wales."

Whatever I was expecting, it wasn't for James to laugh. Certainly not a head-back, stomach-shaking guffaw that stayed with him even after he'd collected himself. "Eleanor, I'm not a superstitious man, but I have lain awake at night considering all sorts of things you might be. Angel, demon, sorceress, changeling . . . I don't know *what* you are. But I definitely know you're not Welsh."

I supposed he wouldn't be laughing if he thought I actually might be a demon or a sorceress. I glared at him anyway. "That's not funny. I don't want to be hanged as a witch any more than I want to be hanged as a goat bandit."

"Good point." But there was still humor in his eyes as he went on conversationally, "Let's leave it at that you are from West-of-Here."

"I have to find a way back. I have parents who need me. And a tourna—"

Dang it, Rob, maybe a gold medal never helped dig a well

in the desert, but I believed that sports could transform a life and that my accomplishments could inspire other women. And maybe it was hokey, but I believed in the Olympic spirit, too.

"I have things to do," I finished. "Things that are important in their own way."

James gazed at me thoughtfully. "What if you have things to do here, in England, in Nottingham. Things that only you can do."

"I don't believe in fate," I said. Which didn't mean I hadn't considered that there was some purpose to my switch to Medieval Relative Time. I was an archer in Sherwood Forest. I'd be an idiot not to theorize there was a pattern here. "What about free will?"

"If I fall into a well, whether I'm fated to or not doesn't matter. I have the free will to try to climb out, or to yell for help, or to lie down and die. Which, if any, of those things will result in my escape—"

"Stop," I said, holding up my hands. "I don't want a philosophical debate, I just want to go home."

"Why do you think it's one or the other?" James said reasonably. "You don't know how to get home, and you don't know what, if anything, you are meant to do here. Maybe they're the same thing."

That didn't help at all. Even if there was a pattern I was meant to trace, I was at ground level and couldn't see it. I was building a house from the inside out with no plans, and with the feeling that if I put a nail in the wrong spot the whole thing would collapse and change the future as I knew it. The pressure of all that made me fold over and rest my forehead on my knees with a groan.

"Here." James put a hand on my shoulder and offered me the canteen. I took it and drank. It was just water, but the normalcy of it steadied me, and the three deep swallows stopped me from hyperventilating. I hadn't realized I'd been shaking.

"Don't think about the war, or even the battle," he said, his hand still spanning my shoulder. "Think about the soldier in front of you. What will be your first step?"

"To not get killed," I intoned flatly.

His expression turned wry. "I hadn't meant literally, but I suppose that still applies." He stood and offered me a hand up. "And it happens to be one area where I can be of some help."

"Right now?" I asked, not eager exactly, but aware that if I was still here in thirty-eight and a half days, I was going to need some new skills in my tool kit.

"Tomorrow." He dropped my hand as soon as I was on my feet. "Today you can exercise your sword arm by helping me put in this gatepost."

CHAPTER SEVENTEEN

∂つC∂

Close combat was nothing like archery.

I mean, besides the obvious. When I was on the firing line, everything had an order—nock, draw, loose. There was nothing measured about fighting. Everything happened at once: swing of sword and spike of fear and spring of muscle.

The sword came down toward my neck, and I leapt out from under it. The weapon swished past me, but that was due more to James's proficiency than my graceless scramble out of the way.

"Eleanor!" he barked, holding the wooden practice sword off to the side, signaling we were in a time-out. "You are supposed to be learning to block and parry. So for the love of the Lord who made you, stand fast and block my swing!"

"I'm trying!" I protested, ignoring Much's laughter. He

was sitting on the wall, watching the lesson, and the only thing he enjoyed more than my clumsy wrestling with the training sword was listening to "Brother" James struggle not to fall back into soldier's language.

James didn't look like a friar at the moment. He was dressed like the day before, in brown wool trousers and a linen shirt that was open at the throat and rolled up to his elbows. Sparring with me hadn't made him sweat, but the day was sunny and warm.

I, on the other hand, was hot and sticky and seriously doubting I was cut out for this.

"Come here," James instructed, and I did. That part was simple. "If you cannot defend against something this basic, there's no point in continuing. Ready." It wasn't a question; it was a warning. He lifted his sword to make the same strike, and I really meant to stay put. But he was intimidating, even in plain clothes with just a stick, and I took an involuntary step back. He cursed. "Stand still. I'm not going to harm you."

"I *know.*" But instinct was instinct.

"Your two options are to engage or to retreat. Pick one and commit to it."

I wasn't too proud to admit that "run away" was plan A if caught off the church grounds by anyone, especially Captain Guilbert himself. Plan B was to stay alive until I could enact plan A.

"Being where the sword isn't seems a pretty good plan to me."

James scowled like I wasn't taking this seriously. "You can

dodge, but don't show fear. Any good opponent and most bad ones will hammer at that weakness." He gestured to the spot in front of him like he was asking me to dance. "And make no mistake, Henry Guilbert is probably the best sword west of Yorkshire."

I moved to where he pointed. "Is he better than you?" At James's quick frown, I reassured him, "Just asking."

"I don't know." His reply was matter-of-fact. "Ready? We'll go through the same defensive sequence." I got my practice sword into position, and he went on conversationally as we began again. "I haven't sparred with him since we were boys. I left for the Crusade when I was twelve."

I dropped my guard and stared at him. "You went to war when you were twelve?"

He didn't pause his swing, saying, like it was no big deal, "I'd been a squire since I was younger than Much."

"Yeah, but you've been at *war* since you were *twelve*," I repeated, as if that would make it less horrifying. James brought his sword around and I managed to get mine over to block him.

"We had to get there first," said James. He picked up the pace as he spoke. "The journey was its own battle, at times, as was living in the heat of the Holy Land or the muck of France."

I figured that if James said something was uncomfortable that meant it was excruciating. "Why did you go?"

"Because that is what you do when you are full of righteous zeal and idealistic enthusiasm." His tone said we were done talking about war, and his next swing came fast at my left side.

I squealed in surprise and jumped out of the way, but he followed through with the motion and smacked me high on my thigh with the flat of the wooden sword. *Hard.* Numbness spread out from the impact, and then, a second later, came a sting like a *mother.*

"Son of a bitch!" I cried, rubbing my leg. "You said you wouldn't hit me."

He didn't apologize. "I said I wouldn't *harm* you." He didn't lower his weapon, either. "That is why you can't flinch from the attack. Anticipate it, and meet it."

I wiped the sweat out of my eyes. My arms were killing me, but I got the sword up when he came at me and didn't let up. It was hard to make my moves purposeful when I felt like I was dancing a beat behind the music and struggling to catch up. I barely made three blocks, and then took another smack, this time on my well-padded arm. "Ow!"

"Look at me," James said, "not my sword." At least he was sweating a little now.

"How am I supposed to block if I don't watch what I'm doing?" I asked.

"How do you know where your arrow is going to go?" he countered as we circled each other. "You look at the bow, do you?"

"I look at the target."

"Exactly." He lunged. I kept my gaze on his face and caught the tiny tells that showed his intent. I knocked his blade aside and went on the offensive. I pictured where I wanted my sword to go and tried to make it a part of me, like my bow.

James went for the high slash that I always ducked. I saw his shoulders shift. When his arm went up, I stepped under it and jammed my padded forearm under his wrist so the sword couldn't come down. My right arm was low, too close to thrust, so I went for a rising slash that would give him a bruise to match mine. With a twist of his arm, he brought his sword down and around like he was taking a golf swing. He blocked my sword, but he had to step back to do it.

Exhilarated at the tiny victory, I went on the offensive. The next thing I knew, James had disarmed me and I saw his weapon coming straight at my heart. He veered, though, and the wooden sword slid very precisely between my chest and my left arm.

Dammit.

We stood there for a moment, breathing hard—well, I was breathing hard—our eyes locked like we'd switched to a staring contest. My pride felt properly skewered, but I wouldn't back away first.

Finally he sighed and lowered his sword. "Eleanor," he began. With his free hand, he brushed a lock of hair out of my face. "Promise me something."

"Yeah?" I breathed, not caring what I was agreeing to.

His hand settled on my shoulder, fingers spread, his thumb resting close to the pulse in my throat. "Please don't get into a sword fight with anybody."

I laughed, even though he wasn't joking. "What about Guilbert's challenge?"

"It won't come to that. I'm more afraid you'll come to trouble wandering off the friary property. You could run afoul of much worse than Henry Guilbert."

"I'll be fine," I assured James.

"Eleanor." He said my name again, and gently squeezed the shoulder where his hand rested. "You cannot even kill a rabbit without tears. How are you going to thrust a sword into a man's flesh? Or an arrow, for that matter."

I honestly didn't know what I would do if it came to that. I figured I would be prepared, and the rest would sort itself out. "What about you?" I countered. "You told me you'd had your fill of killing."

I watched the ghost of battle move across his face and leave him weary. Dropping his hand from my shoulder, he went to collect my practice sword. "My fill and more. Which is why I ask that you please—"

Hoofbeats coming from the village made him break off. Someone was riding fast, not from the Great North Road but from the forest. James and I didn't even exchange looks. He grabbed his real sword, and I ran for my bow and quiver, nocking an arrow as the rider came into sight.

The horse slowed to a trot, and the rider raised both hands to show he wasn't armed. By then I'd already recognized him.

"Will Scarlet," I greeted him by name for James's benefit. "You own a horse?"

"Of course not," he said. "I stole it."

His bravado seemed thin, and his face was drawn. Something was wrong.

James was still in a battle mind-set. I heard it in his voice as he took in Will's tension and his sweating horse and asked, "What's happened?"

Ignoring him, Will addressed me with his answer. "John the Smith," he said. "Little John, you call him. His son has been taken for poaching. The sheriff is going to pronounce sentence at Edwinstowe, where the boy's family can see."

"Poaching deer?" asked James, with that same clipped authority.

Will flicked a blazing look his way. "Do you think I would be coming to you over a few partridges?" To me, he said, "The boy's a young fool, only two and ten, thinking he can provide for all his sisters while his father is outlawed. John snuck back with some game every now and then, but after he brought his share of the roast goat—"

"Little John took the goat to the village?" I asked.

The outlaw gave me a dry look, more like his usual self. "Thanks to your sermon, yes. He was hailed as a hero, which suited John just fine, and young Jack got the idea that if a goat was good, a deer would be better. So I lay this at your door, Robin of the Hood."

That was nice of him, but I could feel plenty guilty without any help. I slung my quiver and adjusted it to make sure it didn't highlight my chest. I'd bound everything up tight, but it was what it was. "Where's Little John now?" I asked.

"Headed to Edwinstowe," Will answered. "I think he's going to do something rash and violent. That's what John does."

I was about to do something rash. Violent, however, remained to be seen. Stepping up onto the wall, I gestured for

Will to bring his horse closer so I could mount behind him. "Hold up a moment," said James. I glanced down at him, expecting an argument. "Shouldn't we have some sort of plan?"

"Plan?" I grabbed the hand Will extended to pull me up. "I thought you'd know me better than that by now."

I settled behind the saddle and found the right angle for my bow. A glance over my shoulder showed James loping toward the horse pen, with Much sprinting after him.

"Your *cher ami* looks different out of uniform," said Will.

"You have no idea," I replied, thinking of the armor and all that. But Will interpreted it differently and laughed. "That's not what I meant," I blurted.

"If you're defrocking a cleric, little Robin, you're a bigger sinner than any of us."

"Just ride," I told him, and held tightly to his belt.

CHAPTER EIGHTEEN

THE VILLAGE OF EDWINSTOWE LAY AT THE INTERSECTION OF two roads through Sherwood Forest. It was big enough to rate a tavern inn, but small enough that the hundred or so people in the village green seemed like a crowd. Nottingham soldiers watched the roads into town, but Will and I hadn't had any trouble blending in with the folk arriving from scattered farms to see what was going on.

"We won't have such an easy time getting out again," Will murmured from behind his mug of ale. The tavern was standing room only, even at the tables outside.

James and Much would be coming along at any moment. We'd left the conspicuous warhorse in the woods and split up there. James had gone full Friar Tuck—his rough wool habit done up properly, rope belt in place of his sword, cowl draped over his shoulders—but he still walked and talked like a Sir James. Whereas no one looked twice at the overdressed William Fitzwhatever and his servant boy.

Will checked out the crowd without looking like he was doing anything other than checking out the ladies, not a few of which were looking him over in return.

I had my game face on too, and all my calculations were going on behind it. "Isn't it weird that Guilbert didn't put any of his rangers on the roads into town? People who would recognize me by sight, I mean."

Because of the crowded tavern yard, I'd spoken in French to foil eavesdroppers, but there was so much gossip and chatter going on, it was hard to hear anyone who wasn't speaking in your ear. But Will replied in the same language, the better to tease me. "Maybe you have an elevated idea of your importance to the dashing captain."

I thought about the look on Guilbert's face when I'd called him a coward, and how he must have heard by now that certain chapel poor boxes and pantries were a little fuller than they were a few days ago. "*My* importance, probably. Robin Hood, on the other hand . . ."

"Robin Hood, did you say?" said a man at a table near us, in thick English. I jumped, but he wasn't talking to me. He drunkenly thumped his ale onto the rough wooden table and leaned on his elbows to tell the man across from him, "That's the cause of this, you know. You think His Honor the sheriff of Nottingham would haul his bony ass up here over a poacher if he weren't . . . weren't . . ."

"Mad as a hornet?" his companion quipped.

There were a few quickly stifled titters from the folks clumped around, and a few warning shushes. Will and I exchanged looks. Mine was sort of a "see," and his was more of a "whatever."

The joker continued, in a not-too-worried tone, "My money says it will be the stocks for the lad."

"What money?" said another man. "The sheriff took all your money."

More laughter, but it was commiserating. "The smith's family is no better off," said a woman who was coming around with refills. "They can't pay a fine. Not with John the Smith down for an outlaw these past five months. It'll be the stocks for the lad, if he's lucky."

A moment of grim silence as that sank in. Then a new voice chimed in, more resonant than the others, with a bit of an accent—rounder on the vowels, softer on the consonants. "Then this troublemaker I've heard tell of . . . he's not just a fanciful tale?"

"Hardly. My own pa was at Nottingham Castle and saw him shoot a plum, naught but the size of a baby's fist, from atop the miller's son's head."

The target in my trial kept getting smaller each time Much brought the tale back to me, which he did after every visit to town. He enjoyed the celebrity.

"And the Marian Sisters at Northgate Priory have plenty of goat cheese again."

There was a good bit of snickering at that. The man with

the accent—was it Spanish? Mediterranean maybe?—went on to ask, "So it's true that he is in love with a lady there?"

Will gave my shoulder a hearty slap, and I jumped. I'd gotten much too involved in listening to my own press. "Boy," he said, in a theatrical voice, "go stable my horse. I think I'll stay and see how the story of this young poacher unfolds."

That was my cue to leave. I murmured something that at least sounded like "Yes, m'lord," then ducked out of the pub's crowded yard, grabbed the reins of Will's horse, and headed one lane over. At the intersection I saw two of Sherwood's forest rangers. I turned like I was fixing something on the horse's saddle, and the pair rode by without pause.

I didn't have to loiter long before Much came down the lane, his sturdy little horse hitched to a stolen pony cart. He didn't stop as I slipped away from the wall, tied Will's horse to the back of the cart, and slid my quiver and bow from underneath the empty grain sacks. All those spy movies were good for something.

After putting up my hood, I slouched, and carried my bow like a walking stick. My quiver, banging against my thigh underneath the cloak, gave a convincing hitch to my step as I joined the flow of traffic headed for the town green. It wasn't rock-concert ground-seating crowded, but as tall as I was, I could only just see the ginormous oak tree, which a lot of kids had climbed for a good view, and the church steeple roughly fifty yards away.

Where the road split to circle the green stood a big stone cross, raised up by three steps. Some people had climbed the steps for a better view of the proceedings, but there was still room and I claimed it.

Now I could see that roughly in the center of the green was a permanent structure that held the village's stocks and enough room for public speeches. The sheriff of Nottingham was already addressing the public. I didn't try too hard to translate his English to my English. The gist was clear.

Also on the platform was an older man, stiffly resentful and not trying to hide it. His clothes looked high-quality, though less ornate than the sheriff's, and the expensive dyes had faded. A local lord, maybe?

There was no sign of Guilbert, and I didn't see any of the rangers on the green, just the guards in Nottingham livery. Two of the sheriff's soldiers stood with him in front of the crowd, and between them was a wiry boy with red hair. The kid was white-faced and his hands were curled into fists to hide their shaking.

The sheriff lifted a hand for silence, his fur-lined cloak framing him. The crowd responded to the dramatic picture and finally quieted. "A boy of your village, Jack, the smith's son, has killed one of the king's deer. You all know that is the same as if he'd stolen from King Richard himself. The punishment must be accordingly severe."

"Your Honor," said the other man on the platform with forced politeness. "Perhaps we should let the boy say how he came to shoot the deer." With approval from the sheriff, the man turned to Jack and gave him a significant nod. "Go ahead, lad."

Some color came back into the kid's face, and he looked like a castaway sighting dry land. "The deer was foraging in the new-sown field. I never did go into the forest, my lord."

In a terribly logical voice, the sheriff said, "But all deer come from the forest, and every deer in the forest—even the ones that wander out—can be said to belong to the king."

Unhappy murmurs started up, and the local lord snapped, "It *could* be said, if one wants to be unnecessarily harsh."

The sheriff narrowed his eyes. "I would love to be lenient, Lord Barnsdale. I don't enjoy punishing the young." His volume rose to make sure the villagers got his point. "But, there has been a rash of disrespect for the king's justice lately and everyone needs to know that stealing from the crown is the same as treason!"

"Treason?" The word erupted from the front left of the crowd, and I climbed a step higher on the cross to get a look. There was Little John, roaring like a bear, with Will and about three other men holding him back. "I'll tell you what's treason, you baby-robbing, sheep-stealing twit!"

"Pa!" cried Jack from the platform.

The soldiers in front of the platform lowered their pikes and raised their swords. Will was saying something to John that was impossible to make out through the crowd's noise, but I bet it was "Don't be stupid."

The sheriff nodded to one of the soldiers, and then two more carried up a big wooden block with ominous-looking stains. The villagers shut up, and a surreal horror floated up inside me and tightened my throat. No way was the sheriff going to chop off a twelve-year-old's head for treason. But then a huge, heavy ax came out next, followed by the dead silence of a collectively held breath.

From my angle, I could just see the smug curl of the sheriff's lip as he spun out the drama. "Jack the smith's son will only lose a hand today, but let that be a warning—"

The rest dissolved under a burst of inarticulate curses from John, and from somewhere came a woman's keening sob, the kind of wail that can only come from a mother. Like someone had cut a cord holding back their voices, everyone on the green started talking—to each other, to themselves, to God. . . .

And where the hell was James?

I stepped behind the marker cross and pressed my back to its cold stone, taking as deep of a breath as dread would allow. Someone was going to have to stop this, and underneath the top layer of wheel-spinning adrenaline, I calculated how it was going to be me.

The cry for mercy went up, picked up from the sobs of Jack's mother and carried through the crowd. It receded like a wave and I slipped back around the monument to see the sheriff raising one hand for silence. "Jack the smith's son will lose his left hand, not his right."

"No!" Little John threw off the restraining hands like a buffalo shaking off flies. "It was me! I shot the deer. Let the boy go."

"Fine," said the sheriff, as if it made absolutely no difference to him. "Release the boy. Hang the bandit."

Well, crap.

The crowd erupted like a pot boiling over onto a stove. I

was pushed back behind the stone cross by people trying to get a better view. I had to judge by the shouts and cries, and the guards ordering everyone back, what was happening.

After all that talking, no one wasted time getting to the hanging. While the soldiers cleared people from beneath the big oak tree, I got my bearings. They'd released Jack, and Will was holding him back as the boy kicked and yelled. Much was at the edge of the green, gripping the leads of both his pony and Will's horse with a white-knuckled fist, ready for a getaway. Lord Barnsdale seemed to be trying to wear down the sheriff with words, since reason and compassion were lost causes.

"Thank God," said someone right beside me. I jumped and looked down to see James standing at ground level. "There you are."

"I could say the same for you." Including the "thank God" part.

There was a new commotion as the soldiers managed to get Little John on the back of one of the horses, hands tied in front of him and a noose around his neck. The soldiers wound the end of the noose around the stoutest tree limb—it took about four loops and two half-hitch knots to hold it in place. It was a thick rope, which was going to make it easier to hit but harder to cut cleanly.

"What do you need?" asked James, not even considering that we couldn't or wouldn't do something.

"Some cover, first." James stepped onto the base of the marker cross like he was just trying to get a better view, hiding me while I strung my bow. The rote action steadied my hands as I pictured the shot I would have to make. My timing would have to be perfect for the rope to snap and not John's neck. "Okay. Now I need a countdown," I said.

James followed my gaze, looked at my bow, then nodded. "You'll have it. Be ready."

Jumping from the marker, he pressed forward through the crowd calling, "Your Honor!" The villagers quieted as he passed between them, so he didn't have to raise his voice. "Allow me to pray for the condemned before you execute him."

I ducked around the stone to where I could see. Lord Barnsdale looked surprised, then seemed as if he was going to greet James by name, but stopped himself. If the sheriff recognized James from my trial, he didn't show it. He just waved his permission to get on with it.

Elbowing to the corner of the marker's top step, I reached under my cloak to get an arrow. If I needed more than one, John would be dead.

The soldiers made room for James next to the horse on which Little John, pallid above his red beard, was mounted. James put a reassuring hand on the man's leg, then raised his right hand to cross himself. There was my countdown.

Forehead.

I nocked the arrow and caught the bowstring in the same motion. Everyone around me vanished, and I focused on the slack rope of the noose.

Chest.

I lifted the bow and drew, pushing against the resistance of the yew, pulling against the spring of the heartwood.

Left shoulder.

From far away came a commotion, but it existed in another universe from me, James, and the rope around Little John's neck.

Right—

James slapped the horse on its flank and I loosed the arrow. The horse took off with Little John clinging to its back, the cut end of the noose trailing behind. A half gasp, half cheer went up from the villagers, and I thought my head was going to float off my shoulders because that was a freaking gold-medal shot.

And then I realized the horse was running away with Little John, whose hands were tied and whose look of terror said he didn't know how to steer the horse even if he weren't flopping around on its back like a hog-tied calf.

"Will!" I shouted over the noise of all hell breaking loose. About twenty Wills looked around, so I shouted, "Will Scarlet!" I pointed at Little John, and Will waved his understanding and sprinted for his horse. He leapt onto Much's pony cart, then onto the back of the horse, like some kind of matinee idol.

"Elli—*Robin,* look out!" shouted Much, and pointed behind me and up.

Oh hell. I'd wondered where Guilbert and his rangers might be. Pouring out of the village chapel on foot and from the churchyard on horseback, they headed for my very conspicuous position.

I dove off my perch and into the crowd, managing not to land on anyone. I ran toward the big oak tree, because that was the last place I'd seen James, but I couldn't find him in the chaos. The sheriff was screaming, the rangers were yelling, the villagers were trying to figure out what had happened, and my racing heart was going to be spitted by some soldier's pike any second, I just knew it.

"Boy!" said the accented voice I'd heard in the tavern. "In here."

The person that went with the voice grabbed my cloak before I figured out where "in here" was. I was pushed into a hollow in the ginormous oak, a space I hadn't seen before, though I'd been staring at that tree harder than anyone.

"What do you—" I poked my head out, getting a look at his dark hair and beard and his golden-brown skin. He was definitely the guy in the tavern who'd asked about Robin Hood, and logic said I should be suspicious. But he was obviously not from around here, which gave us something in common.

With a hand on my forehead, he shoved me back into the niche in the tree.

"I think you may be out of miracles today, my friend, so stay hidden. I'll tell the monk where you are."

I glimpsed a swish of a colorful cloak, but once I edged back, I couldn't see out at all. The tree was so big and old that it had grown around an old injury, curtaining the hollow so it wasn't visible from straight on, and no one much bigger than me would be able to fit.

My breath filled the space, the air thickening with my panic. I braced my free hand on the side of the trunk to keep it from closing in on me. I was hidden, but I was also blind. I could turn, but I couldn't draw my bow. I was a mouse in a cage and all I could picture was a hand reaching in to grab me and feed me to a snake.

Stop that. Focus. You're okay.

I had my bow; I had a few arrows. I wasn't a mouse. I was a fox gone to ground, waiting for the pack of dogs to go by.

The clamor of men and horses was wild enough for a hunt. Then there were the cries of children as the soldiers rousted the village. I heard the sheriff's voice as though he stood right outside the tree.

"Five coins of silver on the head of the outlaw they call Robin of Hood!" he called. "Three on his men Will Scarlet and John the Smith!"

I let my head fall back against the rough wood of the hollow and banged it gently while I waited for the village green to clear. I couldn't blame fate, or anyone but myself. I'd chosen my name, christened Will and Little John. No one made me rob goats from the rich and give them back to the poor. I'd written myself into the story.

I had become a fictional character.

"Scour the forest for this bandit Robin Hood!" shouted the sheriff of Nottingham. "I will see him hang from the gate of Nottingham Castle!"

CHAPTER NINETEEN

❧

I SHOULD HAVE STOLEN A HORSE.

I hadn't gotten very far out of Edwinstowe before I realized that. God, my feet hurt.

My thought had been to avoid the thoroughfare—a horse would need the road—and get through the woods on foot. I'd tried, but I'd gotten lost, and then stuck in the brush so bad I had to cut myself loose. I figured I would be a lot more noticeable blundering like a wild boar through the underbrush than just keeping to the road and taking cover when anyone came by.

I also didn't really know where I was going. I'd headed out of Edwinstowe the way we'd come in, figuring that was my best chance of catching up with an ally. Mapperley was out, because that was the first place anyone would look for me. The second was the priory. Besides, I'd brought enough trouble on the sisters already. And James, well, I hoped he and Much were in the clear. No price on their heads, so maybe the Brother James ruse would continue to hold up with the sheriff—as long as Guilbert didn't tip him off.

Guilbert. Him and his stupid forest rangers. I could hear Nottingham's soldiers coming in plenty of time to get off the road and take cover. But when a pair of rangers nearly rode right up on me, I had to dive into the bushes. My foot caught between two branches, and I wrenched it free to roll into the cold, damp space beneath a fallen log.

Son of a bitch.

The rangers went by, but I stayed where I was as the sharp twist of my ankle became a fiery throb up my leg.

It was dim and cold already—the forest brought dusk on early. The smell of earth and mulch that seemed ripe and nurturing in the warmth of day turned graveyard dank as it chilled. I lay on my belly in the middle of it, shivering and tired and really worried that it would be full dark before I found shelter.

Dammit, Ellie. Whatever Robin Hood is supposed to do here, I'm pretty sure dying of hypothermia while feeling sorry for yourself isn't it.

I'd rolled out from under the log and pushed myself into a crouch when I heard another horse and rider on the road. Like, right on the road, just on the other side of my hiding place. I waited for him to pass, but instead I heard him rein in his horse and two more rangers—the ones that had just passed, I figured—join him.

I was crouched in five inches of dead leaves, and if I so much as shifted my weight, they'd hear it. If they were Nottingham's soldiers, I'd risk rolling back into my hiding place. But not with the rangers. Why weren't they off fighting forest fires or something?

"Any sign?" said the new rider. Guilbert. Of freaking course.

"None that we could see from the road," said one of his men.

"Do you think it's likely he came this way?" asked the other. "Mapperley and Northgate are both to the south. What would bring Hood east?"

"He's not so foolish as to go straight south," said the first ranger.

Only, I was. I thought I *had* been going south.

Guilbert gave what would have been a good answer, if I'd known about it. "Lady Isabel's manor house is this way. Even if she only mentioned it to Hood, he might seek it as a refuge. Keep riding to Ravenswood, but don't give any of the tenants any trouble. Just take a look around."

"Yes, Captain."

Thank God. I was getting a cramp in my twisted ankle that was about to kill me. Two sets of horse hooves went off to the east and one went . . . south-ish. Breathing through clenched teeth, I gave them enough time to get out of sight. I didn't even risk flexing my ankle until I couldn't hear the horses anymore. Only then did I grab my bow from the ground beside me and stand up.

Captain Henry Freaking Guilbert stood, horseless, facing me, arms folded, feet apart.

Shit.

"Don't move," he said.

I made the fastest shot I'd ever made in my life—nock, draw, loose—sending an arrow *ffft*ing by Guilbert's ear. He turned away from it instinctively, and while he was facing one direction, I took off running in the other.

I went for the road, where I could stretch out my stride. I'd outrun him before—in sneakers and without a twisted ankle. Still, I might have done it again, if he hadn't launched himself and taken me down with an old-fashioned football tackle around the knees. I smacked the ground hard, my bow flying out of my hand as everything went numb and gray fuzz crawled across my vision.

Guilbert didn't jump right up, either, but he made it to his feet before I'd gotten my wind back. "Get up," he wheezed.

I ignored him and crawled for my bow, making it about a millimeter before I heard the sound of a sword being drawn. Rolling over to face Guilbert, I found the point of his blade about two feet from my chest.

Pushing myself up slowly, I got to my feet and raised my hands. "I'm unarmed."

"I don't care," he said.

"That's not fair!"

His icy demeanor cracked enough for him to snap, "This isn't a tournament. This is an arrest." A great big fist of fear squeezed my chest. I would never get as far as the dungeons before my head would be the sheriff's new lawn ornament. "It's time for this nonsense to end."

"What nonsense?" I demanded. "Hungry families? Empty livestock pens and grain ... thingies? Cutting off a twelve-year-old's *hand*? You set a trap for me with a *kid's hand* as bait, you asshole!"

A flush of anger rose up his neck but he stayed in control. "You can take that up with His Honor the sheriff once you're standing in front of him."

He whistled sharply, and I heard the clop of horse hooves. Porsche came around the bend. I was too sick of Guilbert to admit that was cool.

"Get over to the horse," said Guilbert.

I edged my weight so that I could make a break for my bow. I was placing a really big bet that he had orders to bring me in alive, and I was desperate. "I don't think I will."

"Devil take it," he spat under his breath, and started toward me. I kept my eyes on his face, not letting his size or his armor or even the sword get into my head. I saw the twitch that said he was taking the sword to my left, and I slid right, coming inside the reach of his blade and up under his arm to brace my forearm under his sword wrist, the way I had with James. As he rolled his arm over to break the lock, I spun in like we were jitterbugging, only instead of dancing back out I punched him in the ribs, throwing all my weight into the jab. I felt at least one crack under my knuckles as I spun out with the follow-through, and Guilbert doubled over.

That I hadn't learned from James. That was all my brother Rob.

Guilbert gasped with the shock of it and I hobbled to my bow, snatching it up. There was a thin strip of cold numbness on my left side, but I couldn't be bothered. Guilbert was after me again. I held on to the bow and kept running, fumbling over my shoulder for an arrow, trying to gain enough distance to fire a shot. I nocked before I stopped, spun as I drew, and ordered, "Stop there, Guilbert."

He didn't stop, and I loosed the arrow, putting the shaft into his thigh.

That brought him to his knees, jarring a roar of pain from him. All the color went out of his face—shock, warned Iron Ellie. He clapped his hand to where the arrow jutted out from the muscle, and blood welled up between his gloved fingers.

I was going to be sick. I needed to run. But I took an involuntary step toward him.

"You actually shot me," he said, when he could gasp anything but curses.

The arrow had missed the bone and pierced the fleshy part of his thigh. When he pressed his hand around the shaft, the arrow shifted. "Don't pull it out!" I cried.

"I know not to pull it out, you madwoman!" he snarled.

"You should have stopped when I told you to." My side had gone from icy numbness to a fiery sting, as if matching my emotions. I put one hand over my ribs and saw blood trickling down my side from a shallow slice as long as my hand. "Oh my God, you could have killed me."

The color came back to his face. "You shouldn't have turned into my sword."

"Hang on," I said, and raised a hold-everything hand while my brain caught up with my mouth. "You knew?"

He pushed himself upright, teeth clenched. "I know a pullet from a cockerel." With a grunt he got his good leg under him. I was all sorts of shocked.

"Don't get up! What is wrong with you?" I looked around like a first-aid kit would magically appear out of thin air.

"Why do you think I didn't drag you straight to the sheriff that first day? I gave you every opportunity to die of a brain fever and reemerge. . . ." He ran out of steam and used the rest of his breath to curse.

I rewound to the beginning and then zipped back through everything in between. "You knew I was a girl when you challenged me to a *duel*?"

"You knew you were a girl when you attacked my men." His glare was narrow-eyed and unapologetic. "I treated you like what you were—are. I thought you'd see sense. Besides, I wouldn't have hurt you."

I made an indignant sound and held up my bloody fingers as proof otherwise. Through the sheen of sweat on his face, he looked more annoyed than chagrined. "That was unintentional."

"You want to take me to the sheriff to get my head cut off."

"You are an outlaw. And the law is—"

"Stupid. Your law is stupid and—"

He held up his hand, which was a lot bloodier than mine. "Be silent."

It was a command, delivered in a commander's voice, and I shut up in an instinctive reaction to it. And also a little bit because, holy crap, he was really bleeding. I'd done that to him. "Guilbert, you need a doc—"

"Quiet." Guilt or no guilt, I was about to tell him to go to hell when I heard what he heard—at least one horse, coming fast. Guilbert listened a moment longer. "That's not one of mine," he said. "That's a destrier."

"What's a—"

"Press here." He grabbed my hand and put it on his outer thigh where the arrow had lodged. I applied pressure, basic first aid, not sure what he was going to do until he took hold of the shaft of the arrow with two hands and quickly, like ripping off a Band-Aid, broke it off a couple of finger widths from the wound.

"Holy shit." That was one way to get the long end out of his way. "I can't believe you just did that."

Guilbert was so pale he looked green in the early dusk of the forest. "Does James know what a blasphemer you are?" He wiped the sweat off his face and threw the end of the arrow aside, then nodded in the direction of the rider. "Speak of the devil . . ."

James cantered around the bend on that SUV of a horse of his. A destrier, I presumed. Guilbert's sports-car ride sidled out of the way with a snort as James reined to a halt and swung down in the same motion.

I left Guilbert to deal with his bloody leg and ran to meet James. He was wearing his sword and dressed for business. "Oh my God, I'm so glad to see you," I gushed, and grabbed his arm on my way to his horse. I didn't want to be here when the next riders down the road turned out to be the rangers looking for their captain and, more to the point, me. I didn't want James here, either. I'd gotten enough people almost killed today.

James caught my other arm and turned me toward him. "You're limping." He took me by both shoulders and bent to look at my face, into my eyes. "What's wrong? Are you hurt?"

"No. Well, yes, but—" My throat tightened and I raised one hand to wipe my face, because I was crying stupid tears of relief. James took one look at the blood on my hand and started checking me for injuries from the top down. "I'm just so glad to see you. Is everyone— Ouch!"

James had gotten to the slice in my tunic, and, with grim-faced efficiency, he examined my side. He got grimmer, and steelier.

He looked past me, toward Guilbert, with righteous fury brewing in his eyes. "James . . ." I knew the cut looked worse than it was—at home they'd just superglue it together—but tell that to a knight defender of victims of their own impetuosity. "Don't—"

Either everything was moving fast or I was moving slowly. James set me carefully out of his path and drew his sword as he locked his gaze on Guilbert and made straight for him. I expected the captain to raise his empty hands and call a cease-fire, but instead he slid the toe of his injured side under the edge of his sword where it lay, flipped it up, and had it in his hand in time to swing at James as soon as he was in reach.

Crap. He *did* have moves.

James ducked it easily and countered. The sound of clashing steel rang through the woods. Guilbert moved so well, was so balanced as he took his weight on his good leg, that I didn't think James could even tell he was injured. It was crazy impressive and totally pigheaded.

"James, stop," I called. "His leg is—"

Will rode up behind me as Guilbert made a feint and then advanced with short, fast hacks that had James on the defensive but didn't betray Guilbert's limp. And all I could do was stand there and wring my hands like some fair maiden. Yelling did no good, I didn't want to shoot anyone else, and I wasn't quite foolish enough to jump between them.

"*Merde,*" said Will, sounding more impressed than upset. "Are they fighting over you, *chérie?*"

"Of course not." At least, not in the way he meant. This had been brewing since the first day at the river, over some fire that must have been lit before James ever left Nottingham. It just needed a catalyst.

James went on the offensive and Guilbert held him off without doing more than touching his left foot to the ground. I couldn't discern much, but Will acted as commentator. "They're both trying to win without seriously hurting the other. We could be here all night waiting for one of them to quit first."

Right. One or both of them needed an excuse to stop

without losing face. *Finally, an idea.* It was clichéd, but I was freaking Robin Hood. Came with the territory.

"I don't feel very well," I said, more loudly than necessary. When they didn't pay attention, I put my hand to my forehead, swayed a bit, and then collapsed onto the rutted road in a graceful faint.

"Ellie!" exclaimed Will, with genuine alarm. I heard his feet hit the ground beside me as he dismounted. "What's wrong?"

The fighting stopped with one last steel-guitar slide of sword against sword. James dropped to a knee beside me and started checking the first-aid ABCs—airway, breathing, circulation.

With my ear on the ground, I heard the next wave of riders coming. I opened my eyes and, looking around James's boot, I saw an ashen Guilbert had whistled his horse over so he could hang on to the saddle. Idiot.

"Those are Nottingham soldiers coming," warned Guilbert. "You"—he pointed at Will—"get over here and help me mount."

As Will went to do so, James looked suspiciously at the captain. "When do you ever need help getting on a horse?" he asked.

I sat up—*ow ow ow*—and snapped, "Because I shot him in the leg! I tried to tell you."

James stood and faced Guilbert. "Why didn't you say so?" he demanded, confused and angry.

Guilbert reined his horse around and looked down his nose at James. "Because I wanted to find out if I could still beat you." He looked over the three of us dismissively and stopped on me. "And you, *Robin Hood* . . . I don't want to ever see you again in this forest."

He rode to head off the approaching soldiers, as incredible as that seemed. Will looked at me with a what-the-hell-just happened expression that I returned with a growing fuzziness. *Everything* had happened, or at least it felt that way.

I turned to James, who watched me with that composure of his, which told me nothing, especially in the darkening forest. When he fought with Guilbert, his power and control hadn't surprised me, but his righteous ferocity had reminded me that he wasn't just Friar Tuck, my sidekick. He was a freaking *knight*. And he stood there with his sword, and that stance, and those shoulders, looking me over, cataloging my injuries and calculating how much trouble I was.

"James," I began steadily. I regretted nothing—well, almost nothing—but I was still grateful. "I know you're probably a little upset with me for getting outlawed and all—"

With no warning, no change of expression, he closed the few feet between us and wrapped his left arm around me, holding me tightly to him, his cheek against the top of my head. Oh God. It hurt. The fire that spiked out from the cut on my ribs was nothing next to the burn that spread out from my heart. He smelled of leather and woodsmoke, of the candles from the chapel and some other scent that had faded from my century.

"You must be more careful," he said. With my head resting on his chest, I felt the words more than heard them. "I said I'd keep you from harm. Don't make me a liar, Eleanor."

I sighed out the last of the fight-or-flight I had left, and my fingers tightened on his sleeve just to keep exhaustion and emotion from knocking my legs out from under me. I didn't think about the next round or the next arrow, I just stood in the moment.

"Excusez-moi, mes amis," said Will from atop his horse, "I hate to break up this tender moment . . ." Funny. He didn't sound regretful. "But we should do as the man said and be going."

"Indeed," said James, releasing me and stepping back to put his sword away. In a fog of tired, I moved to the horses, knowing from experience that I could catnap while leaned up against James's back. He came over, picked me up easily, and placed me—behind Will.

Wait. *What?*

James swung up into his own saddle and Will spurred his horse. I grabbed onto his waist to keep from somersaulting over the horse's tail. Will was shaking slightly, and I suspected he was laughing.

I was pretty sure I'd just been declared an outlaw by the sheriff of Nottingham and friend-zoned by Friar Tuck in the same day. I'll bet *that* had never happened in any tale of Robin Hood.

CHAPTER TWENTY

I WOKE UP ON A SURPRISINGLY COMFORTABLE PALLET IN A
shockingly bright cave—the morning sun came straight
through the opening like nature's alarm clock, with no freaking snooze button. Every single part of me hurt, including my
head, and I had no clue where I was.

Rewind—it had been just after dark when James, Will,
and I had ridden into a small camp in the shelter of a curved
hill. There was a low fire going, and Little John and Much
were waiting for us anxiously. John had dislocated his shoulder falling off the runaway horse; with the help of all three of
us, James popped it back into place. I was surprised John's roar
of pain hadn't brought half of Nottinghamshire to the camp
to claim the bounty on our heads.

Then James—all business—field-dressed my cut, which

involved excruciating scrubbing, slapping a wine-soaked bandage on it, and handing me a cup of the same to take the edge off. Little John had taken off so many edges he was round, but I didn't drink much. I was too worried I'd say something regrettable. I had enough problems with impulse control when dead sober.

I rolled over with a groan and found someone sitting on a small stool, watching me. I jumped, immediately regretted it, and when I finally brought the brown-and-white blob into focus, I'd already worked it out that it was Sister Lady Isabel.

"Good morning, outlaw," she said cheerfully.

"What are you doing here?" I croaked.

She smiled. "We're not a cloistered convent, though, since we're supposed to travel in pairs, Elsbeth the miller's daughter came with me. Much's sister—"

"Is a sister." I pushed my hair out of my face. "I remember now. And he told you how to get . . ." I looked around, baffled by the contrast of cave with everything else. I slept on a pallet of fluffy featherbed and soft woolen blankets. There were carpets covering the dirt floor, a sort of table or desk, and a camp bed with a canopy over it. "Where are we?"

"From what I gather," she said, with a wry lift of her brows, "your friend Master Will Scarlet does not care for . . ."

"Roughing it?" I finished, when she faltered for the word.

"Exactly. Outlaw or not." She rose and went to the table. "Come over here to better light so I can see what these savages have done to you."

I knew better than to disobey. Besides, having survived one fever, I didn't want to tempt fate and end up dying of what was essentially a six-inch paper cut. I'd acquired a clean shirt at some point last night, and I tugged it up so she could see my ribs. "You should look at Little John—John the Smith, I mean."

"I have. He's mending already. James must have put a lot of shoulders back in joint while in the Holy Land."

When I'd asked him about that, James had simply said that physicians weren't always readily available in battle, and then changed the subject.

"You'll live, too," said Isabel, after she rinsed the cut with something herbal and sort of tingly, tying on a clean linen bandage with some kind of salve. "Keep this on it, and you might not even have a scar."

"Oh my God." I grabbed her arm as the rest of my brain woke up. "You have to get Clothilde to go to Nottingham Castle. Guilbert's leg—" My stomach turned over. That arrow had been new, and pretty clean, but with no antibiotics . . .

"She set off as soon as Much arrived at first light this morning." Isabel covered my hand with hers. "Don't you re-member giving him that message?"

Vaguely, before that half a cup of wine knocked me out.

"In any case," said Isabel, packing up the few things she had with her, "she threatened to beat off the barracks surgeon with her wooden spoon if necessary. Henry will be in good hands." She cast a sideways look at me. "You're in for a lecture, though. Something about her expecting better of a sensible young woman, even if she is wearing men's clothes."

I resigned myself to that fate. If Clothilde fixed it so Guil-bert didn't die because of me, it would be worth it. "So . . ."

I needed some gossip, but only so I knew what I was dealing with. "Guilbert and James. What's their story?"

"What's the bad blood between them, you mean?" At my nod, Isabel picked up her little medieval medical bag and tucked it under one arm. "Come along. Elsbeth and I brought breakfast."

We went out to the fire. The space in front of the cave—or rather, caves—was protected on three sides by the hill. On the fourth side, the slope continued down past the natural ledge, but there was a screen of seriously thick forest. Not only was the hideout well hidden, but there was barely a deer track going through all that green. Nothing bigger than Bambi was going to get here without making a racket.

"Rob!" shouted Little John as soon as he saw me. Speaking of making a racket. He jumped off the stone seat he'd taken at the fire circle, and reached me in one giant stride. His left arm was bound to his chest, so his shoulder wouldn't move, but his right arm was free to catch me up in a hug that lifted me clear off the ground. I laughed through the pain until he squeezed tighter. "John ... Can't ... breathe ..."

He let me down immediately, and then placed his big hand on my shoulder. "Sorry. It's just, you saved my boy's life."

Discomfort made me restless. I wasn't sure I hadn't indirectly gotten his son in trouble in the first place. "*You* saved his life, John. I just did some trick shooting."

"Well ...," he said, packing a whole speech into that word. Then he clapped me on the shoulder almost hard enough to knock me over. "My thanks."

"No worries," I managed. I had been fine until his gravelly

voice broke; then I felt my throat tighten, too. I missed my parents and I knew they'd do the same for me as John had done for his kid.

I changed the subject. "This isn't the same camp where Much and I found you."

"Oh no. Those bandits would turn in their own grannies for five silver coins." He jerked his thumb toward the cave. "Will's been working on this place for a while."

"I can tell."

Little John suddenly noticed Isabel, and gestured for her to take his stone seat. "M'lady, you should sit. You too, Rob. I'm going to keep watch for the others. They're stocking up in case we have to stay low for a while."

Well, that answered the question of where everyone was. John took himself downhill, and I sat on one of the stones by the fire circle. I recognized Elsbeth from the priory; she was definitely related to Much, but she'd fared better in the eyebrow department. She grinned shyly as she handed me a bowl of something she'd spooned out of the pot suspended on a tripod over the fire. "Thanks," I said.

Isabel had a bowl too, and took John's seat. The breakfast was some kind of porridge full of honey and dried apples; it was seriously the best thing I'd eaten since I'd been there.

While we ate, Isabel answered my question from the cave. "When they were young boys at my uncle's estate at Huntingdon, James and Henry talked constantly of being knights—planning, practicing, playacting. They only tolerated *my* company if I consented to be rescued over and over. Anyplace we went, if there was a tower, I had to be rescued

232

from it." She rolled her eyes. "Then, when my uncle left for the Crusade, of course James went too, as a squire."

"Of course," I echoed. My mind boggled trying to picture an eight-year-old Henry or James playing at all, let alone with each other. "But Henry didn't go?"

She swallowed a bite of porridge before continuing. "James has family in the Templars, so that was his way in. Henry's family has money, but no noble connections. So his father sent him to squire school in Normandy."

"Wait, squire school?" I'd followed everything up to that. "Like, pay tuition and your kid gets knight training?"

"Exactly. For families like Henry's that have money but no titles or connections. In any case, Henry came back and won every tournament worth winning, which got him noble patronage, which is how he came to his position as the reeve's deputy." She took a huge breath at the end of all that. "And now you know their history."

I knew the facts, but I had to wrap my head around the twelfth-century psychology of it. "So Henry has a chip on his shoulder because his dad essentially bought his knighthood, and James thinks Henry sold out on their dream, especially since he now works for the devil."

She considered that a moment. "I ... think so? Your words are strange, but the tone sounds right."

"And where do you fit into things?"

"Oh, I was supposed to marry James's older brother. Then, after he died, our relatives expected me to marry James. But then my uncle died in Jerusalem and I became a ward of the crown and, well, you know the rest of that sad tale."

I choked on my porridge. I would never have thought . . . They acted way more like siblings than sweethearts. "You were supposed to marry James's brother? And now James?"

"Well, no, because he doesn't want to leave the Templars, so now I'm supposed to marry some horrid Norman in Prince John's court, whose first three wives all died trying to birth a son." She shuddered and stirred her breakfast. "But I have a plan in the works. I've appealed to my godmother." She broke off and glanced at Elsbeth, who had been *not at all* listening to our conversation. With a shrug, she finished, "It may come to nothing, but one never knows."

There was a commotion from the trees downhill. I heard Will's fake birdcall, though, and as the three of us jumped to our feet, I reassured Isabel and Elsbeth, "They're our guys. Or at least, it's Will." I grabbed my bow and quiver, which I automatically kept beside me now. "Stay here and I'll check it out."

I jogged to the path that ran diagonally downhill into the trees. Little John was there, standing with one arm akimbo. Much came out of the woods a moment later, a bunch of rabbits hanging over his shoulder and his slingshot in his hand. He joined John and me, and the three of us watched Will ride into the camp with a man hog-tied over his saddle.

I meant to utter a quip, but all I managed was "What the hell, Will?"

"This fellow was nosing around," he said. "It wasn't hard to spot him in those clothes."

"You should talk," growled Little John, and I snorted.

James followed Will out of the trees, obviously continuing

an argument he'd already started. "What's the point of a hidden outpost if you bring every hapless stranger into it?" He dismounted, and I noticed he was carrying a knapsack and a lute. "What do you plan to do with him now?" he asked Will.

Will swung jauntily down from his horse. "That all depends on how he behaves himself. He says he wants to talk to Rob."

"Get him down from there, Little John," I said, recognizing the captive's clothes. Or the orange tights, at any rate. "I think I know who he is."

"I want to talk to Robin Hood," said the man, his voice muffled by the bag over his head.

"Of course you do," said Little John, easily off-loading the man one-handed, as if he were a sack of grain. "So you can run to the sheriff and collect the bounty on Rob's head."

The man landed orange-tights–first. He wriggled to a sitting position, hands still tied, head still covered. "I don't need the outlaw's bounty," he said, his accent thicker than it had been in the village. "I need his help."

Will hit Little John on his good shoulder. "Do you see what you and that son of yours started? Now everyone wants Rob's help."

"I'm glad you find this amusing," said James, taking the reins of the horses.

Much piped up with "I thought it was funny." James gave him a stern look and handed over both horses.

"Give it a rest, you guys." I crouched in front of the man and pulled the bag from his head. "I am so sorry about that."

He was definitely the man who'd abetted me in Edwinstowe. When I'd very quickly cataloged his outfit, I'd only seen the bright colors, but there was a bit of theatricality to them. Adding in the lute, which I assumed was his, and his lovely speaking voice, I figured him to be a performer of some kind.

As he sat on the ground, hands and feet tied, the troubadour drew himself up straight, looking rumpled but dignified. "I commend your leadership. Your man's loyalty makes him enthusiastic in his defense of you."

"Um, thanks." Yes, definitely a performer. I ignored Much's snort and Will's rolled eyes.

"Your pardon if I do not rise," said the stranger.

"Let him loose." They all gave me doubtful looks. Even Much. "What is he going to do? He's armed with a lute, for heaven's sake. Besides, he had a chance to turn me in yesterday and didn't."

John was the one who crouched and cut the troubadour free. The man gained his feet, rubbing the circulation back into his wrists. "Thank you. And I assure you all, I neither need nor want the sheriff's coin."

Will took the knapsack, opened it, and rooted around with more curiosity now than suspicion. He pulled out a canister sealed with wax. "What is this?"

James took it, examined the seal and the design on the canister, then sniffed it. "Spices from Constantinople." Will had pulled two similar packages from the bag, and James's brows rose. "These are worth more than the prices on all your heads combined."

We all looked at the stranger, who looked expectantly back at me. "Well, you said you had a sad tale to tell," I said. "I guess now is your chance, Alan-a-Dale."

He frowned, confused. "That is not my name."

"None of us goes by his real name here," said Will, handing the man his lute.

I gestured toward the fire circle. *"As-salaam-alaikum."*

He accepted my greeting and my implied welcome. *"Wa-alaikum-salaam,"* he replied.

I had now exhausted all the Arabic I knew, but the look on James's face was priceless.

"Wonderful," muttered Little John. "Another language I don't understand."

"Don't worry, Little John," I said. "We'll stick to English."

"No offense, Rob," he said dolefully, "but I don't understand you half the time even when you do."

I let them go ahead of me toward the fire. Will had shifted into his role as host—he flirted with Isabel and Elsbeth and welcomed to his camp the same man he'd trussed up and thrown over his saddle. He was nothing if not adaptable.

James had hung back with me. "You speak Arabic?"

"That's my whole vocabulary." I looked up at him and asked, "You didn't think to mention you're supposed to marry Isabel?"

I'd finally managed to unravel his composure. He opened his mouth, then closed it, scowled, then cleared his expression—but he couldn't do anything about his blush. "I'm a member of a holy order of knights. I'm not supposed to marry anyone."

Well, there was that. I pieced a few things together and suddenly didn't feel so bad about getting friend-zoned last night. "Not even with special circumstances? Like your older brother dying?"

His eyes narrowed. "I begin to think you *are* a witch."

I was pretty sure he was joking, but still. "I'm not. I think Isabel just enjoys having a friend to talk to about . . . life."

"Isabel has always enjoyed talking." He said it affectionately, though, and turned to go up the path.

"James," I said, and he turned back expectantly.

Don't say anything stupid, Ellie.

"What are you going to do?"

Instead of answering right away, he reached out and tucked my hair behind my ear. "I don't know yet. But I have a feeling it's the least of your problems, Eleanor of West-of-Here."

That was not necessarily true. What if the thing I was supposed to do was get them together, like maybe they were my eleven-times great-grandparents or something. That would make my crush colossally . . . weird.

"I'd kind of just like for you to be happy, James." I went past him on the path, pausing when I was eye level. "Even if you don't think you deserve it."

Then, before I could explode with awkwardness, I rushed ahead to the fire circle, where Alan-a-Dale was waiting to tell his story.

"I was born the fifth son of a minor noble and great merchant in Constantinople," Alan began, as he tuned his lute.

The morning had clouded over, so the fire made a welcome bubble of warmth as the seven of us—eight with Much's sister Elsbeth—gathered around it.

"When my father wished to expand his empire," he went on, "he sent my brothers and me out in all directions—east to Persia, south to Egypt, west to Macedonia. Me, he sent to Spain, where I found a comfortable place managing his trade interests there."

He began to play a romantic tune. I leaned my folded arms on my knees as I listened. "While traveling north from Granada, I met Jocasta, the most beautiful girl in Seville. Hair black as a raven's wing, and cheeks like a crimson rose when she blushes. She is the daughter of a wealthy Norman who married a Spanish woman in order to trade with the Moors who rule Castile. Our passion flourished in the midst of the turmoil in Spain, proving love is stronger than war."

Across the fire from me, Much wrinkled his nose and his sister sighed. Alan-a-Dale strummed a new, harsh note.

"Now her father wants to strengthen his ties to the nobles here in England. He has betrothed Jocasta to an English baron. I followed them here, offering wealth, treasure, trade, whatever he wanted, if he would allow Jocasta and me to wed. She begged her father not to make her marry this aged English lord. But my gifts and his daughter's pleas meant nothing. He sent me away." Alan plucked a jangle of strings. "He kept the bejeweled necklace and a dagger of Toledo steel I had offered, which is inconvenient to me, as innkeepers would rather have copper than turmeric as payment."

"Poor Jocasta," sighed Isabel.

"Poor Alan-a-Dale," murmured Will. "Toledo steel . . ."

"So I have traveled north to Nottingham disguised as a Spanish troubadour." Alan played a flourish on the lute. "It has not been unprofitable. I witnessed the feats of Robin Hood. And I have information to trade for her, no, *his* assistance in saving my lady from this loathsome fate."

There was a moment of disbelieving silence, at least in my head. "You want me to help you rescue your girlfriend."

He nodded. "Jocasta is coming to Nottingham in but a few days to be wed."

"And . . . she *wants* to be rescued?" I asked, just to be sure.

"Of course. She begged me to save her from this marriage so that we could run away together."

"Well, who is she marrying?" asked Isabel, sounding more practical now.

Alan crossed his ankles to sit straighter on the rock where he'd perched. "His name is Lord de Corsey, and he is the new baron of Leas."

Much and I looked at each other, his wide-eyed expression of horror not at all subtle. Mine probably wasn't either. Fortunately, Isabel burst out, "De Corsey!" sounding just as appalled.

Will raised his brows. "That ugly, is he?"

Isabel's cheeks were bright-red flags of outrage. "He's a worse toady than the sheriff. And an extortionist. He made all the old baron's yeomen farmers pay to stay on his land when Prince John awarded it to him. All without bothering to come down from York. He just sent his soldiers."

"That was him?" exclaimed Little John.

"Yes." Isabel saw my frown and explained further. "De Corsey is a member of the prince's inner circle. Prince John relies on him for funds that—"

"I get it. He's Team John, not Team Richard." Which made no difference to me. The guy was a scumbag, from the grave pissing to the threats so filthy I couldn't even translate. I wouldn't let a dog go into his house.

"So what's this information you have to trade?" I asked Alan, like I hadn't already decided to help him.

"Two things." Alan plucked one note on his lute. "Prince John will stop at Nottingham Castle on the journey to his hunting lodge. The sheriff is at pains, they say, to find the money to host him and his retinue and to hold a feast while they're here. At which this humble minstrel has been hired to play," he added with a slight bow. "Which is how I come to know this."

James held up a hand to pause things, and he, Will, Isabel, and I leaned in to consult. "How do we know this man is telling the truth?"

Will added, "That story is direct from any love poem. Tragic love stories always soften women's hearts." He looked at me, implying I would likely be swayed by a love story, or that the troubadour thought I would.

"The royal visit is no lie," Isabel said. "That was the sheriff's excuse to steal the goats, as well as wringing every last coin from every pocket and larder in the shire."

"And it explains his crackdown on crime," I said. Still, I felt like I was missing something. "But all this for a party?"

Isabel sat back before she answered me. "Well, his

entourage will be a hundred people or more. That's not counting servants, horses, and his personal guards. And then there will be all the nobles and barons in the shire, who come for the feast but will also have to be lodged overnight, because of the travel."

That sounded like a hell of a party to have to foot the bill for. But it also meant a lot of traffic, which meant opportunity.

But getting back to the problem of our guest, I said, "In any case, he's not lying about de Corsey coming to Nottingham. Much and I met him on the road."

James looked at me sharply. "When was this?"

"Um . . . when I was in sanctuary and not leaving church property," I said. There didn't seem any point in pretending anymore. Anyway, Isabel knew when it was, because the priory had been the recipient of my ill-gotten gains. But she wasn't going to tell James that, and neither was I.

I broke up our huddle and turned to the waiting troubadour. "What's the second thing?"

He played the next note up the scale. "You will help me, then?"

The others glanced at me for my answer, and I gestured them back into the huddle—John and Much, too, since it concerned us all. "I can't let this girl be forced to marry against her will."

James gave me the frown I was used to by now. "If it's her father's wish that she—" He stopped; my glare dared him to finish that sentence. "I'm saying only that you know nothing about this fellow and— Stop looking at me like that. I haven't said no."

"Very well," said Will. "We know that Rob wishes to help the lady. What say the rest of you?"

Isabel was quick with her opinion. "I'm sure you know what I think."

Much said, "I'll do whatever Ellie wants."

Little John went next. "I'm with whatever Rob is planning."

"Then we are agreed," said Will.

As I turned again to face him, Alan-a-Dale stood and looked at me expectantly. "We'll stop the wedding," I told him. "And if Jocasta wants to marry you, we'll help you."

He burst into a grin, and looked a lot younger. A *lot* younger. The mustache was deceptive. "Thank you, Lady Robin," he said, bowing to me with a flourish. "A million thanks."

"Well," I said, uncomfortable with the dramatics. "We haven't done anything yet."

"But I will give you the information I promised anyway." He paused, prolonging the moment, then shifted his lute out of his way and leaned forward to tell me, "There is an assassin in Nottingham town."

CHAPTER TWENTY-ONE

THE REACTION TO ALAN-A-DALE'S ANNOUNCEMENT WAS clearly not all that he'd hoped for. Will and Little John looked blank and then bored. Isabel glanced at James for his reaction, which was impossible to read due to his game face. Unless you counted that he was wearing his game face. Much and I were the only two who got worked up. He was all about the drama of it, and I was freaked because of Ellie's Second Commandment: Don't change history.

Once Alan-a-Dale got on with the details, though, it was pretty anticlimactic.

"Imagine a shadowed tavern," he said, "and a humble troubadour sleeping near coals, exhausted from having sung for his supper and a space in the rushes. Two voices wake him." He waited until all of us leaned in slightly to hear him. "He hears one whisper. *Poison . . .*"

"That's it?" I asked, when he trailed off after a few more useless, vague tidbits.

That was it. Will rolled his eyes and James fired off questions, and Alan changed neither his demeanor nor his story—though by the fourth retelling he'd dropped the melodramatic reenactment.

Not that I didn't admire his spirit, but I was beginning to think that Alan's story about running his father's shipping concerns in Spain had gotten some dramatic embellishment as well. He wasn't stupid, though, and he finally twigged to the idea that his information wasn't the coin he thought it was.

"You'll still help me?" he asked earnestly. "It is only days until this bishop arrives to wed this *malvado* to my beloved Jocasta."

"Of course," I said, speaking for myself, at least. I'd given my word. But even if I hadn't, I remembered de Corsey's vile language, and how once a woman was married to him, she'd be completely at his mercy.

James took my arm and said to Alan, "If you'll excuse us for a moment—"

He tugged me out of earshot, and I gestured to Little John to watch our guest. "Has none of you thought," said James, once Will and Much joined us, "that this complete stranger might not be as genuine as you think?" He turned to me. "Will had the right of it. This tale is tailored for you, Eleanor.

To appeal to your"—he searched for a word and settled on—
"reckless compassion."

I couldn't argue with that description, or that the troubadour would have me pegged from the events in Edwinstowe.
So he had a point.

"Maybe *he's* an assassin," said Much, sounding bloodthirsty.

I glanced back at Alan, wondering what he was telling
Little John that was earning him so much side-eye. My instincts said he was too earnest to be deceptive, but while
I'd risk myself on my gut feeling, this affected all of us. "He
doesn't need a scheme to get into Nottingham Castle—he's
been invited to play at the festivities when Prince John is here.
He could get near the wedding party with the same excuse."

Will said, "I searched him for weapons before bringing
him here, and we all searched his belongings."

James seemed at least willing to discuss the idea. "This
won't be as easy as walking in and walking back out with the
girl."

"Yes," I said, chewing on that fact. "We probably need to
make a plan."

"Here is my thought," said Will, like he'd been considering it for a while. "The bride's father will be expecting someone to try to spirit her away. Perhaps we can switch out the
groom instead."

Much peered over at Alan, then leaned into our circle
and whispered the obvious, "Not meaning anything by it, but
Master-a-Dale doesn't look much like the baron of Leas."

"Yes, we'll have to replace the officiant as well," said
Will, staring pointedly at James.

246

It took James a moment to realize he was being volunteered. "You can't be serious."

"Why not?" asked Will. "Can't you just—" He made a quick sign of the cross.

"It's not just a matter of blessing the union," James said. "It needs to be witnessed. By people who can attest to it publicly. Which does not include outlaws."

"You're not an outlaw," I said. "Neither is Isabel. And you're both from noble families. Much's family is practically the infrastructure of Nottinghamshire." I looked at Much and asked, "Do you have some relatives who would like to come to a wedding?"

"Do I!" he said excitedly.

"Hold on," said James. "We haven't discussed how you plan to do away with . . . a bishop, didn't he say?"

"We don't have to do away with him," I said. "Or with the groom. Or the bride's family. We just need to keep them out of the way until the knot is tied, right?"

"That's the idea," said Will. I glanced around our tight circle. They all—even James—seemed to be waiting for me to say something.

"All right," I said. It was a lot harder jumping off figurative bridges when you were taking your friends with you. "It's settled. Will, you're in charge of planning Operation Wedding Hijack. Much, your job is to get the intel—whatever details Will needs to know. James will find out what he can from the clerical side of things."

James stood with his arms folded, looking . . . bemused. Especially when Will and Much nodded decisively at my instructions. "And what will you do, Captain Hudson?" he asked.

"Little John and I will be assigned to . . . procurement of resources."

James started to ask the obvious question, then stopped. "Never mind. Better I don't know what that means."

"Probably," I agreed.

Will and Much had moved back to the fire, leaving James and me standing alone in a thickening mist, close enough to touch. "You will be careful, though," he said, making it an instruction, not a request.

"Of course," I said. I always *intended* to be careful.

James gave me a look like he'd heard that silent caveat; then he nodded toward the fire. "Come along, General," he said, promoting me. "Your troops are waiting."

Since I was thinking about assassination and kidnapping, I was already on edge as I waited to get going on Operation Wedding Hijack, and not at all prepared for a complete stranger to suddenly appear at the hideout.

I jumped off my seat by the last of the fire and nearly fell into the cinders trying to get to my bow—then I realized I was looking at Little John with a haircut and his beard trimmed to look less lumberjack-like.

"What do you think?" asked Will, coming out of the cave behind Little John and brushing some invisible speck from the big man's shoulder. "I am a master of all I set my hand to."

"Eh," I said. "You two will do."

It didn't entirely surprise me that a plan of Will Scarlet's involved his cohorts dressing up rather than dressing down. Will would certainly fit in as a wedding guest, and John would fit in his role, too.

"I can't believe we're doing this," Little John said, a common refrain over the past two days.

We'd been busy, and not just because of the wedding heist. With the royal visit and the big feast that Prince John was holding on Saint Egbert's day, the quantity and quality of the traffic on the roads through Sherwood Forest had increased. Some well-heeled travelers had contributed their horses and clothing to our cause, as well as some jewelry to a poor box here or there.

Meanwhile, we hadn't—or at least James and I hadn't—dismissed Alan's melodramatic poison story, but really, between the prince coming to Nottingham, along with bishops and nobles and God knew who else, it would seem far-fetched if there *wasn't* an assassin.

So, first things first. The three of us headed down the path to get our horses from the cave that served as a stable, and I took the time to deliver some last-minute clarification. "Listen, Will. If for some reason the girl doesn't want to marry Alan—she's changed her mind, or Alan is mistaken, or he's been lying to us—but she *does* want to escape de Corsey—"

"I will spirit her away to the nearest nunnery," he said, completing my thought. "Sir Templar and I will have things handled at the chapel. You and Much and John do your bit on the road and don't worry about the bride. In fact, don't worry about anything. Look how lucky we've been so far."

That *was* what worried me. A lot of things had gone our way. The wedding would be in the nearby town of Papplewick, not Nottingham town proper, which meant less chance of the sheriff's soldiers being present. And as for the road, the injured chief forester was conveniently on bed rest thanks to Sister Clothilde's orders.

I didn't mention it to the others, but I also considered it good fortune that Guilbert was, by all reports from the priory, recovering just fine. I didn't want to be responsible for his death.

Will put an encouraging hand on my shoulder. "Relax, Lady Robin. Everything will go the way we've planned."

Right. Because everything had gone *totally* as expected ever since I'd followed that white monk down the rabbit hole to Wonderland.

"They're coming," said Much from his lookout.

I glanced to my right and Little John gave me the all-ready wave. Some riders had passed, and a wagon or two, but after a long time lying impatiently in wait, we finally heard the creak and groan of a much heavier carriage. There was no stealth mode on Middle Ages transport.

The coach that came into view was basically a big box on wheels, pulled by two draft horses. The windows had bars on them and the shades were drawn. Four outriders accompanied the coach, and it was followed by a wagon full of baggage.

We'd picked a spot in the road where only two horses could pass at a time, which meant the outriders had to fall back or go ahead of the coach. I waited until the carriage had reached Little John's position and then I loosed my first arrow into the door and under the latch so it couldn't be opened from the inside. Much nailed the first outrider with his sling-shot, and I clipped the next one in the shoulder so he couldn't lift a weapon. Guard one hit the ground, followed quickly by guard two. I heard Little John drop from the overhanging tree limb and take out the pair of coach drivers with two thunks of his staff.

The guards in the back spurred their horses forward, and I loosed a flurry of arrows—Legolas-style—into the ground right in front of the horses' hooves. Once the horses reared and panicked, bolting with their riders, it was all over except for the crying and the yelling.

The yelling was coming from the coach, but I ignored that for the moment. Little John jumped down and ran back to help Much drag the unconscious guards off the road before any other travelers came along. He intimidated the wounded into joining their comrades. I leapt into action and ran toward the baggage wagon, not expecting any trouble from the pair of wide-eyed, slack-jawed monks who were driving it.

"Over there," I ordered the one with the reins in his hands. "Through that gap. Get off the road—"

I hadn't thought anything weird about two white-robed

monks accompanying a bishop's wagon. The first was horse-faced and sallow, and his big Adam's apple bobbed as he gulped. The other, I'd seen in Nottingham Castle.

His surprise at the ambush shifted to a different kind of bafflement the longer I stared at him. "Who *are* you?" I wanted to hear him speak so I could know I wasn't seeing things. Still. Or again.

His nervous companion was even more confused, looking from me to him before asking, "Brother Thaddeus? What's this bandit talking about?"

Well, that was a relief. If Brother Thaddeus was imaginary, Brother Adam's Apple was seeing him, too.

Brother Adam turned back to face me, and I had almost managed to reconnect my synapses, when Brother Thaddeus coshed his buddy on the back of the head. I stared like an idiot as Brother Adam's eyes crossed and he slithered off the wagon's bench.

What the hell had just happened?

In a pale blur, Brother Thaddeus grabbed something from behind the seat and jumped off the wagon, sprinting back the way they'd come. I ran after him, just like I'd done the last time I'd seen him. He outdistanced me, even in sandals, even while he was wrestling with the bundle in his hands. He reached a break in the trees, and as soon as he hit sunlight, there was a sound like a wood grouse breaking from cover, and then a flurry of blue gray came at me.

I ducked and stumbled, and by the time I got my bearings again, the monk was down the road and the pigeon he'd released was gaining altitude. It would be hidden by the treetops in seconds. I pulled an arrow, nocked, drew, and loosed almost straight vertical. I held my breath as the shaft arced up and speared the pigeon through the heart. It plummeted, hit the top tier of tree limbs, and dropped in the middle of the clearing.

Much reached me. "What are you doing? That's not the plan. Why did you shoot that pigeon?"

I looked at him, not sure what to say. "It seemed important." Brother Thaddeus, or whoever he was, had vanished, but he'd wanted to get rid of something, and now I had it. That was good, right? Much followed me as I picked up the pigeon and examined it.

"What's that on its leg?" he asked, peering over my arm. "A message?"

"I can't think what else it would be. Messenger pigeon, right?" I handed the pigeon to Much to hold while I untied the little slip of paper from around its leg, then held my breath as I unrolled it. Please, God, let it contain the secrets of the universe. Or of this parallel universe, if that was how it worked.

Apparently, the universe wrote in code.

"What does it say?"

"I don't know."

"I thought you could read?"

The side-eye I gave him was not quite a glare but was close to it. "It's not a language, it's jumbled-up letters. A code."

He nodded in understanding, then lit up with a thought. "The assassin!"

"Alan heard them in Nottingham town. These men were coming from Leeds." But it was hard to argue with a secret-agent-ish code and a last-ditch effort to get rid of the message when discovered. Why else run instead of simply staying in character—if a monk wasn't his real character.

Much nudged me back to the task at hand. "Come on. We can talk about it later. John is doing all the work."

I left the pigeon but took my arrow. The message rolled itself back up in my open palm, and I hid it under my tunic, tucking it into the binding that served as my sports bra. It could wait, but it was a concrete lead I could follow, to home or to anywhere.

John had already driven the coach to the turnoff we'd scouted, far enough off the road that a passerby wouldn't stumble across it immediately, but it wouldn't be impossible to find, either. Much and I scooted Brother Adam's Apple into the back of the baggage wagon, and John drove it off the road, too.

Inside the coach, the bishop of Leeds was still yelling, condemning us to hell and other pestilences. Reaching the carriage, I looked in the window. The man was older, but not old, and he definitely wasn't keeping any vow of poverty, judging by his clothes, jewelry, and girth.

"What's the meaning of this?" he demanded when he saw me.

"That monk with you, m'lord. The one called Thaddeus," I asked, trying to sound courteous, because catching flies with honey and all that. "Do you know him?"

The bishop suddenly disappeared from view, and I was looking through the window at a red-faced, spittle-spewing Lord de Corsey. "You! I recognize your voice! You will regret this infamy, you cretin!"

I was still blinking in surprise at his appearance when the bishop came back to the window, his ringed fingers gripping the bars meant to protect him from bandits. The irony wasn't lost on me.

"I know who you are, *Robin Hood*," said the bishop. "I will tell you whatever you want, give you whatever you want, if you will only, please, not leave me in here with this man."

That was unexpected. He meant it, too. I could see the whites of his eyes. "Why is he even with you?" I asked.

"He asked for conveyance. To his own wedding," the bishop said. His Excellency came all the way up to the bars and whispered, "De Corsey never pays for his own travel. And no one rejects his request because he has the ear of the prince." Inside the carriage, the baron was working up to a real frothing tirade. "Please," begged the bishop. "They say you're compassionate, Master Hood."

I gave him a suspicious look and tested him. "How about you give me one of those big rings to put in the poor box at Saint Mary's?"

He immediately took off the biggest one and handed it through the bars as if it were some loose change he was dropping into a tip jar. Since I still didn't open the door, he tried information next. "The friar you asked after—he came from the abbey in Leeds. I do not know who he is. They often send friars who have business where I'm going, to serve as my attendants in exchange for the protection of my entourage." Although pleading, he couldn't resist a pointed "From *bandits* and the like."

I stepped back and glanced at Much. He jerked his thumb at where we'd hidden the wagon. "The other brother says the same. Doesn't know the man. He was of the same order, so he trusted him."

I looked back at the bishop, who really did look miserable as de Corsey let off a litany of French profanity about England, the parentage of all of us, and the particular tortures we were going to endure in hell for this. I *almost* felt sorry for the bishop. But James and Isabel had both told me not to trust him. Whatever ecclesiastic favors the prince needed, the bishop of Leeds was his guy.

"I'll send someone to get you out when we reach Nottingham," I said, untying the leather flap over the window and letting it drop to cover the pair of royal court cronies.

Little John was looking awfully morose, considering the plan had gone off well. "Now comes the hard part," he said.

Much reached up to pat his arm. "I know how it feels. But you have to get back on the horse."

Despite the fact that John and I were both pretty bad riders, we made it to Papplewick without anything disastrous happening. Which was a minor miracle, because I could have ridden off a cliff, let alone into an ambush, I was that distracted. I'd stopped thinking I was crazy a while ago, but that didn't mean I wasn't. While getting home still dominated my thoughts every night when I tried to sleep, not dying and not changing history were hot on my front burners. But I wasn't going to lie—it had occurred to me that rescuing a damsel was a very Robin Hood thing to do, and if filling this role in any way contributed to getting back to my own time—

The monk—Thaddeus—had not recognized me. He'd seemed confused as to how I knew him. Obviously, he was guilty of something, but not of purposefully luring me into the end of the twelfth century for God-knows-what reason. Not to make everything about me, but I was the one who was eight hundred years from home. Did I see him because I was about to come back in time, or did I come back in time because I'd seen him?

Correlation does not equal causation, Dad would say.

Mom would counter with "What we call 'chance' is often the instrument of Providence."

I was kind of relieved when we reached the edges of the village. It was a lot calmer than I had expected—but only because the residents seemed to have gathered in the middle of the town. "Is it all over?"

Much pointed to a big sturdy barn. The doors were closed and barred, but they rattled from someone—a bunch of someones—pounding on them. The shouting was hard to miss, too. "I guess Will and Sir James got all the family guards locked up."

"Come on." I nudged my horse to head toward the church, easy to locate by its tower.

I'd been worried about a disguise, but Little John had gotten a haircut for nothing. No one in the village paid us any attention. There was a loud commotion happening near the church, though. People were crowded around the chapel doors and stretching up to peer in the windows.

I got my leg over the horse and slid down its side to my feet. I lost track of Much and John as I elbowed my way through the crowd and squeezed through the chapel's side door, then through the sacristy, before stopping in the arched doorway.

Apparently, we'd missed more than the fighting. In the middle of the church, the troubadour Alan-a-Dale was kissing a girl in a gorgeous fur-trimmed gown of pale orange silk.

When they came up for air, I saw that he hadn't exaggerated much about how beautiful she was. Like all the women, her hair was covered, but her face was striking and classic, like she'd gotten the very best of her mixed bloodlines. And she was young—probably younger than me. But then, once Alan had shaved his mustache, I pegged him at about my age, too. James had been at war for ten years, and he was maybe twenty-two; Henry Guilbert, the same age as James, was deputy to the sheriff and captain of the forest rangers, or whatever they were really called. No wonder they treated me as an adult. I *was* one here.

James stood a little to the side of the couple, arms folded. Isabel and Elsbeth were near the wall, looking conspicuous in their brown wool habits and plain veils among the guests in bright-colored clothes. Will stood against the wall nearest to me, watching the obviously flummoxed wedding guests, who didn't seem to know how to respond to the lovebirds. A few clapped, but were shushed by others.

"Is it over?" I asked Will. I was answered by a commotion at the back of the chapel, where a furious man pushed his way through the logjam of people in the doorway.

"Halt this farce at once!" he shouted. He was middle-aged, and his wardrobe was so elaborate, so silver-embroidered, gold-studded, fur-edged, and colorful that it made Will Scarlet's look austere. "Where is the bishop? Where is de Corsey!"

Jocasta, clinging to Alan's hand, faced the man and the rest of the crowd. The stubborn jut of her chin increased as she confronted the intruder. "You're too late, Papa. We are married. The friar has given the blessing."

"A lowly friar?" roared her father. "In front of outlaws and bandits for witnesses? This will never stand. You are my daughter and you will do only as I say."

There was a hum as all the guests shifted. Not many of the men were armed—those who were had probably joined the guards in the tithe barn. Alan wore a short curved sword that looked more decorative than functional, but he still put his hand on the hilt.

A sudden dramatic flourish of cloth from the side of the chapel drew everyone's eye. A woman had thrown back her cloak and hood to reveal an ornate and regal gown—one half was fleurs-de-lis on blue silk, the other half gold lions on red. All the guests reacted, and Isabel gasped.

"Godmama!" she cried, hurrying toward the woman and dropping into a low curtsy. James, after a startled moment, bowed deeply, and everyone in the room and all those watching from the door did the same. The exceptions were three women—ladies-in-waiting, maybe—and three men, who undid their cloaks to show they were wearing armor, their tabards the same colors as the lady's gown.

"Your grace!" stammered the bride's father. "I—I . . ."

I recognized the pattern of her dress, even if I didn't quite believe I was seeing it now. I'd done a book report on this woman—if she was who I thought she was—in the second grade.

If Will hadn't grabbed my hand and yanked me down to one knee, I might have fainted.

"Did Isabel just call her 'godmother'?" I whispered to Will.

He slid me a I-didn't-miss-that-either look. "That she did."

The lady motioned for everyone to rise. "I think that the dowager queen of England is a reliable enough witness for this marriage to stand. Don't you, m'lord?"

The father of the bride nearly prostrated himself again. "I . . . yes. Of course, your grace. Naturally."

"Oh my God!" I squeaked it almost soundlessly. I was right. It was Eleanor of Aquitaine, who'd been married to the last king of England and was the mother of King Richard and Prince John. She was in her sixties, at least, but she was still beautiful—the kind of beauty that lay in the architecture of her face. And even if that hadn't been the case, she had charisma. Her presence filled the small chapel.

"Very well," Eleanor of Aquitaine said, settling the matter with the bride's father. "We have traveled quite far, and thought to break our journey with a wedding feast. Having stolen Lord de Corsey's bride, perhaps we should go along to the banquet now and steal his food as well."

She gestured toward the chapel doors, and with those few sentences, she cleared the church, defusing the whole powder keg and leaving only herself and her guards, me and my band of merry men, and Alan and his bride.

Queen Eleanor turned to Isabel next, frowning at her plain brown habit. "What an unflattering outfit for you, my dear. We must discuss a change immediately. As for this one . . ." She turned to James and looked him over. "You seem no more suited to life in a monastery than to life in marriage to my goddaughter."

James paused to consider his answer, but Isabel supplied it for him. "Your grace, as you surmised, this is Sir James Hathaway. He recently returned from the Holy Land, where he served with King Richard."

He bowed again, and the queen's expression turned acerbic. "Well, if you managed to survive my son's command that speaks highly of your luck, or else your common sense." She turned away before James could respond and approached the newlyweds. The bride curtsied, and Alan bowed deeply and with a flourish; he and Jocasta made a graceful pair. "Ah. The happy couple and the reason for the feast. You have my blessing . . . but you may wish to skip the wedding banquet and leave before de Corsey finally appears. He is an insect, but a stinging one."

Alan thanked her effusively, and Jocasta curtsied again, and then they were away.

"Do you think they'll be happy?" I whispered to Will, still close beside me.

He murmured back, "He's rich, and she's beautiful. What do you expect?"

"And *who* are the two of you," Queen Eleanor said to Will and me, "whispering in corners like unruly children?"

I could actually feel my face go pale before a stinging heat rushed in. An unruly child was what I felt like—called out by the teacher. Or worse, by Coach. "I'm sorry, er, my lady . . . ," I stammered. "Your grace, I mean . . ." Behind her, James covered his mouth with his palm, maybe appalled, maybe giving me the sign for "please don't speak madness." Probably both.

"Which of you is the notorious Robin Hood?" she asked.

There didn't seem to be any point in denial. If she'd wanted her guards to grab us, they would have. So I put up my hand. "I am Robin Hood, Lady Eleanor. Your Majesty, I mean."

Her brows, gray but darkened with some cosmetic, climbed to the coif that covered her hair. "Are you, now. Well, this is a very interesting turn. What do people call you when you are not infuriating that weaselly tax collector?"

Don't laugh.

"Robert Hudson, Your Majesty."

Her eyes narrowed impatiently. "Do not play games with me. I mean your *real* name."

"Oh." *That* name. "It's Eleanor, actually."

Her lips pursed and her brows shifted. "Is it really?" It was impossible to judge how she felt about that. "Where is de Corsey? You didn't kill him, did you?"

"No! I haven't killed anyone."

"Hmm. We might have to ask the sheriff's deputy about that." She gestured Isabel over to her side. "Come with me, child. We have much to discuss about your future." With a thin hand, she indicated Elsbeth, and I thought the miller's daughter might faint. "Bring your companion. We won't leave her with these ruffians."

Little John ran in through the front door, calling, "Rob! Nottingham soldiers com—" The guard nearest the door drew his sword and Little John jumped backward, eyes wide as he looked around the chapel. Slowly he edged to the wall and then over, away from the queen and her guards like they were a pack of hungry lions.

Queen Eleanor motioned for her guards to precede her then swept out, leading her ladies-in-waiting. Isabel turned back at the door and smiled at me, sort of sheepish, sort of excited. She caught Elsbeth's hand and tugged her along, otherwise the saucer-eyed girl would still be standing there. Through the open door I saw Much's jaw drop as his sister walked by where he was holding the horses and keeping lookout.

The church seemed very quiet when the eight of them were gone and all that remained were John, Will, James, and me, with Much right outside. I staggered, feeling like I'd just survived a tornado. The guys all looked like they felt the same way. Poleaxed.

"Hey!" called Much from the door. "Soldiers coming!"

Since no one wanted to be literally poleaxed, we jumped into motion, running for the door and then the horses.

CHAPTER TWENTY-TWO

βↃↃϚ

"I'VE HEARD IT'S SUPPOSED TO BE GOOD LUCK IF IT RAINS ON your wedding day," I said, shivering just inside the entrance of the hideout's main cave.

"Where did you hear that?" asked Little John, shaking the water from his hair.

"From a bride who was rained on at her wedding day," James said, straight-faced. He had his moments.

Much frowned, despite his chattering teeth. "But it's the wedding night now. What's *that* supposed to mean?"

James and Little John exchanged a look, and the knight answered, "It means it's a good night to be stuck indoors." It was a pretty tame comment, and I didn't blush, exactly, but how was I not supposed to wonder what James knew about wedding nights? I mean, he hadn't been in the Holy Order of Badass his whole life.

Will returned from inside the cave, his arms full of wool blankets almost soft enough to be towels. I was convinced he'd robbed a cart on its way to Bed Bath and Beyond. "Strip," he said, and handed each of us a blanket.

"You cannot be serious," I said, holding the dry cloth away from my soaking clothes.

"About four bodies dripping on these carpets? Yes. Five, if we count Little John twice." I was about to lay into him about the stupid carpets when, seeing my face, he added honestly, "We can't have a fire inside and it will stay warmer if it doesn't get damp."

"But . . ." Did I have to point out that I wasn't actually a boy?

Will grinned. I was blushing, and everyone knew it. "Take off your shoes and go in, my lady. Shout when you're decent. And no peeking at us out here."

Glaring, I kicked off my shoes and marched into the cave. Will had lit an oil lamp, which provided enough light for me to find my spare shirt and pants among my stuff. I wasted no time stripping off my soaked jeans and tunic and wrapping up in the soft, dry blanket. As I was struggling with the knot on my chest binding, I realized how wet that had gotten, too.

"Shoot." I fished between layers for the message I'd tucked there, muttering, "No, no, no," as I peeled away the wet top layer of the rolled-up strip, and "Please, please, please," as I held the message away from my dripping hair.

"Eleanor?" Sounding vaguely alarmed, James hurried in wrapped in a blanket. Will was behind him. "Did you yell?"

I spared them a glance—and then another, quicker one. James wore his dry blanket like a toga, but Will had his wrapped around his waist like he'd just walked out of a shower. Vain as he was, it didn't surprise me that he kept fit.

Focus, Ellie.

I looked back at the mini scroll I was unwrapping. "I forgot that I intercepted this message. It's in code, and now it's a little wet." The ink was blurred in places and almost washed away at one end. "Dammit."

James picked up the lamp and held it so he could read over my shoulder. "There's still a good bit that's legible." He leaned closer and frowned. "It's going to make decoding it more difficult."

The toga left more of him bare than I was used to, something I couldn't help but notice because his lifting the lamp to read over my shoulder had put me in the curve of his arm. It was distracting when I'd been trying to keep my thoughts closer to the center of the friend zone.

"Here," I said, handing James the slip of paper and carefully ducking under the arm that held the lamp while holding on tight to my blanket. "I don't read your French or English well enough to help."

He frowned, as if he'd been concentrating so hard on the running ink he hadn't noticed me move away. "You can help identify some of these letters, though. The more eyes, the better."

Will—dressed now—draped one of his shirts over James's

shoulder and took the lamp from him. "Maybe she wants to dress herself first and have something to eat before looking at it."

"Hmm. Good idea," said James, barely lifting his eyes from the message. I saw Will's smirk and made a face at him, which made him laugh outright.

"Come over to the table when you're done," Will told me, nodding to where Much and Little John sat. "Much raided the wedding feast and brought back victuals. We may be dressed like paupers, but we will eat like princes."

My stomach growled loudly.

"Bon appétit," said Will, skipping out.

I had spent two nights already on the pallet in my corner of the big cave, so I already knew that Little John snored like a rhinoceros. Much was curled up around a full belly, leaving James, Will, and me hunched over the little camp table.

"I think this is a *D,*" I said, inscribing it on the wax tablet where we had copied down all the letters we could make out on the tiny coded scroll. I'd wrapped myself up in a fur cloak, which felt pretty decadent. The body heat from the five of us gave the cave a little warmth, but the rain outside was making me sleepy.

Will gave a jaw-cracking yawn. "I'm for bed. This cipher will wait for the morning and better light."

"You wouldn't want to develop a squint," said James drily, without looking up from the tablet.

He didn't see the cross-eyed grimace Will gave him before

he left our one circle of light. After Will had gone, James put down the stylus and looked at me. "It is late. You should go to bed as well."

"Only if you come too." My eyelids had been drooping, but not after I realized what I just said. I sat up from my slump, instantly awake. "Only if you also go to sleep in your own bedroll over there, I mean. Not *with* me or . . . anything."

Well, that came out worse than expected.

James gave me one of those long, still-water looks of his, and then a crooked and wry smile. "I wouldn't have thought anything different."

"Of course not," I said, trying to act casual. "I'd never think that you'd thought that I was thinking— Oh, rats."

He chuckled and picked up the stylus again, tapping it on the tablet. It was kind of funny. Tablets here and, eight hundred years from now, tablets again. "I'm going to work on this a little bit longer."

"Okay," I said, sliding back down in the camp chair. "I'll keep you company."

At least, that was what I intended. But that was pretty much the last thing I remembered before I woke up on my pallet, facedown and drooling. There was light outside the cave, but it was thin and kind of watery, like it was still really early.

God, why hadn't someone invented coffee yet?

I heard the others up and moving around, so I rolled off the pallet and pushed myself up from all fours. My jeans had mostly dried, so I put them on. Since I wasn't worried about what kind of tracks I'd leave, I pulled on my sneakers, too.

Robin Hood got the blame for every holdup in Sherwood Forest anyway. I might as well be comfortable.

I headed out to the fire circle, where there was leftover vegetable pie for breakfast. James and Will were discussing whatever was on the wax tablet James held.

"How else would you interpret it?" James asked.

"Not like that," said Will. "But what do I know? I'm not a Knight Templar, keeper of the secrets of Jerusalem."

James took a calming breath and let it out. "The coded date on this message works out to tomorrow. Tomorrow is Saint Egbert's day, when Nottingham Castle will be open and the feast will bring crowds of people, with Prince John in the middle of it—"

"I'm an outlaw," said Will. "I'm only worried about this night and, if we live through it . . ." He paused, as if thinking hard. "No. Tomorrow I still won't give a rat's ass about Prince John."

"What's going on?" I asked, feeling like I'd come into a play at intermission. From what I'd sorted out, James thought there was a plot to attack the prince tomorrow during the feast, and Will didn't want to intervene. Was that it?

Little John sat on one of the stones around the fire, elbows on his knees, chin on his fists. "If Prince John is killed, maybe King Richard will return and things will be better."

"Whoa. Hey. Guys." Finally they looked at me. I was wide-awake now, and while I couldn't untangle my sudden snarl of emotions, I was certain of one thing. "I am not okay letting someone get murdered."

"Assassinated," corrected Will. "A mean man and a bad ruler. Look at what the sheriff does in his name, at what the barons have to put up with, except for the ones who toady up to him and get special treatment."

"And it's not as if *we* are going to kill him," said Little John.

Will added, "I'm surprised someone hasn't done him in already. Surely there have been previous attempts." He shrugged. "Maybe this one will fail too."

His indifference pained me. Wait. No. The pain was because I'd thought better of him. His indifference pissed me off. "Do you really not care if someone gets killed?" There was something else revving up inside me, too, an anxiety separate from my disappointment, separate even from my personal situation. "Not just any someone. A king—prince, I mean. You don't even know all the effects it could have."

Another shrug from Will. "He has guards. It's not our problem."

"But it is!" Forget the moral high ground. This was seriously messed up. Or it would be, if I didn't stop it. "This is *not supposed to happen!*"

The enclosing hill bounced back my shout, and all of them gaped at me. Even James.

Magna Carta, dammit! That's what I wanted to yell. The foundation of common law and limits on government. Western history was changed because King John pissed off the barons enough that they made him sign it.

Don't die. Don't change history. Entries one and two in my twelfth-century handbook. I'd ranked "Don't die" first,

270

but now that I was staring down the barrel of a rewritten past, I wasn't so sure about the order. "How about this?" I asked more reasonably. "What if you end up with someone worse?"

"Could there be anyone worse?" Little John asked.

"Yes." I couldn't tell them how, or who, or what. "Trust me. There's worse."

"Eleanor," Will tried to reason with me, and there was a catch in my heart when he used my whole name. "Nottingham is in a bad place because of the sheriff. The sheriff is bad because of Prince John. And that's just in Nottingham, and not counting the harm he does elsewhere."

"Besides," Little John added, "I don't see what we can do about it. I'm a smith. I don't know what all about assassinations."

"We—at least, I—can't do nothing." How could I be losing my allies over my—Robin Hood's—enemy.

"Go to the sheriff," Will said, a little too cheerily, "and if he doesn't kill you on sight, tell *him* your suspicions."

James had been quiet, but now he shifted his weight, indicating he had something to say. "Going to the sheriff would be dangerous. But intervening ourselves could be even trickier."

Will gestured to James. "You see? The friar knows. If I wanted to stick my neck out for an unlovable tyrant, I could have stayed in Brittany and fought for my father."

"Is this the thing that splits us up, Will?" I asked. "That you won't trouble yourself to stop a man from being killed?"

"*That* man? No. I *won't* trouble myself." He walked over to Little John's side of the fire and sat, stretching his legs out in front of him. "Maybe you should take your theory to Captain

Guilbert. I'm sure he'll be happy to listen to your suspicions while he recovers from you shooting him. After all, he's in service to Prince John, so it's his job to protect him. Not yours, not John's, and especially not mine."

I kept waiting for him to tell me he was kidding, but he just laced his fingers and put them behind his head.

"Little John?" I asked.

He met my eyes briefly. "I'm sorry, Rob. The sheriff put my boy on the chopping block. I'm with Will."

I felt ill, and not from my empty stomach. It came from anxiety and pain and my heart squeezing until my insides flipped over.

If I was supposed to be Robin Hood, could I do that without my merry men?

I had to try. Even if my morals weren't anti-murder in the first place, there was the "Don't Change History" protocol to abide by. The decision was clear. If I let Prince John get killed before he became King John, God only knew if I'd have a home to go home to.

CHAPTER TWENTY-THREE

THE QUESTION OF HOW TO STOP THE ASSASSINATION WAS NOT AS clear-cut. There were just over twenty-four hours to figure it out.

We knew—or, at least, everything pointed to the possibility—that someone planned to kill Prince John while Nottingham Castle was open for the feast. If the specifics had ever been in the message, they'd been lost when the scroll got wet. Brother Thaddeus, the pigeon friar, was one conspirator, but maybe his role had been played out and someone else would take over. Or maybe since I'd shot down his messenger pigeon, nothing would happen tomorrow.

But I couldn't risk it with at least eight centuries of history riding on that.

James, Much, and I left Will and John at the camp and

headed toward Nottingham, cutting through the greenwood and avoiding the highway. Just like old times, except I was on my own horse, and Much was as glum as I'd ever seen him. I felt the same, splitting up from Will and John, but kept focused on the big picture.

"Maybe we should talk to Guilbert," I said, ducking under a tree limb before it could knock me off the saddle. "And by 'we,' I mean someone who didn't shoot him with an arrow. He'd take you seriously, James."

James gave me a doubtful look over his shoulder. "Perhaps. But we also crossed swords the last time we met."

"Look"—it seemed perfectly reasonable to me, which didn't mean it was right—"we all have the same goal here. The sheriff, the sheriff's soldiers—"

"Do we?" James reined in as we reached a clearing where we could turn the horses and face each other. "I will contact Henry. I feel reasonably certain he won't try to cut me down before I tell him what little we know. But even if we could warn the castle or the prince's guard, you're no more willing to delegate this than I am. And you are the only person who can recognize this Thaddeus fellow."

"Which means I need to be inside the castle tomorrow."

James nodded. "I can use my family connections to attend the festivities. But you are an outlaw, and there are more than a few people, besides the conspirator, who will recognize you."

The answer was obvious, at least to me. "Not as a woman. At least, no one will be looking for me dressed as one. So I need to find a dress shop."

"Would either you or I know what to ask a tailor for in the way of fashionable female clothing?" James asked.

"Good point."

"What you need is Isabel's help. And, if we're very lucky, the help of her godmother."

Dressed in a fur-lined robe of lustrous indigo silk, the dowager queen received me—just me, not James, not Isabel—in her solarium. As I explained about the messenger pigeon and the cipher, her brows went higher and higher, and her face grew darker and darker.

"This is an incredible story, Mistress Hudson," she said. "And from someone who has been a great deal of trouble to lawful agents of the crown. Why should I believe you?"

Oh, so many reasons, few of which I could actually tell her. I sat on an extremely uncomfortable needlepoint stool low enough that I had to look up at Queen Eleanor, even with her lounging on a chaise. "Everyone in Nottingham knows that I think His Highness's taxes are unfair and that I support King Richard. So why would I lie?"

She leaned back on her couch and thought about it. "Why indeed. Well, it hurts nothing to be on guard. What do you ask in return for this information?"

"I need to attend the feast tomorrow so that I can keep a watch for this Brother Thaddeus. I would recognize him if I saw him again."

Steepling her fingers, she studied me thoughtfully. "I will save time and tell you what you want—entrée into

Nottingham Castle as Eleanor Hudson. Although, obviously, you will require some transformation. Isabel will enjoy assisting with that." She reached for her cup of wine. "We shall start, I think, with a bath. My ladies-in-waiting will not thank me for letting you join them in your current condition."

When I wrote that book report in the second grade, never in a million years would I have thought Eleanor of Aquitaine would have occasion to tell me that I smelled. My mother was going to die from embarrassment when I told her.

Maybe I would keep the information to myself. All I wanted was to have to make that decision.

I wasn't going to lie. A full hot bath was almost reward enough for foiling an assassination attempt. There was soap—hard soap, as James had called it—and I washed my hair and scrubbed my skin until I was pink. That was the great part. Then there was a lot of pinning and plucking and primping. I had to be instructed on how to put on the dress that Isabel picked out for me. It was a steep learning curve, even more so than with the sword fighting.

After James and Much had left me at the queen's estate, I had no way to contact them before the prince's festivities the next day. At dawn on Saint Egbert's day, half the queen's ladies-in-waiting, plus Isabel and myself, transported her essential baggage to the royal apartments on the top floor of Nottingham Castle. It was torture, and I felt like I'd paid for the pleasure of my hot bath with frustration.

"There's little you would have been able to do before this

in any case," said Isabel, once we excused ourselves from the queen's attendance—which was as soon as we could without raising suspicion. "The festivities are only just starting. Now you'll be able to move among the guests as planned."

I eyed a guard as Isabel and I passed him in the corridor on the way to the stairs that led down to the great hall. The guard had given us a glance, but not a suspicious one. Isabel had been pretty as a nun; as a young lady she was beautiful in a blue gown that followed her figure and showed a bit of her neck. The sleeves draped from her elbows, revealing a red silk underdress. Awfully racy for a nun.

My dress was similar, except green. It was weird to have a shape again. My short hair was covered by a princess-y veil. One of the ladies had tried to cover my face with some powder that would probably give me lead poisoning, so I refused it. Besides, I liked my freckles.

Isabel linked my arm in hers, like a leash to keep me from walking too fast. "Decorum," she said warningly in my ear. "Try not to stride like you're crossing a tournament field."

I wished I were, because then I'd have my bow. I felt naked without it. Worse, I felt helpless without it.

I tried to take in every detail on our way. There was another soldier posted at the top of the circular stairs, and I waited until we passed to say, "Tell me if anything looks unusual or out of place." I wouldn't know what was normal otherwise.

"I haven't been inside the castle since John's last visit." Isabel's expression turned sour. "Given that I was ordered to a nunnery, I take no pleasure in holding on to the details."

That was understandable. At the next landing there was another guard, who acknowledged us with a stone-faced nod. We'd reached the main levels of the keep. The great hall encompassed most of the ground floor, except for a sort of antechamber that connected the big outer doors with the big hall doors, all of which stood open. Out on the grounds were activities for all the townspeople, like a fair, with games and music and an archery tournament I wasn't dumb enough to be lured into. Inside were all the nobles and the top-tier landowners. Both spaces were full of people and smells and music and chaos. I couldn't pick out *anybody* in this mess.

"Ellie," said Isabel under her breath, "you're stopping the flow of blood to my hand."

"I'm sorry." I should have entered the castle disguised as a page or even a soldier. Why had I thought coming in a dress, unarmed, was a good idea?

Oh yeah. I was a wanted man.

But as we walked into the hall, the liveried guards stationed at the doors didn't even glance at us. "You see?" Isabel said. "All is well."

The hall was two stories high, with a gallery that circled the room on the second floor. Musicians played there; on the main level, tables had been pushed back for dancing, though no one was. Warm air came in through the high, narrow windows, and daylight fell on the dais at the far end of the room.

Seated on the throne, sitting upright as nobles approached and paid their respects, was Prince John. The party flowed toward him, keeping the prince at the center of everything.

His clothes were gorgeous—blue silk and heavy gold embroidery and a lot of jewelry—the designer fashion of the day. His looks, though, weren't exactly impressive. His hair was long, his face was long, his nose was really long. He wasn't ugly, but he looked unpleasant. The most distinctive thing about him was his expression. He had the kind of eyes that were always looking for a fault or an insult.

Eleanor of Aquitaine sat slightly behind him and to his left on a smaller throne. Her back was straight, her hands in her lap, and her disdain directed at the prince's rowdy friends. They were raucously drinking wine from large cups, like this was a medieval fraternity kegger. They must be the hunting party, I was betting.

The sheriff circulated among the nobles, who only talked to him if they had to. I could pick out the knights with their coats of arms on their tunics, and there were clergy in fancy robes—including the bishop of Leeds. My heart nearly stopped when he looked right at me, but his attention moved on with no sign of recognition, probably because his eyes never got any higher than my chest.

Another advantage of disguising myself in a dress.

There were a large number of guards. The ones wearing the prince's colors were up by the dais. Nottingham soldiers were stationed at intervals around the great hall, and archers were positioned along the gallery. "Is this a normal amount of guards for a royal visit?" I murmured to Isabel. "I don't know if James even talked to Henry, let alone persuaded him the prince was in danger."

"Why don't you ask him yourself?" she said.

I followed her nod and there was James, wearing civilian clothes, blue and black, with what must be his family crest. The Templar outfit was a lot more badass, but also a lot more conspicuous.

He reached us and bowed to Isabel. "M'lady," he said, with the same familiar affection I'd heard him use before. "You look more colorful than I've seen you since my return. It suits you."

Isabel smiled, showing her dimples. Knowing what I did about their relationship—or rather the expectations of them—I watched her closely. She had a bit of a blush, and when she spoke, there was obvious pleasure in his compliment. "Thank you, Sir James. I can say the same for you."

I didn't point out that blue and black weren't exactly challenging the rainbow. That combination didn't come close to the peacock colors a lot of the nobles were wearing.

James glanced around, frowning slightly. "Is Eleanor not with you?" he asked.

Isabel blinked at him. "She's right here, James."

I deliberately didn't say anything as he looked at me, then recognized me, and then visibly reordered his thoughts. "I—oh . . . um."

Well, that was incredibly satisfying.

"Oh dear," Isabel sighed, on a completely different subject. "The prince has spotted me. I must go pay my respects."

I turned away from a still-flummoxed James and looked toward the thrones. Prince John watched Isabel and James with sharp eyes. Queen Eleanor watched us closely, too, though her expression was unreadable.

"You'd better come," Isabel told James. "You too, Eleanor."

"Me?" I squeaked. "The last thing I want to do is attract the prince's attention."

James finally found something to say to me. "It will be worse if you don't go. He's the type to note who slights him."

Of course he would.

"Just follow us and curtsy like you practiced," said Isabel.

"And don't speak more than absolutely necessary," added James.

For once I wasn't insulted by the advice. James offered Isabel his arm, she laid her hand on his forearm, and they passed through the crowd on the way to the royal dais. I fell in behind them, then moved to Isabel's side when we reached the throne. I made a low curtsy the way Isabel had shown me, and managed to not fall over. Success.

The prince rose from his seat and went to Isabel, lifting her from her curtsy by her hand and kissing both cheeks. "Dear Isabel! How well you look in that color, in *any* color, but brown."

"Thank you, Your Highness," she said. Prince John hadn't so much as glanced at James or me, but Isabel performed introductions. "My childhood friend, Sir James." She didn't stint on his titles. In fact, she seemed to know them pretty well. Then she indicated me. "And this is a distant cousin on my mother's side."

James had called it. The prince gave us both a perfunctory glance, then returned his attention to Isabel and offered her his arm. "What a lovely tune this is, and yet no one is dancing. Shall we change that, my lady?"

She laid her hand atop his without missing a beat, and they

went to the center of the room. Before I let myself breathe, I looked up at Queen Eleanor, who nodded to me, then to James, dismissing us both with a look that was saying *something* . . . but I couldn't interpret what. I just knew that when James offered me his arm like he had Isabel, I felt like more of a poacher than I ever had shooting partridges.

We moved to a spot where we could observe the people watching the prince, and I finally inhaled. Neither of us spoke while more pairs joined the dance. They formed two rows, men in one, women in the other. There was bowing and turning and weaving in and out, and I was sure a whole pattern went by before James said, "You look different."

I let out a loud, surprised laugh, then toned it down. "Obviously," I said.

A glance at him showed a flush rising on his tanned face. "Your hair is covered," he explained. I let that pass without comment. "And you've . . . you're more . . ." I let him flounder until he came up with "womanly."

With superhuman effort, I kept a straight face as I looked at him from the corner of my eye. "Were you this observant on the battlefield, Sir James? Because I am in awe, really."

He turned to me sharply, but unbent a bit when he saw I was joking. His rueful expression made it impossible not to grin. "You should allow me some latitude. I have not been around ladies in a while."

"You did fine with Isabel," I pointed out. "And she's very *womanly.*"

"Yes, but I've known her my whole life."

282

Someone from the fraternity hunting party jostled me a step closer to James, and I didn't immediately back up. "But you're supposed to marry her."

He turned back to watch the room, especially the dancers. The musicians had finished one song and were starting another. "You of all people should know that 'supposed to' doesn't mean 'will.'"

I watched his profile for a moment longer. "So you're going to keep doing penance as a poor friar in the middle of nowhere? Isn't that a waste?"

His gaze slanted my way, for about the same amount of time I'd studied him. "No one would suspect a humble cleric of being the conscience of the notorious bandit Robin Hood. Perhaps that's my godly calling."

It was my turn to look away. Because I didn't know what to do with that. I was going home. Which didn't mean there wouldn't be a Robin Hood to follow me, who would need a Friar Tuck to keep him in line. Picturing it was more painful than it should have been. Thank God something on the dance floor needed attention.

"Isabel seems in need of rescue," I said. Immediately alert, James looked for her. She wasn't in mortal danger, exactly. But a new dance set was forming, and she was about to be shanghaied into partnering with one of the very drunk fraternity brothers. "Go," I said, when James glanced at me.

He went to see to the damsel, and I got back to what I was supposed to be doing, which was keeping a watch out for assassins. Just a little thing.

Nearby, the fraternity hunting party kept drinking, and a bunch of women gathered just behind me talked about raising children or cattle or both. In the far corner were the guys at the company picnic who would a hundred times rather be on the golf course if the boss weren't there taking notes on who ducked out early.

Someone approached from my left, stopping just behind my shoulder. "It's a good thing I'm no assassin," said Captain Guilbert.

"Yes, it is," I answered without turning. "Because I usually am armed with something sharp, as you well know."

There was a weighted pause, then he said, lower and much closer to my ear, "Yes, but where would you hide your bow in that gown."

I forgot about the prince and spun around to make sure that it was indeed Henry Guilbert who just said that, and he was standing close enough to . . . I didn't know what. I'd never been that near to him when we weren't trying to maim each other.

He nodded to the center of the room. "You should have danced with him."

"I don't know the steps," I answered, refusing to be the first one to move back.

"When has *that* ever stopped you?" he challenged. I was having an awful time judging his mood. His voice was benign, but his gaze less so. "What are you doing here? Are you insane? Or are you here to drive *me* to madness?"

"Neither. Didn't James tell you?" I tried searching his face again, but came up short. James must have told him, because Guilbert had opened with a salvo about the assassin.

"He did. And did he not tell you *not* to come here?" While we talked, his gaze scanned the room, then landed on me, then started over.

"I was already committed to the course," I said. "How is your leg?"

He maintained his stoic expression and kept his eyes on the revelers. "It aches when it rains. How is your conscience?"

"Clear." But I blushed anyway. "If you had taken me in to the sheriff, I would be dead by now. You know that. So I'm . . . well, I'm glad you're not dead or dying. But I'm not sorry for doing everything I could to escape you."

I'd kept my voice down, but there was nothing I could do about my intensity. Guilbert's next glance at me contained a warning. "People are taking notice," he said, then took my hand and placed it on top of his, catching my fingers between his thumb and palm when I tried to snatch my hand away. "We'll walk, and people will know from my limp why we aren't dancing."

"I don't want to walk with you," I said, leaning back when he took a step.

His black eyes flashed, finally, like he'd come to the end of his patience, and he ducked his head close to speak in my ear like before. "Do you want the sheriff to take a closer look at you? Or the bishop of Leeds? Try to look like you're enjoying my company."

"Does anyone?" My tone was caustic, but I left my hand in his, and when he started walking, I went with him.

"A few." He kept at a stately pace. "Tell me if you see this mysterious monk of yours."

Oh. Right. Eventually, he and I would make a slow circle of the room, like a few other pairs were doing. Maybe he wasn't doing this just to torment me. "I haven't seen any sign of him."

"It's early afternoon yet." Guilbert's hold on my fingers lightened but didn't disappear. The most uncomfortable part about this was that it didn't feel uncomfortable. This . . . ass-hole had manhandled, threatened, arrested, and sliced me with his sword. And, okay, I'd punched, insulted, escaped from, and shot him with an arrow. But when I slanted a look at him—

"Oh my God," I said, choking my voice to a whisper. "Are you checking me out?"

"I don't know what that means. But I expect I was, yes." He only looked embarrassed at having been caught.

This time I did yank my hand away. "You are . . . so . . ." I nearly burst trying to hold my voice down. "Infuriating!"

"Now you see my point." We'd reached the doors of the hall. Instead of continuing around the room, Guilbert abruptly pulled me out of the hall, into an adjoining stairwell, and up enough steps so we were between floors, hidden from view. He placed his hands on my shoulders and ordered, "Leave. Leave now and go back to your greenwood, or wherever it is you came from. I have men to protect the prince. Sir James is here to protect the royal family, too. No one can protect *you* if you are discovered."

"I can't leave this to someone else, Guilbert."

"Have you considered that your being recognized might make this more difficult? And more dangerous for your friends?"

No, I hadn't thought of that. But I set my jaw, unbudging, and with an annoyed sound, Guilbert let go of me. Then he reached up and straightened the circlet that held on the princess veil. "You'll only look more conspicuous, I suppose, if you hide more of your face." I froze until he had it all straight. "Go up these stairs to the gallery and keep watch from there. You'll see better *and* be seen less."

"Why are you helping me?" I demanded, feeling stupid for not slapping his hands away.

"I'm not. I'm helping James and doing my duty, guarding England's ruler in absentia." Then, when I kept glaring at him, his shoulders dropped in an almost apologetic shrug. "And because I feel bad about how I treated you. I thought if I dealt with you as the boy you pretended to be that you would see sense."

"You thought you could scare me off, you mean."

A glimpse of annoyance reassured me this was the same Henry Guilbert. "If you want to quibble. You would disappear, and I would not have a war between my duty and my conscience. But James was right to come after me with his sword of righteousness."

That . . . was a lot to absorb. I didn't know whether to challenge this half-assed apology, accept it, or pretend to accept it so I could get on with the business of halting the revision of history.

I exhaled in frustration and turned to continue upstairs. "Your timing sucks, Guilbert. I'm going to go stop an assassin. I'll deal with you later."

Leaving him in the stairwell, I went to the gallery and found a spot to stake out. Across from me were the musicians. They made me think of Alan—I hoped he and Jocasta were safely off to their happily-ever-after, and I made him a small mental apology for blowing off his assassin tale.

Besides the musicians, I shared the gallery with watchful guards, who I avoided, some couples promenading, some baronial types talking.

Downstairs, a new dance had started and Prince John was partnering a new lady. Guilbert had reemerged, and he resumed his watch without looking up at me. Isabel was still among the dancers, and still with James. I watched them for a moment, then got back on task.

Guilbert was right about one thing: I could see a lot better up here. Maybe not faces, but I could see the patterns of people moving around—the dancers in the lines and squares they made, circling each other, then moving to a new position. It was easier to read body language, too. The sheriff stood apart, looking disgruntled. He was like that kid who only gets included in parties because his parents leave their liquor cabinet unlocked.

Something small finally pinged my subconscious. I had to wait for it to ping again before I could figure out what my pattern recognition software was telling me.

There. That man in the dance, two spots away from

Prince John. He was moving a little stiffly, just a hair behind the others. Maybe he was just a bad dancer. But the couples shifted and now he was only one space away from the prince.

Was it the monk—Thaddeus—in civilian clothes?

I saw the man move his hand strangely, and I was certain. The messenger monk was the assassin, and he was slipping something down his sleeve and into his palm. A few more bars of music and the dance would bring him right up to the prince.

I looked at Guilbert and then at James, but neither returned my stare. None of the guards could see from ground level what I could from the gallery. If I yelled, the assassin could easily strike in the chaos before the guards could make it through the ranks of dancers.

I needed telepathy, but that wasn't my superpower. There was an archer, though, posted just a few feet from me. Moving toward him with my eyes still on the dancers, I knew I wasn't going to have time to point out the target, and that was if he believed me.

Not all my quick-fire decisions are good ones.

I grabbed the bow from the archer and an arrow from his quiver, nocked, drew, and . . . and hesitated. Just for an instant, until the assassin was clear in front and behind. I left myself room to miss—

And I did.

The arrow whiffed between the prince and the killer and thunked into a table behind them, vibrating where it stuck out from the wood.

Total pandemonium. Exactly what I hadn't wanted. The dancers reeled back and the royal guard pushed forward, and then someone screamed, "The prince is bleeding!"

The mass of people dispersed, the royal guard shoving them back. Prince John lay on the floor, crimson spattered on the blue silk of his tunic. There was no sign of a weapon or of the man who'd wielded it. Only my arrow, stuck in the table and pointing up to me like an accusing finger.

"*Fils de putain!*" It was a voice I recognized, and its owner had recognized me. De Corsey looked up at me and for just a moment he was speechless. "*Fille de putain!* That is Robin Hood."

I should have used the moment to run. But by the time the thought had worked its way through the crackly static of *I missed, I missed, I missed* it was too late. Soldiers wrenched the bow from my hand and hauled me up by my arms. I didn't struggle. My mind had frozen over, preserving the image of the once and future king of England lying bloody on the stones of Nottingham Castle's great hall, and Isabel, James, and Guilbert staring up at me with expressions of disbelief and betrayal.

CHAPTER TWENTY-FOUR

𝔅ↄ𝔠

I HAD NEVER BEEN TOTALLY ALONE BEFORE.

I'd felt alone with Rob missing, but even so, I always had an inkling he was out there. That one person made up of the same DNA as me was in the world somewhere, and that maybe I could tap some quantum spiderweb of atoms and he would feel it a whole world away.

I'd been by myself, but my parents were only either a phone call or text message away. Same with Coach, and my teammates, and my grandparents.

If I were in modern jail, there were a lot of people who would come bail me out. Will and John were off in Sherwood Forest, though, and Much was safe at his father's house. But Isabel's shock and James's expression of betrayal had clipped the strings of our association, and I'd felt them fall away as the soldiers dragged me into this stinking hole under the castle.

There were other prisoners with me in Nottingham's dungeon, but I was utterly on my own. The smell was foul, the straw on the ground was foul, the slime on the stone walls was foul. But the foulest thing of all was the sheriff.

"The Robin of Sherwood Forest is a girl." He stood outside the barred door and gloated.

Everything I'd seen of him made him a cruel, petty, and narcissistic despot. I don't think he enjoyed making people miserable. I think he just enjoyed how powerful that made him feel.

"I've known that for a while now." My voice shook, despite my best efforts. I was cold and terrified, but as scared as I was to be inside the cell, I was happy *he* was outside of it. He might have looked directly at me two whole times when I'd been a boy, and that included when he was calling for my death. Since he'd ordered the soldiers to carry me down here, he'd been cataloging my features like he was doing an IRS audit.

"This explains why you were able to fool my soldiers, my foresters—even my deputy," he said. "You think irrationally, like a woman. Erratically, like a woman."

"Intelligently, like a woman."

That went straight over his head, but it made me feel better.

I kept thinking someone must have seen what had really happened. That I had tried to save the prince. That I'd be pardoned. But I had been shivering in this dank cell, enduring the sheriff's sneers and leers long enough that I knew that wasn't going to happen.

I hated pleading my case with him because it put me at his nonexistent mercy. But he was the law in Nottingham. "I didn't aim for the prince. There was a man with a knife. An assassin."

"Was it a magic knife? Could it disappear into the air?" He was a sarcasm amateur. I could endure his mocking. There were worse tortures than trying to reason with someone who knew only his own logic.

The sheriff strode back and forth in front of the cell. "If you can produce this knife from the air, I might believe you." He waited. Looked around for a knife to appear. Faked disappointment. "Then it's the executioner's ax for you."

Stay focused. Don't let him into your head.

"Eventually," the sheriff amended, and left me to imagine what would happen between now and then.

The idea was a worm that burrowed in and ate through my courage. I was going to die here and I might even be happy about it by the time it happened. I had no rights, no money to bribe someone, no one—no *man*—to speak up for me. I had no guarantee that anyone would protest anything that happened down here in the dungeon, because I literally did not exist right now.

I didn't even know if my parents existed right now. And if they did, and I died here, I'd doomed them to a life of never knowing what had happened to me.

Don't get killed. Don't change history. *How had I screwed this up so badly?*

As soon as the sheriff had left, Iron Ellie sank like the *Titanic.* My knees gave up, my nerves gave up . . . my badass gave up. I knelt on that horrible floor, gathered the skirt of my dress, and sobbed into the balled-up fabric.

All my life, I'd never failed at anything. But that was because I'd never tackled anything I wasn't good at. I should have been good at the twelfth century, thanks to Mom and Dad, but I'd crashed and burned and soon I'd be taking modern civilization down too.

I cried myself out quickly and then spent an eternity listening to rats scrabble and water drip. Now and then there was the sound of iron on stone.

Maybe I should get some perspective.

What could I actually do something about? If I had some time before I joined Sir Aethelstan over the bridge, I could ask for parchment and ink. Something durable. Would it be possible to leave my parents a letter and somehow direct it to them care of the twenty-first century?

That sounded like a really far-fetched plot twist.

The sound of a key turning in the outer door brought me to my feet. There must be a rule that dungeon doors had to squeal like a tortured soul. I braced for the worst, and then Henry Guilbert stepped into the meager torchlight.

"Thank God," I breathed, surprising myself. When had I started being glad to see Guilbert?

He wasn't expecting that reaction, either. "That's not the usual thing traitors say when they see me."

I had a pretty good explanation. "Well, you're not the sheriff."

"No," he said grimly, "I'm not. I suppose you might see it as a blessing that you won't have to deal with him once you're transferred to the Tower."

The floor seemed to take another elevator plummet. I only *thought* I'd been terrified before. "The Tower of London?" I grabbed onto a bar of the cell and used it to slow my drop to the ground. "Is that where people are drawn and quartered for killing a prince?"

"If they're lucky."

I was going to throw up. My heart was going to kick its way out of my chest like a horse out of a stall.

"Fortunately, the prince is not dead."

"What?" I was still screwed, but maybe history had a chance.

"He got a cut on his arm, and he fainted." Guilbert's arms were folded as he looked down at me. "The prevailing theory is that your arrow nicked him when you attempted to kill him."

I got my legs under me and stood again with the help of the cell bars. "I didn't nick him. That must have been Brother Thaddeus—the monk—with a knife."

Guilbert nodded slowly. "Isabel spoke up for you. She said she saw a man lunge at His Highness, and that she thought he had something in his hand, like a knife."

Not daring to hope, I asked, "Does the prince believe her?"

"No one quite believes her."

I heard the clank of metal as Guilbert chose a key on the giant iron ring in his hand, and unlocked my door. "However,

I do," he said, pulling the cell door open with another clang. "If you wanted Prince John dead, you wouldn't have missed."

Don't be so sure.

I tried to leave that thought behind in the cell. My legs still trembled as I walked out, half expecting the door to slam closed on me. But Guilbert held it open, and when I wobbled, he steadied me. I hated to look weak in front of him. But I'd look stupid if I shook him off and then face-planted in the dungeon filth.

"You know what this means?" I said, gaining strength and resolve. "The assassin is still out there. And no one will be expecting him because they think the culprit—me—is safely locked up." I bounced on my toes, and my knees didn't fail me. "I wouldn't put it past someone to plan it that way."

Guilbert almost smiled. "Now you're starting to think like a Norman noble."

Some of the buoyancy went out of me as I got up the courage to ask, "Does James think I tried to kill the prince?"

The captain's air of command settled back around him, and he gestured toward the door. "Let's discuss it outside of the dungeon, in case anybody comes."

CHAPTER TWENTY-FIVE

I WASN'T SURE WHAT TO EXPECT WHEN WE EXITED THE DUNgeon into a shadowed corner of the castle bailey. Full dark, yes. A phalanx of guards? I hoped not. But it definitely was not James, wearing his friar's habit and standing in a circle of torchlight with two unconscious guards at his feet. His smile was downright subversive. "No one ever suspects the cleric," he said.

Somehow I stopped myself from rushing over to him, and restrained myself to a smile. "Especially not a paladin," I said. Then I gave him a closer look, because he definitely seemed a lot more Friar Tuck than usual. "Have you put on weight?"

He shucked off his brown robe and cowl. Underneath he wore armor, and he was back in his Templar-blazoned surcoat. I'd missed it.

"Good to see you again, Sir James," I said, choking on too many emotions to sort out.

He took a full quiver from his back, pulling the strap over his head. "I thought we could use God on our side tonight."

"To save Prince John?" said someone from the shadows. "I think the devil looks after his own."

Will stepped into the light, wearing the livery of a Nottingham guard. I grinned, my heart lightening despite the dire fix we were in. When Little John appeared as well, I looked up at my two comrades in my short-lived crime spree and my throat tightened on what I wanted to say. "Will, John, I . . ."

"Don't start crying all the time just because you have on a dress," said Will, breaking the tension. He handed me my bow, and James gave me the quiver.

Guilbert held the dungeon door open. "Drag those two in here," he said, nodding at the unconscious men. Will and James grabbed one guard and deposited him in the prison, while Little John managed the other by himself. Then the captain closed and locked the door.

"That can't be all the guards," I said, because the bailey had been swarming like an anthill before.

"My rangers have locked the Nottingham regulars in the guardhouse," Guilbert said. Will and John looked at him with varying amounts of distrust and dislike but didn't say anything. "There's still the royal guard to deal with, and the sheriff's personal men."

"Oh, no problem, then." I faked a confidence I was far from feeling. I took a practice draw with my bow, and the last intact underarm seam of my gown split. The elbows were still too tight for a full draw, though. "Who has a knife?"

Will took his from his belt and cut my sleeves where I pointed, over the elbow, and then gave the cloth a good rip so my arms could bend freely.

I caught them up while Will did his tailoring. "The assassin is still here and will probably try again, especially since I got blamed. I have to find him, or figure out his next move and intercept it."

"Just to be clear, Ellie," said Will, in a last-ditch-effort sort of tone. "You're risking a sword in the gut for a man who is right now planning your execution. Your *gruesome* execution. Are you sure you want to do this?"

"Look at the thanks you got the *first* time you saved his royal backside," said Little John.

James, when I looked at him, said, "I am sworn to defend even the likes of Prince John. So is Henry, as an agent of the crown. But you are not. I would rather you go with Will and John and be safe."

As much as I didn't want to be beheaded by the sheriff of Nottingham, it had been the thought of execution at the Tower that was the real gut check. Cruel and unusual punishment was not against the law here. And the punishments were exactly that—cruel and unusual.

Maybe I'd done enough. Maybe I'd foiled the assassination attempt, done my duty, and the tunnel would be open. Or, if it wasn't, well, as long as I was alive, there was hope I'd get home.

Did I honestly want to risk certain death for a bad prince who would be a negligible king except for that *one thing* he did that was important?

But what if this was my one thing?

Guilbert weighed in last. "You're no longer the only one who can identify the assassin. Isabel had a look at him."

"Here's what I think," I said with finality. "Everyone will be off their guard believing I'm locked up. An assassin would be stupid to miss this opportunity. And Thaddeus—the assassin we know about—he was sending that message to someone. So he may have a conspirator. Or a backup plan. Or, who knows, maybe blame-the-outlaw has always been plan A." I waved a hand, as if swiping those things away. "But I have to stay, whether or not you do, Will and John."

They didn't even glance at each other to confer. "If you need to stay, then we do, too," said Will, and Little John nodded. "Though I'm not sure what two extra men will do against all the prince's guards and the sheriff's brutes."

"Fewer may be better," said James. "We should keep this quiet, and keep the assassin complacent."

"The sooner the better, too," said Guilbert, nodding up at the parapet. "The sentries are still at their posts and they'll be around in a moment."

"What about the caves under the castle?" I said. "The secret passage. Can we get into the keep by that route?"

Guilbert and James exchanged startled glances. "I did not tell her," James avowed, raising one hand to ward off Guilbert's accusatory look.

The captain turned back to me. "Is that what you were doing the day you were here? A reconnaissance?"

"Hardly." Though I guess I had been on an exploratory mission when I headed down the tunnel back in ... Wow. It felt like it really had been eight hundred years ago. "I never plan that far ahead."

Guilbert looked surprised, then offended. "You and your band have evaded my rangers this whole time and you just ... just ..."

"*Wing it,* is what we say where I come from." Though, it was more a case of knowing my strengths so I didn't have to intellectualize too much. Medals are won on the practice range. It wasn't like I didn't have *goals.*

"How do you stand that?" Guilbert asked James.

"I stand her very well," he said simply, his shoulder next to mine. Little John was on my other side, and Will Scarlet flanked him. My band of brothers.

Guilbert took the point and, hardly mocking at all, pressed his hand to his chest in a sort of salute. "My apologies, captain of the greenwood. Tonight, I stand with you, too. But I would rather not stand here all night."

"One more moment," James said. "Since you spoke of reconnaissance—" He gave a sharp whistle. A servant girl appeared from around the corner. She wore a shabby dress and apron, and her hair was covered by a kerchief. And she looked familiar.

"Elsbeth?" No, *he* was close enough that I got a look at the eyebrows. "Much! You're dressed like a girl."

Even in the torchlight I could see he was blushing. "I got the idea from you."

"What did you find out?" asked James.

Much dragged the kerchief from his mop of hair and answered the knight. "The royals are all in the best rooms in the keep, way up top. Prince John retired for the evening, on account of his grievous injury. The queen and her ladies-in-waiting are at one end of the great hall, and the knights and lords as are here for the hunting are at the other, drinking all the ale in Nottingham, says the cook, who says she doesn't know what she'll give them to drink tomorrow."

"Where's the sheriff?" I asked.

"Moaning and wailing because the prince has taken himself to his bed after all the work Nottingham did to host him." Much seemed to enjoy the sheriff's displeasure most of all. "He nearly licked the floor for His Highness, trying to get back in his good graces, but Prince John says his nerves are in tatters, just like his sleeve. The sheriff sent for the physician to attend His Highness. Probably going to bleed him," he added, with bloodthirsty glee.

Ugh, leeches was my first thought. My *second* thought was more to the point. "Couldn't a physician easily kill someone by letting them bleed too much?"

James shook his head. "He wouldn't be left alone with the prince for just that reason."

Little John cleared his throat. "You know, Rob, when Alan was telling us what he heard in that tavern . . ."

He trailed off leadingly, cutting his eyes distrustfully

toward the deputy sheriff. Guilbert gestured impatiently, not at Little John, but to me.

"He mentioned poison," said James. "It was a very vague story."

"Just because something makes a good story," said Will, "doesn't mean it's *not* true."

"Poison." I looked from James to Guilbert. "That seems like something a physician could definitely do, and under everyone's noses."

Guilbert turned, obviously expecting us to fall in behind him. "Come. We'll discuss while we walk."

I put the kerchief back over Much's hair and gave him a hug. "Stay safe."

He grinned up at me cheekily. "Okay, Captain Ellie."

Little John had picked up a guard's helmet that had fallen to the ground. "Are you coming?" Will asked him.

"I don't like tunnels. I never fit." He put the helmet on and mashed it down on his hair. "I'll see you inside."

Will and I had to jog to catch up with Guilbert and James. Despite what the captain had said, there was no talking as we crossed the castle's ground level. We moved quietly, falling into the shadows once as a sentry walked the parapet above us. Then, at Guilbert's gesture, we moved silently on to the low door where I'd emerged ages ago. My eyes had adjusted to the moonlit courtyard, and there were fires lit in the bailey close to the keep. But the tunnel was pitch-black.

"A torch will give us away." Guilbert stepped into the tunnel and offered me his free hand. I ignored it, then found out the sloped ground was covered in gravel and loose dirt. I ended up grabbing his hand after all. Once I had my feet under me, Guilbert moved my hand to the sandstone wall. "Keep your right hand on the wall, and you won't get lost."

I had a moment of déjà vu, from when I'd stumbled through the swallowing darkness between my *then* and this *now*. This dark, though, stood still and didn't turn me upside down. There was no sense of an open door, either. I slung my bow and hurried after the captain, keeping my hand on the wall.

"You're wrong about the physician," said Guilbert as we went. "Jerome Arden is a respected man. He's attended the sheriff and the barons of Nottingham and Derbyshire—the ones who can afford him."

"Then he'd be the first called if something happened to the prince, right?" There must have been a little light from somewhere, because when I glanced back to make sure James and Will were behind me, I could see the white of James's surcoat as a patch of light gray, as opposed to Guilbert, who was basically invisible in his dark-colored clothes. "The sheriff and the barons are not stellar references."

"But the sheriff enjoys his power because of the prince," said Guilbert. "He's John's man through and through."

"Lackey, you mean." I let it drop when I smelled a smell that still gave me nightmares. "Are we near the river?"

"This tunnel is used to transport supplies arriving by river up to the bailey." Guilbert had stopped—I felt the subtle change in the air currents and halted before I ran into him.

"We're here," he said, and I heard him feeling along the wall.

James had stopped behind me, his hand touching my back as if to keep track of where I was in the dark. "Do you remember how to open it?" he asked Guilbert.

"Of course I remember. I'm the one who's been in Nottingham all this time."

"I beg your pardon. I hadn't guessed the bowels of the castle were on your sentry rounds."

"Boys," I chided, though sarcasm was better than swords when it came to their hacking at each other.

Will's voice came from behind James. "Does anyone in Nottingham *not* know how to get into the castle by the secret door?"

James, missing the point a little bit, explained, "Henry, Isabel, and I discovered the door when we were children. There's a combination of levers and counterweights—"

There was a soft click and a whisper of movement, and a slice of warm light cut through the dark. The two knights exchanged one of those looks, the one that said they were thinking the same thing, and whatever that was made them plunge ahead through the narrow portal, one after the other. I managed to catch the door before it swung closed, and Will and I followed. The only sign of the other two was James's heel disappearing around a curved stair.

The passage was just wide enough to swing a sword, with shallow steps carved into the sandstone. "The torches are lit," Will said. "Someone has been through this way."

We exchanged looks of our own, and ran up the stairs, unshouldering our bows as we went.

CHAPTER TWENTY-SIX

WHEN THE PASSAGE ENDED, WILL AND I FINALLY CAUGHT UP with Guilbert and James. The door opened inward and was hidden behind a tapestry. The knights didn't even confer about a plan, just pushed back the wall hanging and strode out like they hadn't been apart for ten years, let alone fighting with freaking broadswords less than a week ago. I glanced at Will. "Should we just charge out after them?"

"Your *chers amis* didn't hesitate."

My look turned into more of a glare. "Not the time, Will Scarlet."

There was always time for some things, apparently. He gave me an obvious ogle and a smirk. "Well, that *is* a well-tailored gown. I am not the only one to notice."

"Stop distracting me." I listened for noise, and heard only muffled voices. Peering out, I saw a corridor lined with more tapestries. At regular intervals, big iron candleholders, as tall as me, lit the hall. The dowager queen's apartment was up here, too. I'd walked down this way with Isabel about an age ago.

I slid into the corridor, where I could hear from around the corner someone challenging James and Guilbert to stop where they were. Will and I pressed up against the corner and listened to the answer. "Stand aside," ordered Guilbert, in a voice even I might have obeyed. "We have a message for his grace."

"On whose orders?" demanded a sentry.

"Captain Sir Henry Guilbert, chief forester and deputy sheriff of Nottingham."

It sounded impressive to me, but not to the guard. "A backcountry deputy and a Templar Knight." The guard's sneering tone and his "backcountry" crack made him sound like one of the royal guards, Prince John's own retinue. "We know how you churchy types think of His Highness. Give me the message and go back to your forest."

I got low and peered around the corner. I could have warned the guard that Guilbert had a temper. But then he wouldn't have been so surprised when the captain punched him in the face. The man reeled back, blood streaming from between his fingers as he clutched his nose.

"Come on," said Will. "We're missing the fun part."

The other guard brought the business end of his pike down and James knocked the spear to the side. Will and I had arrows ready as we stepped out into the corridor, just as six Nottingham soldiers came up the hall from the opposite direction, led by the sheriff.

"Stop there!" the sheriff said, but as soon as he saw Will's arrow pointed at his chest, he jumped out of the way. One of his solders was Little John–sized, and once he bashed two of his comrades' heads together, everything got kind of crazy.

"Get to the prince," Will said. "John and I have got this."

He sounded kind of excited about it, so I took him at his word and ran up the hall. The two sentries were on the ground and I had to step over them as I followed Guilbert and James to the royal apartment. It was a good thing I was okay with winging it, because *maybe* the guys had a plan, but I didn't know it.

Guilbert, still with a full head of steam, rapped quickly on the prince's door, then threw it open without waiting for an answer. "Your grace," he said. "There's danger of another attempt on your life."

That was rich coming from the guy who'd just taken down two royal bodyguards.

Prince John reclined on a divan in front of the fire. A servant—slack-jawed with surprise—stood with a cheese board in one hand and a knife in the other. And over His Highness bent a sinister figure in a black robe with bell sleeves, perfect for hiding things like knives and poisons.

Whoever he was, I'd never seen his face before.

"What's the meaning of this?" demanded the prince, half rising from the divan.

"Your grace," soothed the physician, and there was something desperate in his tone. "Your tonic—here, take it."

He held an embossed gold cup toward the prince. He'd been holding it since Guilbert and I had burst in. Everyone else had jumped, but his hand had never wavered. Whatever was in there must be really important.

"James," I said, my nocked arrow pointing to the physician. "The cup . . ."

The wide-eyed man looked from one knight to the other, then back to me. I saw his decision to flee before he even moved. I fired, and pinned one bell sleeve to the timber mantel above the fireplace. The arrow never touched him, but he screamed anyway. So did the servant and the prince. The physician didn't lose his grip on the cup, but a glass vial rolled from his sleeve. It tumbled end over end and smashed on the stones of the hearth.

Guilbert strode over and took the cup before the man could drop as well. The physician shrank against the wall, reconsidering a move to pull himself free.

Prince John had leapt to his feet, wrapping tight his fur-lined robe. "Guards!" he screamed. "Seize this traitor! Seize all these traitors!"

The two royal guards limped in. James was waiting, and backed them into a corner, half with his sword, half through intimidation. "We have matters to discuss with his grace," he told them. "Stay out of things until they are clear."

One guard was bleeding from his nose, and he pointed accusingly at Guilbert. "The sheriff's man attacked us, your grace! He took us by surprise."

"Only because of the threat on your life, my liege," said Guilbert, pointing to the hearthstones. "What was hidden in this man's sleeve?"

Prince John's face got even redder. "Are there conspirators all around me?"

"It's nothing, my lord," groveled the physician. "A harmless sedative, most efficacious, but very expensive, so I hide it in my sleeve in case of robbers."

The sheriff entered, flanked by two of his own guards and looking as panicked as he was angry and bewildered. The prince turned, the heavy hem of his robe flaring. "What's the meaning of this?" he demanded of the sheriff.

"Traitors, Your Highness. Treason and deceit—" He nearly fell over himself with excuses. Then he saw me and froze, realization creeping glacially over his features. "How ...?" Spotting Guilbert, he demanded, "Did *you* let this creature out of the dungeon? Guards!" he said to his own men. "Seize them both. And the Templar, too."

"Stop!" yelled the prince, then pointed at his own guards. "You! Seize the sheriff's men! Seize *everyone* or I'll have all your heads on spikes!"

No one wanted their head on a spike, so everyone pointed a weapon at someone else, seemingly at random, in a kind of medieval standoff.

As the one with the projectile weapon, I had the advantage. I picked the sheriff. At this distance I could skewer him with half a draw and no aim. Into the quiet of the stalemate, I told him, "Send your men out to make sure no one else comes near."

The donnybrook in the hall must have been over because Will appeared in the doorway. "Guard the door," I told him.

"I am the prince and regent for the king in absentia!" roared Prince John. "*I* give the orders here! Sheriff's men, go out. Keep anyone from approaching. You," he said to Will, "guard the door."

Looking happy to get out of there, Will, for the first time since I'd known him, left without comment.

"Sire!" said the sheriff, seething with desperation. He'd taunted me with threats just hours ago, and now he was just as trapped as I'd been, facing someone just as unreasonable.

The prince cut off any excuses. "This witch just shot the physician that you sent to me, and your deputy has accused him of assassination. What do you say to that, m'lord sheriff?"

The physician and the sheriff spoke at once to defend themselves. The sheriff was barely coherent, blustering that Master Jerome was his personal physician and he could vouch for his skill. The physician vouched for himself with "Your Highness, I have been this shire's physician for five years! I've attended to nobles and knights, and I was trained by the most learned medical men in Paris."

"Paris!" The prince made the word both an accusation and a curse. He waved an imperious hand at Guilbert. "You . . . whoever you are. Give me your sword."

Guilbert looked uncertain. "My lord?"

"Give it to me! I am your prince!"

There was a moment when everyone seemed to be searching for any better idea than giving a sword to a crazy man. Then Guilbert handed over his weapon, with a slightly

311

mocking ceremoniousness that the prince missed entirely. Prince John took it, his arm dropping under its weight. Then he pointed the sword at Master Jerome and said, "If you weren't trying to poison me, then drink the tonic yourself."

Boy, I hoped my instincts hadn't been wrong this time. If the physician drank from the cup and didn't die, I'd be back on the chopping block, and I'd have brought Guilbert and James there with me.

Guilbert was one cool customer. He wrapped his hand around the arrow holding Master Jerome's sleeve to the wall, yanked it out, then offered the ornate little cup to the man.

The physician had broken out in a sweat. "My lord," he pleaded with the prince, "these ruffians could have poisoned the tonic to frame me for their treason."

"Drink," growled Prince John. He pressed the point of the sword against the man's chest until the physician whimpered.

"Wait," I said to stop that sound, and the sound of my conscience. "Your grace, if you kill him, you can't learn who sent him."

Prince John turned to the sheriff. "*You* called for him. Your own man, your own expense, you said."

The sheriff stepped back. Bad move, with a prince who loved to hunt. The sheriff had made himself the prey. The royal guards watched their liege advance on the sheriff and exchanged glances.

"Highness," said the sheriff, begging for reason, "I have known Master Jerome for years. If he has some fiendish treason in mind, I have no knowledge of it."

The prince kept advancing, his robe sweeping majestically. "Then you must be an ignorant fool."

The sheriff stopped with his back pressed against a tapestry depicting a wild boar hunt. "No, my lord."

"Then you are incompetent." Prince John was enjoying himself. "A fool, or a traitor." He offered the cup to the sheriff. "Prove your loyalty and drink."

The sheriff's lips were white and bloodless as he licked them with a tongue so dry it seemed to stick. I finally pitied him, and apparently so did James. "Your grace," he ventured.

"Quiet, Templar. If I want a sermon, I'll go to church. Besides, if he's innocent, then God will protect him," said the prince, "and the poison will not kill him."

I dragged my eyes from the sheriff and looked at the physician. Master Jerome had no poker face; it was clear that he didn't expect God to prove the sheriff's innocence. The sheriff stared at the cup. I could see him reasoning it out: If he refused, he was dead anyway. So he gambled on the drink and took the cup from the prince.

Everyone's eyes were on the sheriff as he sipped.

"All of it," ordered the prince icily.

But before the sheriff could comply, the physician cried out in alarm. Then I heard a sound that I knew like I knew my own name. I glimpsed a flash of swan-white fletching just before it was spattered with crimson as the broad barb of an arrow sliced through the poisoner's neck. His mouth worked in a wordless gurgle as the last pumps of his heart sprayed blood over the hearth.

I gasped as the hot, salty copper smell filled the room, and only the slump of the body onto the ground bumped me out of my shock.

The shot had come from the door. Someone had silenced the physician, eliminating a conspirator. I knew the fletching on that arrow, too. It was Will's, and Will was guarding the only way in.

CHAPTER TWENTY-SEVEN

I WAS CLOSEST TO THE DOOR AND THE FIRST TO MOVE. I RAN out and nearly tripped over Will, who lay in a pool of scarlet on the cold stone floor.

The hallway was otherwise empty. I slid to my knees beside him, dredging my dress through the blood. "Don't be dead," I begged, pressing my hands to the gash in his side.

"I'm not dead," he moaned. So much blood welled up that I knew he wasn't. Not yet.

"James!" I yelled. "I need your help!"

He was already coming out of the royal chamber. From inside the room I could hear Guilbert shouting out one of the windows for the guards to close the gate and secure the keep. Meanwhile, Prince John complained loudly about the sheriff being sick in his royal chamber pot. Guilbert came out of the

315

room, sliding his sword into its scabbard as if he wished he were silencing His Highness with it.

James replaced my hands with his and used his surcoat to stanch Will's bleeding. More armed soldiers were headed our way. The clatter of steel and creak of leather didn't sound foreign anymore.

Will pointed down the hallway. "He took my bow. After all the trouble I took to steal it. He looked like the man you described. The pigeon friar."

Guilbert asked, "Did you see where he went?"

"No," Will said, his eyes squeezed shut. "I was busy holding in my spleen."

He was so pale. His eyes were sunken, his lips bloodless. I looked at James, who had probably seen more wounded people than I would in five lifetimes, and he avoided my gaze.

"Take him to the barracks, James," Guilbert said. "Our surgeon will see to him. No one will notice an extra man just now."

A mixed group of royal guards and the sheriff's men reached us, and Guilbert gave rapid-fire orders for some to protect the prince and others to spread out and search for the assassin.

I was getting to my feet to join the search, when Will grabbed my hand. "Ellie, listen. The man had on the tabard of the royal guard. That was how he was able to approach me."

I looked at the guards in the corridor with us, searching their faces. James murmured, "He's eliminated his conspirator. Either he'll flee the castle or he'll do away with witnesses next. You have to find him, fast."

Realization gave me a solid, painful punch. "Isabel." I jumped up. "How many people heard her say she'd seen the man?"

"Anyone and everyone," said James grimly. "Much said she's with the ladies-in-waiting and the queen in the great hall."

"Right." Grabbing my bow, I wiped the blood off it with my skirt. "I'll start there."

"Eleanor—" said James, and I paused midstep. "Try not to kill him. I would like very much to know who sent him."

"I'll try," I promised. Then I pointed at Will. "You, don't die."

I thought he'd fallen unconscious, but he smiled and said, "I knew you loved me best of all."

When it came to uncomplicated love, I did. If Will died, I'd be losing another brother, and if I let that spark of insight catch fire, I wouldn't be able to stay in this moment. So much for the focused athlete who avoided interpersonal drama.

Speaking of interpersonal drama, Captain Guilbert had finished delegating duties and fell into step with me as I hurried to the stairs. "Where are you going?"

"The great hall. Isabel told the whole world she saw the assassin, right?"

He followed my reasoning and nodded. Then he suddenly stopped and grabbed my arm. "You can't go down there like that."

"There's no time—"

"This will take but a minute if you stop arguing." As he

said it, he was already approaching the two castle guards standing sentry at the top of the stairs.

"Captain Guilbert!" said one, snapping to attention.

"You," he ordered the first man. "Go to the great hall and tell the commander of the royal guard to protect Queen Eleanor—that there's been a threat to her and her ladies-in-waiting." When the first soldier had gone, he turned to the second. "Give me your clothes."

"I— What, sir?"

"Your uniform," ordered Guilbert. "Now."

The bewildered soldier rushed to comply, leaning his pike against the wall and pulling off his mail coif so he could unlace his leather tunic.

Guilbert switched to French to tell me, "You need to move through the hall without attracting attention. Even if you weren't covered in blood and dungeon filth, you're a wanted woman. *And* a wanted man, which may be a precedent, even in Nottinghamshire." The soldier handed over his jerkin and Guilbert gestured for him to fork over his pants. The man was wearing a full undershirt that covered his thighs, but I turned around anyway.

"Even after I saved the prince's life." I shook my head sadly, taking the trousers Guilbert handed me. I put them on under my dress, then bent to pull the heavy gown over my head. I'd forgotten to unlace it, but Guilbert grabbed the fabric and yanked. I emerged, and tugged my chemise so it covered everything important. More or less.

"Arms up," he told me. I complied and he dropped the leather jerkin onto me, pulled it into place, and tightened the laces under my arms so I wasn't swimming in it. Medieval clothes were a lot easier to put on when you had help.

"You shouldn't expect mercy from the prince merely because you saved his life." Guilbert kept his eyes on his hands, not on me. "At best he'll grant you a quick and clean execution."

It was definitely weird having a guy talk about your execution while his fingers were moving so close to the ticklish sides of your ribs. "I don't plan to be here for that," I said.

"Good." He nodded as he straightened and met my gaze. "I would truly hate to see your head taken off. But what I wish were justice is not always so in this shire."

I didn't have time to sort out why I was blushing, so I finished tucking in my chemise and picked up my bow from against the wall. "Let's go, before you overwhelm me with your flattery."

He switched to English and told the guard, "Give me your helmet." When the poor guy handed it over, he added. "Say anything of this, and I will cut out your tongue."

"You have a real flair for command," I said, adjusting my quiver as we hurried down the steps.

Guilbert gave me a wry look. "Whatever he's thinking, it's probably not as strange as the truth."

We hurried to a staircase that spiraled down one of the corner turrets with no exits until the bottom, which made it easily defensible and quick to navigate. Even without Guilbert, I would have found the great hall easily. As we rounded the last turn, voices and torchlight overflowed into the stairs. And so did smells—the smell of straw and mud and people and dogs, and also the scent of roast meat and savory vegetables and sage and onion and baked apples.

After all I'd seen that day, I didn't think I'd be hungry. But I was wrong.

I tried to look soldierly as Guilbert and I walked into the hall. Things had been rearranged for the feast, with giant heavy tables moved into rows, each set with more food than the people of this shire probably saw in months. There was definitely a rating system, rank-and-file landowners at one end of the room, lords in the middle, and local barons closest to the U-shaped head table. In the very center was Queen Eleanor, next to an empty seat for the prince. Along the sides of the table were a bunch of well-dressed, mostly well-fed men, including the bishop of Leeds and Baron de Corsey. The royal fraternity buddies looked pretty drunk on wine and rich food.

Isabel sat beside one of the hunting party, and I was relieved to see her safe. She nodded at whatever her dinner companion was saying, but she hadn't eaten the food in front of her. I didn't know if anyone had been able to get word to her that they were going to spring me from the dungeon, but I was sure no one had had a chance to update her since then.

"Any sign of him?" asked Guilbert.

"No," I said, scanning the faces of the royal guards stationed behind the dowager queen. I saw no one I recognized, so that was good. But I did identify the serving girl standing behind the barons with a flagon of wine—Much, in his disguise, literally watching Isabel's back.

I looked around for the biggest guard in the room and

found him positioned midway down the hall. Little John was keeping watch, too.

"Keep an eye on the gallery," I told Guilbert. "He has Will's bow, and he seems pretty good with it. If he's going to shoot someone, it'll be from there. I'll watch faces down here."

"As you wish, m'lady."

I didn't spare him a glance. There were so many bodies moving around, even with most of the guests seated—servants bringing food, guards patrolling, pages delivering messages, and giant wolfhounds getting the scraps from under the table. There were five servants circling the head table. Each carried a wooden board with different cheeses and fruits on it. Another servant worked his way down the table pouring wine.

If I were going to be an assassin, a servant would be the best disguise. No one paid attention to them. Their heads were down as they moved behind the dinner guests, so I couldn't get a good look at them.

"I can't see their faces," I said.

Guilbert turned to me. "What?"

"The servants." One approached the queen's side with a flagon of wine, easy to poison. One moved closer to Isabel with a tray and a cheese knife. Both servants had weapons; both women could be targets. "Poison or knife?"

Guilbert followed my gaze, and I pulled an arrow from over my shoulder. I was just a soldier next to the captain right now. But as soon as I raised my bow, I would be smothered by a mountain of bodyguards. "Which is he?" asked Guilbert. "Poisoned wine or cheese knife?"

"I don't know." My eyes flicked from one to the other as

each moved closer to a target. "I can't see their faces!" I said again.

If I shot the one with the wine, and I was wrong, the assassin could strike with the knife and be gone in the chaos. If I shot the one with the knife, the queen would be distracted and not drink her wine—and I'd have shot an innocent man.

"The one with the knife," said Guilbert. He grabbed the closest page and told him to run and tell the queen not to drink.

But what if, what if, what if—

The fletchings were stiff against my fingers as I nocked the arrow. Both men moved one person over, as if choreographed.

Stay in this moment, Ellie.

"Pick one, Hudson!" ordered Guilbert, and I obeyed that voice.

"Thaddeus!" I yelled down the length of the hall.

One of the men looked up.

I shot the one who didn't.

"Protect the queen!" shouted the guards, surrounding her. "Protect the queen!"

As soon as my arrow hit, I dropped the bow, almost before anyone screamed. The moment expanded to hold a thousand details as they rushed toward me. The points of swords and pikes. The slide of steel from scabbards. The creak of timber above and boots on stone below. The smell of armored men, musty and salty with old sweat.

There was a splintering crash and I thought the gallery floor had given out under the weight of the price on my head. It hadn't, but the dining tables cleared as a mob rushed at me. Guilbert called "Hold!" over the chaos, and it was echoed—"Hold!"—at the ends of the hall.

But it was as though every soldier and good citizen in the place wanted to capture Robin Hood and they all looked giant as they came at me. I squeezed me eyes shut and got ready to tuck into a ball so I wouldn't be pulled to bits. But the first one to reach me wrapped the hard band of his arm around me, picking me up around the waist and tucking me against him.

"Stop," commanded James, his voice vibrating through me as he held me with one arm, his other free for his sword. "I have her. Come no closer."

I opened my eyes and tried to sort out what was going on. I'm not sure I had any better luck than anyone else.

The soldiers and good citizens had fallen back, all except Little John in his disguise, protecting James's back. A path cleared between us and the head table, which had been over-turned by the royal guard to better surround the dowager queen. James set me on my feet, Little John picked up my bow, and we followed Guilbert forward.

The assassin was sprawled on the floor, wine soaking his clothes along with the blood that seeped from around the arrow shaft protruding from under his collarbone. More royal guards surrounded him, their pikes at his throat.

It was certainly Thaddeus, of the messenger pigeons, dagger, and arrow.

The commander of the royal guard stepped over the

wreckage and picked up the flagon of wine, dipping his finger in the dregs still in it, and touching it to his tongue. He spat immediately. "Poison, your grace."

The lords and ladies at the head table who dove for cover started to pick themselves back up. Much helped Isabel to rise. She saw me and smiled, covered her heart with both hands, and mouthed "Thank you."

"Lady Isabel," said Queen Eleanor, coming out from behind the table as well, looking as regal as ever. The guard had pulled the assassin to his feet, and the queen gestured to him. "Can you confirm for Commander Boyer that this is the man you saw make an attempt on the life of the prince today?"

Isabel took a good look, then nodded to the commander. "That's him. He drew a knife from his sleeve and tried to stab Prince John in the back."

That news rippled through the hall. Queen Eleanor ignored it and touched Isabel's shoulder. "I am very sorry I did not believe you, my dear. One hates to think there are so *many* bandits and cutthroats running around Nottinghamshire." She added drily, "Someone should have a word with the sheriff."

As a smattering of quickly stifled chuckles erupted among those close enough to have heard her, Eleanor approached the assassin. Commander Boyer lifted his sword, pointing it at the traitor's chest, ready to strike if he should lunge at the dowager queen.

"So," she said, standing at the commander's side. The assassin had eyes as blank as a shark's, and he blinked expressionlessly at the queen. "What have you to say for yourself?"

I definitely wanted to hear what he had to say for himself.

I felt like I had a vested interest for a lot of reasons, in this century and my own. But he didn't speak, and a moment later the doors to the great hall opened with a crash. Prince John strode in, his fur cloak sweeping behind him.

"What do I hear?" demanded his grace. "These fools have actually caught him?"

As he approached, the guests all took a knee, lowering their heads. I was slow to react—not grudging, exactly, just slow.

It was hard to tell what happened next, while everyone was bowing and not looking. It seemed the assassin grabbed his chance for escape. The guards grappled with him, and by the time everyone looked, the tussle was over. The assassin sank to his knees with the commander's sword buried between his ribs.

Only James moved quickly, reaching the man in time to take his weight as he collapsed, easing him to the floor. I followed and knelt beside him, surprised that the guards didn't stop me, until I realized that Guilbert had my back. Isabel edged closer, too.

James leaned over the dying man and whispered, "Confess." But the assassin only breathed once more, then took his secrets with him.

The hall was so still only the drip of spilled wine proved time hadn't stopped. The bishop had come forward as well, and he intoned a solemn but short prayer in Latin, with James joining in on *"In nomine Patris, et Filii, et Spiritus Sancti."*

The rustle of sleeves filled the hall like sighs as everyone made the sign of the cross.

Even Queen Eleanor, with her arthritic fingers. What would she confess? Would *I* ever confess that I knew she'd pushed the commander's sword forward and silenced an assassin?

In that moment when all the assembly was bowing, and I was catching up, I'd seen Eleanor's hand on the elbow of Commander Boyer's sword arm. She might say it was in revenge for treason, but I *knew,* in a way that I couldn't explain, that my namesake had conspired to have her son killed and to blame it on the local troublemaker.

And when she saw me watching her, she knew that I knew. Maybe that would put an end to this. She would go home to Aquitaine. Prince John would go on his hunting trip, keep angering lords and barons, and if anything got in the way of that again . . . it wasn't my job to fix it.

Because I also knew it was time for me to go home.

CHAPTER TWENTY-EIGHT

I COULDN'T EXPLAIN MY CERTAINTY ANY MORE THAN I COULD explain how I'd come to be in the twelfth century in the first place. One moment I knelt beside the dead man, wondering which of his faces—monk, soldier, courtier—was the real one, and what it meant that I'd seen him in Nottingham. Was it a premonition or was the vision an effect of the same anomaly that had brought me here?

Then, with a feeling like that of going down in an elevator, all the things that had become so normal that I'd stopped noticing them became strange again. I felt like my body didn't quite fit in the space around it anymore.

So much was happening that when I pushed to my feet and walked to the door, no one stopped me. I listened to the talk, and every person I went past had a different version of what had happened. The Robin Hood legend would stay as contradictory and unlikely as it had always been.

It should have felt weird to walk out of the castle with no one stopping me or ordering me around. Outside, the bailey was bright with torches haloed by the damp air. I smelled horse manure and wet stone and ... exhaust fumes. The fumes smelled as real as the monk had looked on my side of the tunnel. Premonition or a glimpse of where I was going, I took it as a sign.

I wanted home with all my heart, but I didn't know how I could bear to say goodbye.

"You left this."

I turned to see Guilbert holding my longbow. "Thank you."

He came down the steps from the keep's main door, and I took the bow from him. "Are you going to run?" he asked.

"No," I said, with enough spirit to chase away the feeling I was going to cry. It came right back. "But I am going to leave."

His brow rose. "Without saying goodbye? I didn't think you were a coward."

"I am *not* a coward." He raised his other brow, and I set my chin. "I'll start with Will, if you'll show me where the barracks are."

We walked there in silence until I noticed he wasn't limping. "You exaggerated your limp when we were in the hall this afternoon, didn't you?"

"Only a little."

"How did you heal so fast?"

"My strong constitution and the excellent care of Sister Clothilde."

He held the barracks door for me, which was even weirder than being able to walk in silence with him. The inside was surprisingly not disgusting for a bunch of men living together in the Middle Ages. But that was relative.

Will was sleeping in one of the cots, all bandaged up. Just when I was thinking this might be easier than I expected, he opened his eyes. "Have you rescued the prince from the dragon, m'lady?"

"What kind of drugs are they giving you?"

He laughed, then groaned. "Not enough."

I laughed, too, and then didn't. "Will . . . I have to leave."

He sighed. "Of course you do, you strange creature. Is it back to fairyland with you?"

Laugh, cry, what was the difference? "Is that what you think? James debates between angel and demon."

"It depends on the mood."

His hand reached for mine, and I held it. "I just wanted to say . . . ," I began, and swallowed before I could continue. ". . . that I have a brother somewhere. And he's lost to me. But now I have another."

"Who will never be lost to you." He squeezed my hand. "But please make the Will Scarlet you take with you better dressed than this."

"You're not dressed at all, you rogue."

329

"All the better." He lifted my hand to his lips and kissed it. "Little John can't bear goodbyes. I'll tell him for you."

He closed his eyes and pretended to go to sleep so I'd be able to leave.

Guilbert was waiting outside for me. He didn't say anything, just started walking back toward the keep, pretending not to hear me sniffle. There was a lot of pretending going on. Whatever it took to get through.

"Do you realize," he said, idly, "that you have never told me your real name?"

"Really? It's Ellie Hudson."

"No it's not." He stopped, and of course I did, too. "It's Eleanor Nikola Hudson, of South Bend, Indiana, born in what I assume to be the year of our Lord two thousand—"

"How do you *know* that?" Shock knocked everything off-kilter. I swore the whole of Nottingham Castle turned sideways.

Guilbert reached into his jacket and pulled out my passport and cell phone. "Did you not realize you lost your satchel on the bridge before you jumped? I'm afraid the bag and other items were scavenged. But the guards left these as worthless."

I took them like they were precious artifacts. Which I guess they were. Artifacts of the future.

"How—? What in the world have you been thinking this whole time?"

"That whatever sorcery brought you here would take you away before the sheriff could remove your head." He frowned, like he found that annoying. "I do believe in justice appropriate for the crime. But I suppose I have to let you go, regardless."

The discomfort of somehow not fitting in the space around me had gotten worse since I'd taken back my passport and phone. The pull was tangible but not yet irresistible. "Do you have something to write with?"

He exhaled in annoyance. "Why didn't you say something at the barracks?"

Good to know I could still irritate him.

We went back to the barracks, and Guilbert found me a scrap of parchment and a pencil that looked more like a crayon. I jotted down a date, time, and place and rolled the note up. "Now I'm ready."

He stopped at the door of the barracks. "You know the way from here, I suppose?"

"I think I can manage." I paused, though, because he seemed to have something he wanted to say.

It took him a moment to work up to it. "I am sorry that I was rough with you when you were Robert Hudson."

I gave him a suspicious side-eye. "Did James tell you to apologize properly?"

He looked indignant. "I would have anyway. It has been weighing heavily since you *shot* me."

This was getting awkward. "Don't make me start liking you now that I'm never going to see you again."

He raised one damned eyebrow and nodded to my passport. "That small parchment in your hand bears the seals of governments I've never even heard of. How can you possibly say for certain we'll never meet again?"

That was a fair point.

"In that case," I said, taking a step back, "I won't say good-bye."

I turned and left him in the barracks. My walk was purposeful this time as I headed again to the keep. I wasn't entirely surprised to see James coming down the stone steps to meet me. I stopped to watch. He really was something else in his mail armor and surcoat, sword at his side. That was something I'd take with me, too.

We met at the midpoint between the keep and the stables. He looked concerned, then bemused, then just confused by whatever was on my face. I came close to him and pressed the rolled parchment into his hand.

"What's this?" he asked.

"It's where I actually come from." I kept our hands clasped together. "Don't look at it now. I don't know what you'll do with the information, but . . . it's yours. So you know."

Maybe I was so confident that I'd done what needed doing that I wasn't afraid of changing the eight hundred years between us. Maybe it didn't seem to matter since Guilbert knew, or it didn't seem sporting that one knew and the other didn't. In any case, it was done.

"You're leaving." It wasn't a question.

"Yes." I felt so strong saying it, but I was shaking. I stepped back so he wouldn't feel it. "Maybe you should find a way to retire all this holy order business and marry Isabel. Being a farmer and a just and fair landlord would suit you. Living a good life is an atonement, too."

One more step, and he stopped me with my name. "Ellie."

He crossed the span of my two steps with one of his and held my gaze in the torchlight. "I'm sorry."

"For what?" I asked.

He raised his hand and swiped his big, callused thumb over my cheek, holding it up to show tears I didn't know I was crying. "I told you I wouldn't allow any harm to come to you."

I gave him a watery smile and said, "You didn't." I wasn't conflicted about going home. It wasn't his fault that going someplace meant leaving someplace else behind.

Well, someone.

Some ones.

"Tell Much . . ." There, I finally faltered. "Think of something, will you?"

He stepped back, making it a little easier for me. "Of course. Be careful, Eleanor, back there in West-of-Here. Maybe learn to look before you leap off bridges."

I made a face. "What? Have you never met me?"

I waited for his laugh, then headed for the stable. The doors to the tunnel stood open. I could smell damp sandstone and I could smell coffee, and I burst into a run, not even breaking stride when I reached the pitch-freaking-dark.

CHAPTER TWENTY-NINE

"MISS! YOU'RE NOT SUPPOSED TO BE IN THERE." A LADY IN A blue polo shirt pointed at me with her furled umbrella. "Only tours can go into the caves."

"Oh." It took me a moment to get my bearings. I had a certainty of *when* I was, but I was still a little confused about *where*. And how to get out of there.

I finally did what I had done to get in and climbed over the gate between the terraced top of Nottingham Castle's cliff and the path leading to the caves beneath it. The Nottingham Castle lady complained some more but then stopped when she looked at my clothes.

"Is there a reenactment today?"

"I don't know," I said. "What day is it?"

"Tuesday."

"The date, I mean." People always got weird looks when they asked that in movies and, unsurprisingly, that's what I got from her.

"The fourteenth."

The day I left. Or at least the date I left.

"Are you quite sure you're all right, dearie?"

Somehow that was even funnier in her thoroughly modern accent, and I had to stop laughing or she was going to call someone to take me away for psychiatric evaluation. I didn't want that happening now any more than I had then.

The lady went back into the tea shop and suddenly I was starving, but I didn't have a cent on me. At least I had my passport and my phone. That, and a really cool outfit for the next Renaissance fair. I smoothed the front of the leather jerkin and my fingers found the sling I'd fashioned for my bow.

My longbow.

I pulled it off my shoulder and checked to make sure. Yep. There was even some of Will's blood on the string notch. We were still the same as we were back then.

Now what?

I took out my phone. The last thing I expected was any charge, but when I turned it on, there was a tiny bit of red in the battery indicator. According to Vodafone, I'd come back within five minutes of when I'd left. Multiply that feeling of flying for nine hours and getting somewhere before you left by about a hundred, and that's how I felt.

I supposed I should call Mom with the last of my charge. But my thumb was out of practice, and I hit the picture app instead.

There was the last picture I'd taken. Me and Robin Hood. I couldn't help a hysterical laugh. It wasn't even *close* to a likeness.

Then an accidental swipe took me to the next picture. Still at the statue. Still me. And beside me . . .

I staggered and had to sit in one of the wire patio chairs outside the tea shop.

Beside me in the picture was Rob, and we were making like archers in front of the Robin Hood statue.

I shot out of the chair and ran around the big building that wasn't a castle and down through the garden that had once been the barracks and out through the gate where Henry Guilbert had ridden up and said to throw me in the dungeon and down to the street that hadn't been there at all. I ran downhill to the inset concrete space where Robin Hood was now, and where the river had been then. Where James Hathaway had pulled me out of the muck.

No one was there. Lots of people on the street, but no one at the statue. I circled it, then went around to each of the murals from the legend, and then I went back to the street.

"Ellie!"

I swung around. There was Rob, the real Robert Hudson, coming up the hill toward me. My God, he was so thin.

I ran, threw my arms around him, and didn't let go.

"What is wrong with you? God, you smell. What are you wearing?" He pried me off him and looked at me. "Where did you get this getup? Is that a yew longbow?"

"Yes," I said. I wiped tears from my face, and my hands came away not just wet but muddy. And my lost brother had

336

just said I smelled. And it was the most beautiful thing ever. "I'll tell you, but I'm just so happy to see you!"

He gave me a look. "You saw me thirty minutes ago."

I laughed a little hysterically and said truthfully, "It feels longer."

It had been, for me. Last I saw him was six months ago, plus Medieval Relative Time.

Rob gave me an annoyed-big-brother look and I hugged him again. He pulled me off him and examined my face. "You were supposed to meet us at the pub."

"Sorry!" I couldn't stop smiling.

Now I got the side-eye from the other direction. "Who are you?"

"I'm Ellie. Ellie Hudson." It felt wonderful to say.

Someone spoke behind me. "Glad to meet you, Ellie, Ellie Hudson."

It was a male someone. A male someone with a British accent. I turned and saw . . .

No one I knew. But for a second I thought I did.

"Ellie," said Rob, a little amused and a little annoyed, the way brothers were, "the most bizarre coincidence just happened. I want you to meet the guy who literally saved my life."

"Pleased to meet you," said the handsome, tanned, caramel-haired, blue-eyed male someone with a British accent who put out his hand.

"An honor, your grace" was what came out of my mouth.

He laughed. "I'm not a duke. The only rank I've got is lieutenant."

"Oh." I laughed awkwardly. "I had to practice that line for a play and it pops up at the weirdest times." Nothing in Rob's or the stranger's expression said they believed that, but I didn't care.

Rob performed a proper introduction. "Jamie is part of the search and rescue squad that found my group out in the desert. Jamie, this is my usually *very* serious sister."

"Jamie?" I asked, not startled, really.

"James. A family name." He looked me over. Not in that way. In a why-are-you-dressed-like-a-complete-nutter way. "Are you a living-history enthusiast, Ellie?"

"No. I've just had a really strange day." I went to put my hands in my pockets, but I had none. Middle Ages pants. My jeans and sneakers, I realized, were in the past. Oops.

"Do you ever have one of those days," I said, "where it feels like it's been a month or two?"

"Clearly you've never been in the army or you wouldn't have to ask." Jamie's smile slipped and he peered closer at me. "Do you have blood spatter on your face?"

I ran my sleeve over it, although I wasn't sure that helped. Rob held something out to me, and I took it automatically.

It was a breath mint.

"Oh my God, seriously, Rob? What the hell?" He just gave me a speaking look, and I popped the mint in my mouth, saying around it, "You were saying about coincidence?"

He was still looking at me funny. Maybe because every time I looked at him I grinned. "Just running into Jamie here. He doesn't even live in Nottingham."

When I turned back to Jamie, he was checking out my longbow. Also not in that way. "Is that a longbow?"

"Yes, it is. It's actually my favorite bow."

Something in my tone—maybe I'd picked up Will's flippancy—made him smile. And yes, in *that way*. "This is going to sound mental, but my family has this letter from the beginning of the thirteenth century—1215, actually."

"Are you serious?"

He nodded, and yes, he looked completely serious. "It's written by an ancestor of mine. Do you . . ." He gestured up the street. "Do you want to have a coffee or something?"

"I . . ." I stumbled, wanting so badly to say yes, but my brother had just come back from being lost and I didn't want to waste a second with him.

"She does," Rob said, and I finally wrapped my head around the fact that what was new for me wasn't new for him.

"I really do," I assured Jamie, real name James, a family name. "I haven't had a coffee in ages."

He turned and I fell into step beside him. We were walking past the unflattering Robin Hood statue, Rob following us. "Well, the thing is, the letter has today's date on it. And this place."

"Anything else?" I asked tentatively. Fragilely. Because what was old for him was new for me.

"Nothing. No explanation, just a note that if there's anyone left in the family, they should be here."

"And here you are."

Jamie had a face that looked good smiling. "And here I am."

339

MIDDLE AGES NOTES

1. Boil everything.
2. Whatever it is, don't ask what's in it.
3. If it's the king's deer, don't shoot it.
4. All deer are the king's deer.
5. Common Law: Don't even try to figure this out.
6. At least remember these guys →

WILLIAM I
(aka William of Normandy, aka
William the Conqueror)

HENRY I
(the one I don't know anything about)

HENRY II ──────── ELEANOR
(the one Peter O'Toole   OF AQUITAINE
played in that movie)   (the one I'm named after)

Three kids   Three more kids
who don't   who don't rule
rule England   England

RICHARD I   ## JOHN I
(aka Richard the Lionheart,   (aka Prince John,
aka Good King Richard)   aka John Lackland)
• Must have had a good press agent   • Not a people person
• Spent about six weeks in England   • Signed the Magna Carta

ACKNOWLEDGMENTS

How do I even begin to thank everyone who has kept me going as I wrote this book? Boy, did my life go off the rails. Luckily, I have the most marvelous people to get me back on track.

I particularly want to thank my agent, Lucienne Diver, for her friendship and support, not to mention her mojo; Krista Marino for having faith in this book (and me) and Monica Jean for batting cleanup; all the Penguin Random House folks, especially the design team that gave me this awesome cover.

God bless Sandy Seavers, who bugged me for a time-travel book for.ev.er.

Thank you to my friends and colleagues and those who just put up with me at the DFW Writers' Workshop. I'm so glad that Rosemary brought me to meet you. In special particular, A. Lee Martinez, Brooke Fossey, Shawn Scarber, and . . . You know what? If I start naming people, I'm going to accidentally leave someone out, so . . . all of you awesome people.

I don't know what I'd do without Jenny Martin, whose talent keeps me on my toes; Kate Cornell, whose sarcasm keeps me on my toes; Sally Hamilton, who gets me out of my cave with equal parts love and intimidation; and Cheryl Smyth, who just gets me.

Then there are my blood relations, who would love me even if they didn't have to—Mom, Tante Meitie, Oma, Tracy, Tavish, et al. I love you ad infinitum.

Finally, I know people always say this, but I literally would not have been able to write this book without these people: K. Hutson, Archduchess of Awesome; Greg the Terrible, King of Supania; and Rachel Caine, Our Lady of Morganville.

As for Peter the Greatish . . . thanks for not telling the parental units how you broke your arm that one time.

ABOUT THE AUTHOR

Kara Connolly loves history, though she's never time traveled. She lives and writes in Arlington, Texas. To learn more about Kara and her books, visit karaconnolly.wordpress.com, or follow @karaconnolly4 on Twitter and @readkaraconnolly on Instagram.